ONE

SUMMER WINE

Joe Loxley turned up the air conditioning in his white BMW X7 as he pulled away from the Beaulieu Motor Museum in the New Forest. The country was in the middle of a sizzling heatwave, giving the B3056 road back to Lyndhurst a vague dusty haze. It had been a busy morning at the museum. He had been employed there part time for the most part of the twenty years since he had moved down to the New Forest after retiring from the police force. The three mornings a week suited him fine. Today was Thursday, his last working morning of the week. He liked to think that he was a valuable member of the staff, imparting his vast wealth of knowledge and enthusiasm for cars to the thousands of visitors who attended every year. He enjoyed working there, even mucking in with the polishing of the rich collection of classic automobiles when the mood was upon him. He found the act of polishing reassuringly therapeutic, while also giving his ageing body the added bonus of keeping himself reasonably fit. He felt very fortunate that even though he was now in his mid-seventies, he was still physically active and, he liked to think, mentally alert. Sure, he occasionally fell victim to the occasional senior moment, not to mention the intermittent aches and pains that came with advancing age, but unlike most of his less fortunate, retired compatriots in the Met, he had managed to reach his senior years without the aid of significant medication.

He slowed up as a small group of New Forest ponies ambled lazily across the tarmac in front of him, tails swishing. He and his wife Janet had originally moved down to Lyndhurst to be nearer to her parents, who lived in Bournemouth. Sadly, Billy and Jenny had now passed away, but he had no doubts that it was the best move they had ever made. He was vaguely aware of a voice on the car radio talking about possible hosepipe bans and climate change. He quickly changed the channel to Greatest Hits Radio. Even before the enforced isolation of the global pandemic a couple of years back, he had already got to a stage in life where he much preferred the closeted existence of the New Forest. He had increasingly grown to love this peaceful, forested oasis that existed just off the M27. Seemingly far away from what seemed an increasingly troubled twenty-first-century world, where the tone had seemed to be set at the very beginning by the 9/11 atrocities in 2001. Apart from the sports news, he now preferred to avoid as much outside noise as possible. He was one of the few people he knew who still possessed a mobile phone with no internet access. Not for him, the divisive hornet's nest of social media and the chattering classes. Janet's unstinting devotion, Sky Sports and an occasional pint at the pub was all he needed nowadays.

It occurred to him that it now must be the best part of two years since he had last ventured down to London to meet up with his old police colleague James Cumber. They had spent a pleasant day reminiscing about the old days while taking in a tour of the new Tottenham Hotspur stadium. That fond recollection reminded him that James was coming down that evening to stay with them for a few days on one of his occasional visits. As always, Loxley looked forward to it, their solid friendship having been forged in the common experience of working closely together for years in the force while both being long-suffering Spurs supporters. Though James was only ten years younger, Loxley had always felt he was more like the son he'd never had. So much so that he had felt James's personal-life disappointments of divorce and career-ending injury almost as keenly. Poor James had also an extra cross to bear with his troublesome son Jason. Thankfully, Loxley's own daughter Clare had never given him much grief, apart from a brief period in her university days when she seemed to lack any directional drive. Her lucky break had been meeting Tom. A builder by trade and totally practical, he had already started his own painting and decorating business by the time he met Clare. They now lived in a big house in Cuffley, Hertfordshire, so Loxley had no worries there. Sadly, they had shown no interest in blessing him and Janet with the gift of grandchildren, but they had consoled themselves with the thought that you can't have everything in life. Tom was always polite and civil enough; though, if he was being picky, he did not find him the most sociable. Still, there was no denying he was a good provider and, most importantly, Clare had always seemed happy enough.

Loxley turned right into Southampton Road as a fire engine pulled out of the fire station on its way to yet another tinderbox outbreak in the forest. The hot weather was certainly keeping the firefighters busy. Shortly after turning left into Queens Road, he pulled up on the drive of a large, detached, red-brick house. Janet was in the front garden pottering with some plants. Loxley never failed to get a good feeling whenever he returned home. It was a house that went some way to justifying all those long days he had spent chasing criminals when he could have been spending more time with Janet. They had been married for over fifty years, but they both knew that it was only in the last twenty that they had spent enough quality time together. Back in those adrenaline-charged days when he had been hunting down the desperate and the dangerous, she had always been there in the background, solid, dependable, uncomplaining. He loved her dearly.

He remained in the driver's seat for a minute or so watching Janet absorbed in the plants. It was one of her many interests. She had dealt with the relatively recent loss of her two parents by keeping herself busy. In addition to her voluntary work for the charity shop in the town, she also had her Pilates classes, book clubs and coffee mornings to keep her active and interested. After getting out of his car, he took the time to enjoy the strong scent of honeysuckle and appreciate a good stretch of his long, angular frame. It was coming up to midday and he felt in need of some refreshment.

He called out to Janet, 'Hi, pet, fancy a Pimm's?'

Janet looked up with interest. 'Sounds like a good idea.'

Loxley smiled. 'I had a feeling you might be tempted; I'll bring it out to you.'

He went through the front door while Janet rose from the flowerbed and made her way to the wooden bench that sat at the front of the house. Loxley soon joined her and handed over the freshly prepared drink, while he settled for a glass of chilled San Miguel. They sat there contentedly in silence for some time, savouring the refreshing drinks in the hot sunshine. It was Janet who eventually broke the peaceful tranquillity.

'Was it busy at the museum?'

Loxley took a quick swig of his beer before replying, 'It was absolutely rammed. At one point I thought they were going to ask me to stay on a bit longer, but I managed to slip away sneakily when no one was looking.'

Janet commented, 'You never know, they might have offered you some overtime if you'd stayed on.'

Loxley laughed. 'I doubt that very much. Anyway, you know full well that if they'd offered, I wouldn't have been interested.'

Janet smiled in agreement. Fortunately, they'd reached a financially comfortable stage in life when their personal time would always be more valuable than any potential monetary reward.

Janet changed the subject. 'What time we expecting James today?'

'He said he hoped to get here late afternoon.'

'I wonder what he's been up to.'

'Knowing him, he's probably spent all his time trying

to get his golf handicap under sixteen. He'll manage it one day; he's a determined little bugger.'

Janet finished her Pimm's and rose from the bench. 'It will be nice to see him. I'll go and get his bed made up.'

Loxley remained seated and lingered for a little longer, enjoying the beer and lightly dozing in the heat. Some obscure noise stirred him, and he opened his eyes. He caught a brief glimpse of someone who appeared to be lost, passing back and forth on the street between the bushes at the front of the house. Seeing an unfamiliar stranger on the quiet residential street was unusual, but he supposed it could easily have been an Amazon delivery driver looking for an address and thought no more of it. He eventually rose from the bench and entered the house. Janet was busy in the kitchen preparing a cheese salad. He picked up a couple of unopened letters left on the table in the wide hallway. He recognised one of the letters as being a pension update, but it was the other one that caused him a growing unease. The sky-blue vanilla envelope with the Sellotaped seal had a familiar look. Loxley slipped on a pair of leather gloves that he kept near the front door. He felt an involuntary shaking of his hand as he opened the envelope. Inside was a single sheet with a three-word message that read:

REASON TO HATE.

Loxley went straight to a chest of drawers and pulled out an identically stamped, addressed envelope, written in the same neat, precise, copperplate handwriting. Everything about the letter looked the same except for the message, which read:

HOW DO YOU SLEEP?

He'd been sent the original letter a week before and had kept it on the off chance that there just might be a follow-up. There were plenty of cranks out there and there was no doubt he had made plenty of enemies in his highly successful police career. He had thought about mentioning it to the desk sergeant at the local Pikes Hill station, but he had dismissed the idea in the hope that it was a one-off from some pea-brained nut job who'd heard that Loxley was an ex-policeman. Loxley had thought no more of it until now. Looking at the two letters side by side, he began to feel some of the old anxiety that had dogged him in his last years in the force.

Not surprisingly, he could not disguise his uneasiness from Janet over lunch. Suddenly losing his appetite and picking indifferently at his salad, Janet asked him what was wrong. Loxley was reluctant to burden Janet with any of his worries. He always felt a touch of guilt on the rare occasions when his past career impacted on her peace of mind. At the same time, he realised that she should not be kept in the dark if these messages were serious. He rose from the table and returned with the two letters, before placing the two written notes in front of her with his gloved hands.

Janet studied them for a few seconds before looking up. 'You should take them to Pikes Hill Station immediately. You can't take any chances.'

Loxley looked apologetic. 'I'm really sorry for all this hassle, pet. I guess it's just not possible to totally wipe out your past.' He picked up the notes from the table and gently kissed Janet on the forehead. 'I'll get down to the station straight away.'

*

Loxley pulled up in front of Lyndhurst Police Station at Pikes Hill. He had kept up his contacts with the police force and he was still an admired and valued figure within the policing community. From time to time in his retirement, he had even done a little work for them. Jobs like going around the local community advising on home security or, even better, giving the investigative officers the benefit of his vast experience on difficult cases. He was buzzed through the security door into the public reception area.

The desk sergeant, Tom Fallon, looked pleased to see him.

'Hello, Joe, what can we do for you?'

Loxley gave a grimace before placing the two letters on the desk. 'I'm not sure, Tom, could be something or nothing. I've had these two Sellotaped beauties land on the mat in the last couple of weeks. Obviously the sender's sealed them with tape instead of licked so as not to leave any DNA.'

Tom Fallon gave the envelopes a brief scan without touching them, before passing comment.

'First class, Brockenhurst postmark, standard post office stationary.' He looked enquiringly at Loxley, before asking, with a touch of irony, 'I gather they're not good news?'

Loxley picked them up with his gloved hands and showed Fallon the contents. 'They're not the worst threats I've ever had by any means, but it's the why now? After all, I've been a long time retired.'

Fallon picked up a forensic bag and held it out for Loxley. 'Shove them in there, Joe, and we'll get the boys to check for dabs at least, just in case the sender slipped up.' He paused reflectively before asking, 'How do you want to play it, Joe? Obviously we'll go with your instincts.'

Loxley took a deep breath. 'I'd like to think it's a harmless idiot, but that's not my feeling. I think I should take it seriously, but at this point, Tom, I don't want any visible police presence so prefer it to be off the record. Don't worry, I'll be vigilant, and you'll be the first to know if I see anything suspicious.'

Fallon nodded. 'It's your call, Joe. In the meantime, I'll get these fast-tracked by forensics.'

'Much appreciated, Tom.'

As an afterthought, Fallon asked, 'Do you want me to inform DCI Jennings?'

Loxley hesitated. David Jennings was a good friend and would be sure to escalate the case.

'No, leave it at the moment, Tom, I'll take it at my pace if that's OK?'

'No problem, Joe.'

*

On the short drive back to his house, Loxley was deep in thought. He suddenly remembered the solitary stranger who appeared lost in front of his house earlier that day. Was he being overly apprehensive? In his last years in the force, he had suffered periodic bouts of depression and anxiety. It had never stopped him working, but there was no doubt that, at the time, he was beginning to show increasing signs of mental and emotional fragility. By the time he got to his early fifties, the job was really beginning to get to him and the early retirement came at just the right time. He hadn't had those feelings for twenty years until today. He felt a deep hostility towards the sender of the letters for making him feel that way again, resented his intrusion into the idyllic existence that he shared with Janet. This was personal! With a steely resolve, he made up his mind. He had never been one to back down in the face of intimidation and was dammed if he was going to start now.

*

James Cumber repositioned his set of golf clubs in the boot of his black Audi A6 after loading his luggage. He stood back and surveyed the packed items. Satisfied that he had not forgotten anything, he swiftly pulled down the tailgate. He was running late. His morning golf session of nine holes at the West Essex Golf Club had gone on far longer than he'd expected. The exceptionally hot weather had naturally slowed things down, but most of the delay had been caused by a fellow member's birthday celebrations in the clubhouse afterwards. To be fair to old Harry, he'd put on a good spread, and it had saved Cumber having to worry about lunch. He went back inside his well-appointed two-bedroom apartment in Chigwell to make sure he had not forgotten anything. Joe and Janet were expecting him early that evening. There was no way he was going to make that now. He would ring them on the way there. After using his iPhone to select a favourite playlist of Brandon Flowers and The Killers, it was not long before he was pulling out of his drive and passing Grange Hill Tube Station on his way to the M25. He was looking forward to his visit to the New Forest. He had noticed that these pleasurable stopovers in Hampshire were becoming more frequent. It must be three or four visits a year in recent times. He blamed Joe and Janet Loxley. They made him feel so welcome. The routine was nearly always the same: long walks in the forest, leisurely pints with Joe in his local, plus the occasional meal out with the two of them in Lyndhurst. Best of all, there was the golf – nowadays far and away his favourite pastime. The Peter Alliss Golf Course at Ferndown was not too far away and he would always squeeze in a few rounds while he was there. Golf was so much more than a hobby to him; in many ways, it had been his saviour. He had started playing the game after his painful and messy divorce from Susan. His two children, Kelsey and Jason, had taken it badly and his life was a mess. The absorption of rolling that little white ball into a hole momentarily took him away from all of that. Since then, he had found the game a useful crutch to help him get through bad times, from the death of his beloved parents to his injury-forced retirement from the force. Those had been dark days. After all these years, he still had flashbacks of the car speeding towards him and the pain in his leg before mercifully blacking out. After several operations on his smashed limb in an unsuccessful attempt to get him back into active service, he was left with a noticeable limp and a generous early pension in his mid-forties. At least he had survived. His partner, DS Brian Parrish, had not been so lucky. The poor sod had never stood a chance. The Met had offered an office job, but he was never going to be happy with that tedious scenario. The Bravery Medal he was subsequently awarded for his actions in the incident was appreciated but was scant consolation. The stark reality was that the job he had loved most had been taken away from him in his prime, never to return. He remembered it as a time that the light in his life massively dimmed. It had been the innocent trivial pursuit of golf that had kept that fading light glimmering. He gave out an involuntary sigh; now in his sixties, it would be fair to say that his life had not quite turned out as he had envisaged. As he joined the M25 and headed west, he searched for Joe Loxley's number to tell him he was going to be late.

*

Loxley had returned to his house in a pensive mood. After telling Janet how he'd got on at the police station, he had gone to his study, which housed his career memorabilia, to go through a stack of his old case notes. His optimistic intention had been to see if he could find some significant clue as to who might be sending the threatening notes, but it was an impossible task. It was like looking for a needle in a haystack; there were so many cases in which grudges could still have been held and vengeful thoughts festered. It came as a welcome interruption when his mobile rang, and he saw it was James.

'Hi, James.'

'Hello, Joe, I got a bit delayed at the club this morning, so I'm running a little behind time. The traffic on the M25 is doing its usual to make things worse.'

'That's alright, James, you get here when you get here, no need to rush.'

'I'm still hoping to fit a pint in with you tonight at the pub.'

Loxley looked at the clock on the wall of his study. 'You should be good for that. I'll tell Janet to keep the grub warm.'

Cumber protested, 'No need, I can easily get a takeaway later on.'

Loxley laughed. 'She wouldn't hear of it; she's bound to have one of your favourites on the go.'

Cumber paused for a moment. It was true that Janet pulled out all the stops on the cooking front whenever he visited.

'Well, in that case… how can I refuse?'

'You daren't.' Loxley chuckled.

'I know I've said it before, Joe, but you got yourself a real cracker there.'

'I know; I'm lucky.'

Cumber changed the subject. 'How're you managing in this heat?'

'Loving it, though I don't think the firemen would agree. They've been in and out the fire station like a fiddler's elbow.'

'Not surprised; this hot spell doesn't look like it's ending any time soon.'

Loxley hesitated slightly before saying, 'There is something I want to chew over with you when you get here.'

'That sounds ominous.'

'It's just a little local issue but I want to run it past you if that's OK?'

'I'm at your service as always.'

'Thanks, James, I'll catch you later.'

Cumber's Audi trundled a few yards further forwards in the line of traffic before stopping once more. He'd be lucky to get there tomorrow at this rate. The rush hour seemed to be getting earlier and earlier these days. He wondered what Joe had to discuss. He knew him well enough to know that it couldn't be that trivial. There had been that familiar tone in his voice that he knew of old. Something was troubling him.

*

By the early evening, Loxley was feeling a lot better. Not surprisingly, one of Janet's homemade lasagnes followed by a long cool shower had revived his spirits considerably. Maybe he was emboldened by the fact that his old fellow crime cracker was coming down to join him. Either way, he had made up his mind that he was not going to be changing his routine just because of some numbskull with a grudge who thought he could scare him. It was his normal habit to go to the pub on Thursday evenings and that was what he was going to do. When he had said this to Janet, he was not sure if she was happy with it or not. Typically, as she had always done in his career, she kept her worries to herself, quietly steeling her inner resolve and putting whatever anxieties she might have felt to one side.

It had been a couple of hours earlier when a frustrated James Cumber had made another call saying there had been an accident on the M3 and the traffic was at a standstill. It was now gone seven o'clock and he had still not arrived. Loxley joined Janet in the lounge.

'James will be starving by the time he gets here.'

Janet sounded sympathetic. 'The traffic must be bad. I'll do my best to keep his lasagne warm, but it won't be at its best.'

'I'm sure he'll be grateful whatever, pet. Looks like I'll have to go to the pub without him.' Loxley looked at the clock on the mantelpiece. 'Phil will be calling anytime soon.'

Phil Shaw was Loxley's neighbour and regular drinking partner. Long retired from his job as a geography teacher, Loxley found Phil's simple honesty and lack of side refreshing; besides which, he was easy, undemanding company.

Janet feigned sarcasm. 'Heaven forbid you keep Phil waiting for his pint; it would be the end of the world as he knows it!'

Loxley laughed. 'James will understand. Remember, he has met Phil.'

'Don't forget to take your mobile with you so I can let you know when James arrives.'

'No worries.' He felt she needed some reassurance. 'We're only going for a couple, but probably sensible to be on your guard to unexpected callers just in case.'

She nodded understandingly. 'I know the drill. Remember, I was a copper's wife for thirty years.'

Loxley gave her a hug. 'What's more, a bloody good one at that.'

Not long after, Loxley and Phil Shaw were making their routinely short walk along the Southampton Road, towards Lyndhurst High Street. They were confronted with the usual familiar sights: Janet's favourite Italian restaurant, the quaint wood-clad bus stops and the fire station. The regular highlight for Loxley before entering the pub was the glossy Meridien Modena car showroom, with its impressive selection of Ferraris on the forecourt. Loxley could never help momentarily pausing at this point. Phil would begrudgingly tolerate this small interruption to their progress on the understanding that Loxley would buy the first pint. Before moving on, Loxley caught his reflection in the showroom window and self-consciously straightened up. For someone in his mid-seventies, he liked to think he carried his six-feet-two frame with the physical presence of a much younger man; hunched shoulders in someone so tall was never a good look. Certainly, Phil Shaw had no such problem as his shorter, thickset frame pushed Loxley up to the bar after entering the pub. The Prince was a popular pub with the locals, with Loxley being on nodding terms with most of the familiar faces that frequented it. Most of all, it was a comfortably familiar venue, one in which he and Phil had shared a pint and some worldly wisdom for many a long year. As was their usual custom, they liked to stand at the end of the bar. Loxley liked to position himself so that he could see the customers coming in and out. He guessed it was a policeman thing; something he had always done. It was only on the odd occasion when they stayed for a third pint that they'd feel the need to go and find a seat. The landlord, Jack, was already pulling their favourite pints as they reached the bar.

'Good to see you, gents, great drinking weather.'

Loxley glanced around the crowded bar. As was the modern trend in pubs, the dining space had been expanded at the expense of the public bar area. On summer evenings like tonight, it didn't need a lot of people to make it feel busy.

'Great atmosphere, Jack, you must be doing something right.'

Jack looked pleased. 'You know me, Joe, I do my best.'

They both raised their glasses to him before Phil took a long swig of his favourite, Old Speckled Hen, before turning to Loxley.

'So, your old mate is still stuck on the motorway?'

Loxley had stuck to his regular pint of IPA and made sure he took a long swallow before nodding his head.

'Poor sod, it sounds like the M3 is completely snarled.'

Phil shook his head sagely. 'I try not to go near motorways nowadays, too dangerous. Too many cars driving too close together, and as for those so-called smart motorways with no hard shoulder... don't get me started.'

Loxley's love of fast driving prevented him from totally agreeing, but he had to admit Phil had a point about the smart motorways.

'You've got to have the motorways; how could you get anywhere in a reasonable time without them?'

Phil looked pointedly at his watch. 'It's certainly not helping your mate much.'

Loxley had to concede Phil had a good point there. 'When they work, of course.'

Phil was not deterred. 'That's what's wrong – the modern world's got too fast. Everything has got to happen yesterday. Hopefully this heat will slow everything down.'

They were interrupted by a group of people at the other end of the bar laughing loudly. Loxley glanced in their direction.

'They sound like a happy bunch; must have something to celebrate.'

Phil pulled a face. 'They obviously didn't tune into the news today. It's official, we're all going to hell in a handcart. I don't know about you, Joe, but the more time I spend on this mortal coil, I think that anyone who's happy is either mad or dangerously deluded.'

Loxley laughed. 'The news was that bad, was it?'

Phil confirmed, 'It was worse than bad!' He took another long swill of his beer as if to banish the memory.

Loxley smiled. 'Then I'm glad I don't watch it anymore. You should do the same.'

Phil shook his head. 'Believe me, I've tried, but I'm a hopeless case. I think I'm a news junkie.'

Loxley laughed. This was why he liked these light-hearted drinking sessions with Phil. He was so uncomplicated. Everything in Phil's world was satisfyingly black and white, so different to the harsh grey realities that Loxley knew existed out there. He looked across at the noisy crowd at the end of the bar. He recognised a few faces; one of them he knew as Roger Turnbull. Their eyes met and Roger came out of the crowd and approached them.

He offered his hand. 'Hello, Joe, how're you keeping?'

Loxley knew him from the various social functions that he had attended through the years, but he would also see him from time to time in The Prince. He was never sure what he did for a living exactly, but he was well respected in the New Forest area for his charity work and animal welfare. A smart-looking man somewhere in his early fifties who he knew lived a few miles down the road in Ashurst; he was always unfailingly polite and friendly to Loxley.

'Hello, Roger.' Loxley shook his hand and nodded in the direction of the laughing crowd. 'Celebrating something?'

Turnbull smiled. 'It's my nephew's birthday – twenty-one. Those were the days.'

Loxley stared across and looked wistful. 'Different world when I was twenty-one, that's for sure. Are you keeping busy?'

Turnbull stared amusedly at Loxley with his steely blue eyes. 'I'm always busy, Joe. I don't like to be idle.'

Loxley thought there was something slightly unsettling in the stillness of his gaze. It was as if he was scanning his features for why he asked the question. In Loxley's long experience of criminals, that normally meant they were up to something. In Turnbull's case, he'd never had any reason to doubt he was one of the good guys. A keen inquisitiveness could just be a part of his character; he was obviously an intelligent man.

Turnbull went on, 'Are you still giving the boys in blue the benefit of your experience, Joe?'

Loxley gave a chuckle. 'You know how it is, Roger, I like to keep my eye on them, make sure they're keeping up to scratch.' Loxley changed the subject. 'Are you going to carry on the celebrations somewhere else afterwards?'

Turnbull gave a wry smile. 'I think some of the younger ones might be going into Bournemouth. Not for me; I need my beauty sleep.'

'I don't blame you.'

Another man whom Loxley recognised beckoned Turnbull back to the crowd. Turnbull offered his hand to Loxley once more.

'It's good to see you, Joe.' He directed a brief cursory glance towards Phil Shaw before rejoining the party.

Phil Shaw had been quietly following the conversation. 'It's funny, I've seen him countless times in this pub, and he's never said a word to me. He obviously likes you.'

Loxley smiled. 'Now, Phil, I hope you're not getting jealous.'

'Maybe just a little bit. Seriously though, there is something about him I just can't put my finger on. I can't fathom it. You know him better than I do.'

'I know what you mean. He's been a well-respected member of the New Forest community and charity circuit for a long time, but I still don't really know much about him or what he does exactly.'

'My thoughts entirely.' Phil looked across at the crowd once more. 'It's the same with that guy who called him over; I've never liked him. There's something of the weasel about his features.'

Loxley laughed once more. 'That's Jack Foster, worked on the council for years. Bit of a social climber, I believe.'

Phil finished off his pint. 'I rest my case.'

*

James Cumber drummed his fingers on the steering wheel. His Brandon Flowers playlist had looped for the second time, and he was still only just outside Winchester. The journey had been an absolute nightmare. It had obviously been a bad accident, with the traffic not moving for a couple of hours and air emergency helicopters buzzing overhead. Now the traffic was in a stop-and-start mode as delayed rush-hour traffic merged with people travelling down to Bournemouth to make the most of the sunshine. His mobile phone rang. He saw that it was his daughter Kelsey.

'Hi, Dad, where are you?'

'You really don't want to know. I've been stuck on the motorway for about four hours.'

'Sounds bloody awful. Where are you going?'

'The intention is to get down to see Joe Loxley and his wife.'

'That's a shame, I was coming down to meet you at the flat and stay for a while.'

'I'll be here for about a week. You can have the run of the flat if you like. I gather you've still got the spare key I gave you?'

'Key? What key?' She laughed. 'I'm only joking. Have you got plenty of food in?'

'Lots in the freezer… fill your boots.'

'Ah, thanks, Dad. I plan to still be around when you get back.'

'I'll look forward to seeing you. Have you seen anything of your mum?'

Cumber thought he detected a slight bit of hesitation in her answer.

'Not recently, hopefully she's not fallen off the wagon again.'

A few years after the divorce, it seemed that Susan had turned increasingly to drink. It had got to the point where it was seriously affecting her health and Kelsey had stepped in and referred her to a doctor. The last he'd heard was that the treatment was working well, and she was getting her life back on an even keel.

'I really hope she's not undoing all the good work.'

Kelsey replied, 'She's good, don't worry.' She changed the subject. 'Have you met anyone yet? Please say you have.'

Cumber shook his head. She often fussed over him and worried that he was on his own.

'I've met plenty of people; why do you ask?' he teased.

'You know what I mean, a nice lady to look after you.'

'As I've said before, I'm doing fine on my own. Don't worry yourself.'

'I just think it would be nice.'

Cumber laughed. 'Well, think on; it's probably not going to happen.'

'I could get you on Tinder.'

'No, thanks.'

'Spoilsport.'

'Besides, you probably wouldn't get on with her and it would make my life a misery.'

It was Kelsey's turn to laugh. 'That wouldn't happen; I get on with everybody.'

Cumber snorted. 'That's debatable. Anyway, when are you going to settle down and stop gadding about enjoying yourself?'

'We're talking about you, remember?'

Cumber laughed once more. 'How can I forget? I'll call you tomorrow and see how you're settling in.'

'Love you.'

Cumber was pleased to see that the traffic was finally showing signs of freeing up. The bursts of speed between the stops were getting longer. He thought back to the conversation with Kelsey and smiled to himself. Now in his senior years, he was comfortable with the thought that if an attractive lady did happen to come along, it could be purely recreational and did not need to lead to anything serious. There was a time when he used to envy Joe Loxley in his relationship with Janet and wanted to emulate it if the right partner ever came along. Those days had long gone. Through painful experience, he had slowly come to the realisation that he was just not suited to a committed union. And though at times it could be lonely, on balance he found he was happier on his own.

He thought back to his failed marriage. Had he really loved Susan? After all that had happened since, it was difficult to know for sure. Things had seemed good enough in the early years, but when it came, the breakup had not come as a total surprise. Extremely attractive, flirtatious, easily bored; in retrospect, he could see that Susan was never going to go the distance as a long-suffering copper's wife. After the children had reached senior school, she was left on her own for far too long and it was not long before disillusion with a policeman's long, antisocial hours set in. The split was acrimonious and bitter, with Kelsey and Jason unfortunately being caught in the emotional crossfire.

In adulthood, Kelsey had proved the stronger of the two children. Inheriting her mother's stunning good looks, she'd had the intelligence to turn them to her advantage, carving out a career in modelling and bit-part acting in television. Fiercely independent and single-minded, so far she had showed no signs of being interested in long-term relationships. As for her poor brother Jason, he never seemed to get over the split. His life had been one long tale of misery and woe. It started with rebellion, anger and drugs, small-time crime and debt, followed by more drugs, before finally cutting himself from the family. The last Cumber had heard was that he had contacted Kelsey a few months previous and was living in Australia. He had left no contact number. As a consequence, Cumber lived every day in fear of bad news; he could see no other outcome.

*

The evening air was warm and still when Loxley and Phil left the pub. Loxley noticed that there was still a shaft of light on the horizon that gave the summer night sky a tint of inky-blue. Phil had wanted to stay for a third pint, but Loxley declined, preferring to get back to Janet. Looking up into a clear night sky twinkling with stars, Phil was discoursing in some depth the mathematical probabilities of UFOs.

'Did you know that some scientist has come up with a theory that there is a forty-five per cent probability of intelligent life out there?'

Loxley was unimpressed. 'That sounds surprisingly low.'

'You notice I said intelligent life; sixty per cent is the figure for any type of life.'

'That's still surprisingly low.'

Phil looked a bit put out. 'You think so? I do sometimes look at the mess in the world and wonder what the percentage of intelligent life is on this planet.' He pulled a face. '000.1 per cent I reckon.'

Loxley laughed. 'You're an old cynic, Mr Shaw.' His trained eye was immediately drawn to a movement on the opposite side of the road near the bus stop. He couldn't be sure, but it looked like a man who was deliberately keeping himself low-key. A car went past and illuminated the bus stop for just a few seconds. It was enough to give him a good look at the man. What he saw surprised him. It was Roger Turnbull. What was he of all people doing on his own at a bus stop? He was going in the wrong direction if he was going home to Ashurst. Perhaps he'd had a change of heart and decided to join the birthday party in Bournemouth after all. Then he realised that it was well past nine o'clock and the Blue Star bus service had finished an hour ago. What was he doing there? As they walked slowly on, Loxley realised that Phil's conversation had moved on a pace, and he was now waxing lyrical about the mathematical probabilities of a meteorite striking the earth. As they approached the turn into Queens Road, Loxley could not resist one more look back at the bus stop. A black sedan had pulled up at the stop. Loxley could not quite make out the make and model in the gloom. After a short and animated conversation, a back passenger door opened, and Roger Turnbull got in. Loxley's first thought was that he had arranged a lift to take him home, but the car carried on in the opposite direction. It looked like he might be travelling into Bournemouth after all.

Meanwhile, Phil was warming to his subject. 'I make a meteorite strike a one in 1,750 chance, so get your crash helmet on.'

Loxley was still thinking vaguely about this doomsday scenario as he entered his house, before being quickly snapped out of his reverie by Janet telling him that James Cumber had still not arrived.

*

Cumber had finally turned off the M27 and onto the A337 Lyndhurst Road for the final leg of his long and tedious drive. It had been an absolute stinker of a journey! He struggled to remember one that had been worse. He felt hot, tired and hungry. Janet Loxley had assured him in his last phone update that her reheated lasagne would still be fit for consumption. He could not wait to get stuck in! Not surprisingly, the long time spent in the car had aggravated his old injury: his left leg felt stiff and ached like hell. At one stage, he'd had to pop a couple of paracetamol, but it felt like their effect was beginning to wear off.

He tried to take his mind off the pain by focusing his thinking on food, sleep and golf. Then, suddenly and alarmingly, it all happened! Just ahead of him, a car sped out of the Minstead Road on his right and turned widely and recklessly towards him. For a couple of horrific seconds, the headlights of the two vehicles were locked directly onto each other. Cumber's police driving school training kicked in and he instinctively swerved to the left, all the time fully aware that there was a whole bunch of trees just a few feet away on that side. The gap was perilously small as he squealed the brakes and braced himself for impact. Mercifully, there was none! Cumber opened his eyes and looked in the rear mirror to see the red tail lights of the vehicle disappearing speedily into the distance.

He shouted loudly, 'You bastard!'

His car was tilting slightly to the left, so he had some difficulty getting out of the driving seat. After finally managing to scramble out, he leant heavily against the chassis and drew in some deep breaths. He swore several more times in both anger and relief. His limp was more pronounced than normal as he walked round to the passenger side. He noticed the car had slid off the road into a slight dip just a few feet away from a large oak tree. He'd had a close call. Back in the day, it had always been Joe Loxley who had been the driving ace at Scotland Yard. Cumber had the feeling his old boss would have been proud of him.

A car coming from the direction of Lyndhurst stopped on the other side of the road. A middle-aged couple got out.

The man asked, 'Are you alright?'

In explanation, Cumber pointed vaguely in the direction of the Minstead Road.

'Some maniac came out of that turning like he was on a rally. He almost forced me into the trees.'

The man tutted sympathetically and shook his head.

As Cumber limped heavily back round to the driver's side, the woman asked again, 'Are you sure you're OK?'

Cumber realised she was referring to his limp. 'It's alright, it's an old injury. I'm fine.'

Finally satisfied, the couple got back in the car and gave him a concerned wave as they drove off.

As Cumber clambered back into the driver's seat, he muttered to himself, 'It's nice to know that there are still some decent people out there.'

TWO

MURDER UNEXPLAINED

'So you didn't manage to get much of a look at it?' Loxley asked as he handed over another bottle of chilled San Miguel to James Cumber.

'Not a chance, it was all I could do to keep the car on the road. All I know is that it was a big unit, could've been a BMW or a Merc.'

They were all sitting in the Loxleys' spacious lounge after Cumber had done full justice to Janet's warmed-up lasagne. Not for the first time in Cumber's occasional visits to the Loxleys, he looked around him appreciatively. The room was tastefully and comfortably furnished, with just the correct amount of coloured prints adorning the fashionably neutral walls.

Loxley had his detective head on. 'They must have been heading for the M27. With any luck, Pikes Hill might be able to get something on the CCTV, some number-plate recognition.'

Cumber stretched out his stiffened left leg on the

pouf that Janet had thoughtfully provided. What with the long, wearisome journey and the near-fatal collision, he had been feeling pretty rough and not a little shaken up by the time he'd finally arrived at the Loxleys'. Now with a full stomach and enjoying his old friends' company well into the night, he was feeling a lot better. He had taken some more paracetamol and thankfully they were just beginning to kick in. The melodious tunes of the alternative rock band Keane were playing softly in the background.

Thinking back to the incident, Cumber felt an involuntary tightening in his abdomen. 'Wherever they were going, they were certainly in a hurry, that's for sure.'

Loxley sat down next to Janet. 'I'll have a word with Tom Fallon at the station. He might be able to get hold of some footage.'

Janet changed the subject. 'How's Kelsey getting on? I haven't seen her on anything lately.'

Spotting Cumber's daughter playing small parts on the TV was always a pleasurable pastime for both Joe and Janet.

Cumber always felt a sense of pride whenever Kelsey and her small-part TV career came up in the conversation.

'I think she has been doing a bit more modelling recently, though the last time we spoke about it she did say there could be a bigger TV part coming up in the autumn – some new drama.'

Janet could see that Cumber was looking a lot better than when he first arrived. He was obviously enjoying the conversation, so she thought it would do no harm to enhance his feel-good factor.

'I thought she was very good in that series about the supermarket; she came over very natural.'

Cumber looked pleased. 'Do you really think so? She will be chuffed to get that positive feedback, especially coming from you, Janet.'

Janet smiled.

Not for the first time, Cumber was reminded of what a fine-looking woman Janet Loxley was. Even in her seventies, she radiated a handsome elegance; those strikingly blue eyes, which he had always felt were her best feature, still twinkling and alive.

Joe Loxley reflectively swirled his Armagnac around the glass before taking a sip. Over the years, the rich brandy had become his chosen nightcap. He was going to ask James about his troubled son Jason, but he thought better of it. Instead, he chose a subject where he knew he was on safer ground.

'Dare I ask about the golf?'

Cumber let out a resigned sigh. 'I just can't get under sixteen. I think it's too late; I'm going to have to accept it.'

Loxley scoffed. 'Since when have you ever quit a challenge, James? It's unheard of.'

Cumber pointed despairingly at his leg. 'I think I would've got there if it wasn't for this.'

Loxley smiled. 'I bet it's not going to stop you getting down to Ferndown Golf Course while you're here though.'

Cumber grinned and spread out his hands out as if he had no choice. 'It has to be done.'

Loxley suddenly looked serious as he took another sip of his Armagnac. 'I mentioned that there was something I wanted to run past you.'

Cumber remembered the conversation in the car and could not fail to notice Janet's concerned expression.

'I'm all ears.'

Loxley took a deep breath. 'The long and the short of it is that I've been sent a couple of threatening notes, both in the post from Brockenhurst. Pikes Hill is taking a look for dabs and DNA, but the seals were taped so I very much doubt they'll find anything.'

'Just how threatening are they?'

'Nothing too spine-curling, but it looks like it could relate to a past case.'

Cumber questioned, 'But after all this time?'

'It's not unknown… dish served cold and all that.'

'I know, but in this case the revenge must be freezing.'

'It did get me having a look at some old cases in my archives. See if anything jumped out at me.'

'Have you got any ideas?'

Loxley held out his hands. 'Not a blooming Scooby.'

Cumber asked the obvious question, 'Have Pikes Hill offered you any protection?'

'I haven't asked for any so far. At the moment it's purely off the record; even David Jennings doesn't know yet.'

Cumber looked concerned. His old mate was in a tricky situation. It could be some harmless nutcase causing mischief; on the other hand, it could be more sinister, and Joe did have Janet to consider.

'So how're you going to play it?'

Loxley looked across at Janet for support. 'We're going to brazen it out and go about our business as usual. We'll be keeping our eyes open for anything suspicious, of course.'

Cumber nodded his approval. 'I think that's what I would do. Of course, if you get another note or threat, that could be a game changer.'

'I really don't want to put any further strain on police resources if I can help it; they're pretty stretched already.'

Cumber agreed, 'You're not wrong there, Joe, but at the same time, you've more than paid your dues through the years. They owe you big time.'

Janet stood up. 'I'll second that.' She looked at the late hour on the mantelpiece clock. 'I think it's about time we got you two old reprobates to bed. That is, if we have any serious intention of getting up at a reasonable time in the morning.'

She didn't get much argument.

*

Lucy Turnbull swallowed one last spoonful of her muesli breakfast before picking up a glass of freshly chilled orange juice. She was sitting out on the patio overlooking the garden of her large house in Ashurst. Though it was still early morning, the heat was already starting to get up and the sun glared brightly off her white garden gazebo. Her husband Roger had not come home last night. Though he did not make it a habit, it was hardly the first time. What was different on this occasion was that he had not even bothered to give any reason. On his last phone call, he had told her to expect him. She told herself that he had probably changed his mind at the last moment and gone on to Bournemouth to continue celebrating young Ben's twenty-first. When would he realise he was getting far too old for boozy nights out? He was probably sleeping it off somewhere in a hotel bedroom. She had tried ringing him on his mobile several times, but it kept going to voicemail. After one more attempted call with the same result, she eventually gave up and went back inside to shower and get dressed. Though she told herself not to worry, it was not like him. As she went upstairs, she was aware of a pessimistic uneasiness growing in the pit of her stomach.

*

Joe Barnett was not far from finishing off his morning constitutional. He was coming to the end of his walk earlier than usual, as he had made sure to set out before the heat of the sun fully kicked in. It was the same daily route he had taken for many years, but he never tired of it. It never failed to wake him up and get his appetite going. He felt his step quickening at the thought of some cooked breakfast at the café in the village. He was walking through the wooded area alongside the approach road into Minstead when he saw two foxes ahead of him. They seemed to be getting stuck into some carrion or animal carcass, but they scurried away when they heard him approach. On reaching the spot, he came to a startled halt. The shocking sight that he was confronted with caused him to take a sudden intake of breath. At first, he doubted what his eyes were telling him. But there was no doubt about it. It was the body of a man lying face down with a mass of dried blood on the back of his head.

*

'How's the leg holding up?' Loxley asked Cumber as they came to a halt alongside a conveniently fallen log.

'Not too bad. The doc says that the exercise is good for it, but I could do with a break.' He sat down on the log and massaged his leg.

They had been walking in the New Forest for a good hour, so Loxley did not look too displeased as he settled down alongside his old friend. After rising fairly early that morning, they had accompanied Janet on the short walk into Lyndhurst to the charity shop where she worked. Situated at the end of the High Street near the church and just opposite the old Crown Manor House Hotel, the shop was a small but busy outlet which provided a good local social hub for Janet. After leaving Janet in the shop, the two men had retraced their steps and entered the forest. It was a route they both knew well, as it was a regular morning ritual whenever Cumber visited.

They both sat there in silence for a while, enjoying the quiet solitude. The heat was already getting up, so they were more than grateful for the cooling wooded shade that the forest provided.

It was Cumber who finally broke the silence. 'I should do more of this. Get in touch with my inner forest.'

Loxley laughed. 'It would be much less stressful than the golf course.'

'It might improve my golf.'

Loxley nodded. 'Possibly, though I'm not sure you'd find the time for both.'

Loxley pulled out two small bottles of water from his rucksack and handed one over to Cumber.

Cumber took a grateful swill. 'I was sorry I couldn't

make Bill Kemp's funeral, Joe, there was no way I could get to the Cotswolds that week.'

Loxley gave a sad smile. 'I'm sure he would have understood.'

Both he and Janet had managed to get to the funeral at Moreton-in-Marsh a few weeks previously, but it had merely left him feeling guilty that he had not seen enough of his old boss and mentor in the years after his wife Ann died. In his experience, the finality of death often did that; either guilt for things that shouldn't have been done or guilt for things that should've been.

'What year was it that Bill retired?' Cumber asked.

Loxley remembered it well. '1986. It was just after the Marcus Varney case.'

'Oh yeah, I remember it. The old Falklands hero who we saw shot in Oxford. What name did the press label it?'

Loxley didn't hesitate. 'The Oxford Trinity.'

'That's right, three murders.'

'It was a case that certainly left its mark on Bill. There were mistakes made, and it was a real high-profile investigation.'

It was all coming back to Cumber. He remembered a well-known Tory politician being one of the victims. Could it really have been all of thirty-odd years ago?

He commented, 'I remember there not being many bigger cases at the time, that's for sure.'

They were interrupted by the sound of branches and twigs being snapped on the ground behind them. A group of New Forest ponies came out of the trees and trotted purposefully past them. Momentarily fascinated, the two men watched them until they disappeared into the depths of the forest.

Cumber asked, 'Have you had any more thoughts on the threatening notes?'

Loxley's jaw looked set as he stood up and stretched. 'Nope, other than I refuse to be intimidated by them.'

Cumber also rose slowly to his feet and gave Loxley a pat on the back. 'I'm with you all the way on that one.'

Loxley's mobile went off. It was Janet ringing from the shop.

'Hello, Joe, just heard some shocking news.'

'What's that?'

'It's not confirmed, but I've heard that a body has been found in the forest just outside Minstead. They say it could be a shooting.'

'Christ!' Loxley thought instantly of Cumber's near collision in that area the night before and felt a stirring of excitement that he had not felt since his days in the force. 'OK, pet, we'll start making our way back – meet you at the shop.' Loxley put his phone back in his pocket and stared at Cumber. 'Well, James, I've a hunch it's just possible that you might have been in the right place at the wrong time last night.'

*

DCI David Jennings brought his car to a halt beside the blue tapes. DC Paul Mason and PC Matt Packer were talking to a short elderly man, who, judging by his slightly glazed expression, seemed to be in a state of shock. Mason and Packer were dressed in paper suits and masks in the manner of CSIs. Jennings got out of the car and took a paper suit from the boot of his car before climbing into it.

He took a good look around him. Though the road was not overly busy, there were some occasional cars slowing. Not surprisingly, there were curious expressions on the faces of the vehicles' occupants as they passed. Jennings ordered another uniformed officer to regulate and speed up the traffic. He approached DC Mason and PC Packer.

'Tell us the story so far, Paul.'

Mason introduced him to Joe Barnett, the man who had discovered the body. Jennings was looking at a man somewhere in his sixties, pale-lipped and very shaken.

'Sorry we've kept you hanging around this morning, Mr Barnett, but can you tell us how you discovered the body?'

Barnett stuttered slightly as he answered, 'Yes, it was as I was coming to the end of my walk. My attention was taken by two foxes having a nose at something. They ran off as I approached and that's when I saw the body. I immediately rang the police station.'

Jennings turned to PC Packer. 'What time did you get the call, Matt?'

'Around about 8:55 this morning.'

Jennings looked at Joe Barnett. 'That will be all for now, Mr Barnett. We'll need you to come down to Pikes Hill at some stage to make a formal statement.'

He looked at the traumatised figure in front of him with some sympathy. The man's cosy routine existence that he had always known would never be quite the same.

'I bet you could do with a strong coffee.' He turned to the gathering crowd of people from the village standing outside the blue plastic ribbon. 'Can someone see that this man gets a coffee or something stronger?'

There was a brief murmuring amongst the crowd before someone offered to take him back up the road to Minstead.

Jennings glanced at Mason. 'It's time to show me the worst, Paul.'

Mason grimaced. 'I warn you now, it's not a pretty sight.'

They made the short walk to the dead body lying face down on the ground. Jennings could see straight away that it was nasty. He slipped on some latex gloves and examined the horrific wound on the back of the head. There was no doubt it was a one-shot execution. The man had been wearing a light-coloured summer jacket, but the top half was now soaked in dried blood. He slipped his hands into the man's jacket pockets. They were both empty. There was still the possibility that there could be some credit cards in his inside pocket, but at this point he could not disturb the position of the body. The fact that there was no sign of a mobile phone already suggested to Jennings that the man was likely to have been stripped of his ID. He'd heard that was not an unusual occurrence in the case of a professional hit. This whole scenario was beginning to have the look of something very heavy and deadly serious. Crimes like this were not supposed to happen in the New Forest.

He turned back to Paul Mason. 'We'd better get Doc Bowyer down here and the full CSI team.'

*

'You have to admit, James, it's a big coincidence. From the way you describe it, that car was trying to get away from someone or something as quick as possible.' Loxley had to talk loudly over the constant stream of traffic that routinely passed through Lyndhurst. It was midday and Loxley, Janet and Cumber were sitting at a table outside a coffee shop under a shady canopy on the high street. Though no new details of the discovered body had yet been revealed, they were discussing the horrific news that had spread around Lyndhurst like wildfire.

Cumber had to agree, 'They came out of that turning like a bat out of hell. They were definitely getting away from something and almost took me with them.'

Janet took a sip of her coffee before urging caution, 'I don't want you two thinking you're twenty years younger, back in the game, and jumping to the wrong conclusions. Surely it's no hardship to wait a little longer to be doubly sure before you potentially make fools of yourselves.'

Loxley and Cumber looked across at each other and could not help laughing before Loxley said, 'Thanks for the vote of confidence!'

Janet stared back at him as if to say it was no laughing matter.

After a short silence, Loxley took a deep breath. 'Fair enough, we'll wait to spare you any potential embarrassment, but I can bet my bottom dollar that we'll be helping the police with their inquiries at Pikes Hill by the time the day's out.'

*

It was mid-afternoon at Pikes Hill Police Station and DCI Jennings was with DI Ed Farrows, DC Mason and

Doc Bowyer in a small, partitioned workspace situated at the side of the spacious open-plan office. The clunking and sometimes erratic air conditioning in the office was working overtime. The CSI team had completed their work quickly and efficiently in the rising heat and the man's body had already been transported to the mortuary of the Lymington New Forest Hospital.

Doc Bowyer was giving his report. 'I'd say the time of death was anything between 10:00pm last night and 2:00am this morning. I'd say a single bullet to the back of the head from a 22-calibre handgun, probably with an integrated silencer.'

Jennings asked the burning question, 'Obviously a professional hit then?'

The doc nodded. 'It has all the hallmarks.'

It was supposed to have been Ed Farrows' day off, but he had been called in immediately because of the seriousness of the case. He was looking at the case notes.

'So, as yet, we don't have the identity of the victim because there was no trace of any ID or mobile phone found on the body. We should be able to get the DNA, prints and dental records in a day or so. If he is known to us, we should have his ID very soon.'

Jennings agreed, 'It shouldn't take long. The body was dressed quite smartly as though he was going out. Somebody is probably already missing him. On the downside, there's been a little animal activity, so he's not a pretty sight.'

Paul Mason chipped in, 'We've got a couple of officers doing the house to house in Minstead... see if anyone spotted anything. It's going to take some time, as we're spread pretty thin.'

Jennings looked to reassure him. 'This case has a good chance of going higher up the food chain, so you never know. We may get some extra resource.'

*

After Lucy Turnbull finished her phone conversation with her nephew Ben, she felt a desolate morbidity beginning to envelop her. Roger had not gone to Bournemouth to continue Ben's birthday celebrations. Roger's phone had been switched off all morning. She just knew that something bad had happened to him. She steeled herself as she rang Pikes Hill Police Station.

*

It was late afternoon in the Loxley household and Joe was making a cup of tea in the kitchen when the landline rang. Janet and James Cumber were out in the garden, so he answered the phone. He could not help feeling a slight quickening of his pulse when he saw it was from the police station.

'Hello, Joe, it's Tom Fallon.'

'Hi, Tom.'

'Not good news on the forensic, I'm afraid, Joe, nothing on the database that matched. The dabs they did find on the letters probably belonged to the postman.'

Loxley was not surprised. 'Oh well, it was always going to be a long shot. It was pretty obvious the sender was forensically aware.'

'What do you want me to do with them, Joe?'

Loxley hesitated for a moment. He had a strong feeling there were more threats to come.

'It would be appreciated if you could keep them safe for the moment, Tom.'

'No problem, Joe. I suppose you've heard about the shooting last night?'

'I've heard rumours – so it's true?'

'No doubt about it. I'm sure you understand I can't give out too much info yet, Joe, but what I will say is it looks like it could be big.'

'Now you've got me interested.'

'You know it was up on the Minstead Road?'

'I know that much. I assume the victim was a man?'

'You assume correctly.'

'Can you give me an inkling of the time it was supposed to have happened?'

'It was estimated to be around sometime after ten o'clock last night.'

Loxley felt his excitement mounting. 'I take it David Jennings is running with the case?'

'He is so far, though the feeling is it could go higher.'

'I might just have something that could be useful.'

Tom Fallon could tell that Loxley was not joking. 'Really?'

'I've got my old Scotland Yard colleague staying with me, James Cumber. I think he might be able to offer something useful to the investigation.'

'I think you've mentioned his name before, the one that got pensioned off with honours?'

'That's the one. Tell David we'll be calling into the station later this evening.'

'Certainly will, Joe.'

'See you later, Tom.'

Loxley put the phone down and went out into the garden to give the news.

*

Lucy Turnbull was feeling numb and listless after returning to her home from the morgue at Lymington General. PC Sarah Harrison was sitting in her lounge directly opposite her, offering some sensitive policing. Lucy was not even noticing; the policewoman might just as well not have been there. She thought back to when she had reported her husband missing, to the devastating moment when the police had told her that a body had been found at nearby Minstead and was waiting to be identified at the hospital morgue. After being taken to the Lymington hospital by police car, she had eventually managed to identify her husband. But the lifeless, disfigured body lying cold on the slab in front of her bore little resemblance to the man she had spent her life with for the last twenty-five years. Now, sitting back home in her lounge, the stark realisation began to hit. The numbness slowly lifted, and the tears began to flow. Sarah Harrison stood up and put a comforting arm around her shoulders. She sobbed uncontrollably for the next ten minutes before she finally stopped. She'd been told that the police would be coming around to question her when she felt ready. But what could she tell them? A lot of her life with Roger had been as much of a mystery to her as his sudden, brutal death was now. In truth, she was as much in the dark as the police. She knew he was widely respected for his public works and philanthropy. She had certainly never wanted for anything. But against this, she had always felt detached from a large part of his life; a part of his life that had been strictly off limits. She had learnt over the years to accept this and not delve too deeply. It had not been ideal, but they had made it work for them. Until now.

*

'I would never have recognised him.' David Jennings was sitting in the small side office at Pikes Hill talking to Ed Farrows and Paul Mason. It was now late afternoon, and he was still getting over the shock of Roger Turnbull's identification. Though he did not know him well, he had met him on many occasions through the years at countless social gatherings. He remembered him as a smart, good-looking man, even of feature and distinguished. The death mask of the man lying in the morgue had taken all that away from him.

Farrows spoke. 'The big question now is why would a man like Turnbull end up the victim of what looks like a professional hit?'

'To even begin to get the answer to that we'll have to start with the wife. PC Harrison is going to let us know when the poor woman's ready to talk. Unfortunately, the early reports from the CSI boys are not promising. They didn't have much to work with at the murder scene.'

Paul Mason confirmed, 'The execution is what you would expect from a pro killing, pretty much as clean as a whistle.'

Jennings gave it some thought. 'It's looking like one for the Homicide and Major Crimes Unit. Scotland Yard might well want to get involved in this one if they can spare the resource.'

Farrows informed them, 'It's going out this evening on both the regional and national news so someone might come forward and throw some light on it.'

'I don't suppose there's anything interesting yet from the house to house in Minstead?'

Mason shook his head. 'Nothing so far; it's going to take some time.'

Jennings made up his mind. 'I'll have a word with Area Commander Cobbold, see if we can squeeze out some more manpower. After all, it's not every day that we get a fatal shooting in the New Forest.'

They were interrupted by a knock on the door followed by Desk Sergeant Tom Fallon popping his head in.

Jennings beckoned him in, 'Come in, Tom.'

'Sorry to interrupt, sir, but I've just had Joe Loxley on the phone. He thinks he might have something useful regarding the murder.'

For a brief moment, David Jennings looked taken aback. 'Well, I didn't see that one coming. I wonder what he's got for us.'

'We'll soon find out, sir, he says he's coming over tonight with James Cumber.'

Jennings grinned widely. 'Not Cumber his old sidekick. I'm told there was a time at the Yard when they were called "the dynamic duo". Their clear-up rate was seriously impressive.' He turned to Mason and Farrows. 'This case is getting more interesting by the minute.'

*

It was early evening and Loxley, Cumber, Farrows, Mason and Jennings were all packed tightly around the table in the small office space, sipping from cardboard cups of machine coffee.

Jennings could hardly keep the eagerness out of his voice. 'So, Joe, what's this all about?'

Loxley leant forwards. 'Well, am I correct in hearing that the murder was pitched sometime after 10:00pm last night?'

Farrows confirmed, 'That's right.'

Loxley turned to James Cumber. 'Do you want to take it from here, James?'

Cumber then told his story of the near collision the night before, close to the murder site. After he'd finished, Jennings, Mason and Farrows all looked at each other before Jennings spoke.

'It definitely sounds too much of a coincidence. From what you say, you probably didn't get a chance to see what car type?'

Cumber tried to replay the incident back in his head. 'All I can say is that it was big and dark-coloured, probably black, maybe a BMW or a Merc.'

Loxley added, 'It was going towards the M27, so traffic footage is a definite possibility.'

Jennings agreed, 'We'll definitely get onto it.' A sudden thought occurred to him. 'You must have been on more than nodding acquaintance with the victim, Joe, have you got any theories?'

Loxley looked puzzled. 'Remember, David, I'm not in the loop anymore. I've no idea who was murdered.'

Jennings immediately realised that the news that Roger Turnbull was the victim had not quite reached the public domain yet.

'Of course you don't. Sorry, Joe. It was Roger Turnbull.'

Loxley's head reeled for a second before he could get the words out. 'What? I only saw him last night.'

It was Jennings' turn to lean forwards. 'Where was that, Joe?'

'In The Prince—' Loxley stopped abruptly. He recalled the sight of Turnbull at the bus stop looking shifty before getting into the dark sedan: a Merc or a BMW? Then the realisation hit him like a lightning bolt… it must be the same car that James had narrowly avoided crashing into. He went on to tell Jennings of the short conversation in the pub, and the strange episode of seeing him being picked up at the bus stop by the dark sedan.

'What time was that?'

'It would have been around 9:45 last night.'

Jennings looked across at Cumber. 'It's got to be the same car that nearly put you in the ditch.' He asked Loxley, 'How did he seem to you in the pub?'

Loxley thought back. 'I would say pretty relaxed, didn't sense any uneasiness or anxiety.'

DI Farrows asked, 'What did he do for a living exactly?'

Loxley answered, 'That's a good question. He was obviously comfortably off, giving money to good causes and being well-in with the local dignitaries.'

Jennings enquired, 'Was he a mason of some sort? He seems to have all the right credentials.'

Loxley shrugged. 'Now that's something I wouldn't know, but I see your thinking.'

Jennings looked at the clock on the wall and turned to Ed Farrows. 'Can you get in touch with PC Harrison and see if the wife is ready to talk to us?'

Farrows gave a nod and left the office.

Jennings could not help shaking his head as he looked at Loxley and Cumber.

'Looks like you two have still got the old magic. What were the odds of the two of you seeing the suspect car in different places on the same night?'

Loxley laughed. 'Johnnies-on-the-spot, I guess.'

Jennings could not help giving a brief smile before adopting a more serious expression.

'It's blindingly obvious that this killing has all the hallmarks of some heavy stuff. There's more than a good chance that your old Scotland Yard successors could be called into the investigation.'

Farrows poked his head into the office and interrupted. 'The wife's ready to see us, sir.'

Jennings stood up. 'Good news. Now let's see if we can get to the bottom of it.' A thought occurred to him. 'Did you know the wife, Joe?'

'I've met her a few times.'

'Fancy a trip to Ashurst? Be nice to get your input. No pressure.'

Loxley hesitated. He was sorely tempted but with the recent bit of trouble at home, he was reluctant to leave Janet alone for too long.

Cumber picked up that his old partner was conflicted and read his thoughts.

'Go for it, Joe, I'll get back and keep the home fires burning.'

Loxley looked relieved. 'If that's OK with you, James?'

Cumber put his hands up. 'No problem. Means I'll get the bigger portions of Janet's cooking,' he added with a smile.

Loxley laughed. 'Try to leave some for me, you gannet.'

David Jennings further reassured him as they rose to leave the office, 'It shouldn't take too long, Joe.'

*

'Take your time, Mrs Turnbull, we're not here to make things any more distressing than they already are.' David Jennings spoke soothingly. He was seated in the spacious lounge of Roger Turnbull's house, along with Ed Farrows, PC Sarah Harrison and Joe Loxley. Jennings repeated his question, 'So it was around seven o'clock yesterday evening that Roger left the house?'

Lucy Turnbull dabbed at her red-rimmed eyes with a handkerchief and nodded. 'He was getting a lift to the pub in Lyndhurst for young Ben's twenty-first. His friend Jack Foster picked him up. He never liked to use the car when he knew he would be drinking.'

Ed Farrows was writing it down. 'So Ben is your nephew?'

She nodded again. 'Roger knew that Ben was likely to go on to Bournemouth afterwards, but he told me he wasn't interested and said he'd be home before midnight.'

Jennings pressed on gently, 'So were you concerned when he failed to get home by twelve?'

'No, not really. He was always changing his mind. He was a law unto himself in that way.'

'When did you start to worry?'

'When I woke up around four o'clock in the morning and realised he was still not home, and he'd left no message. It was not unusual for him to stay the night somewhere else, but he would always let me know when that happened and where he was. After waking, I tossed and turned for the next couple of hours but couldn't get back to sleep.'

'What did you do then?'

'I got up and rang his phone, but it kept going to voicemail. I think I left a couple of frustrated messages. It was then that I started to get a bad feeling that something was seriously wrong. I tried to kid myself that he had gone on to Bournemouth and had been out on a bender. It was after lunchtime that I finally managed to speak to Ben and found out that Roger had left the pub early. That was when I rang Pikes Hill Station.'

'Can you give me any idea of his movements throughout the day? Anyone he may have met up with?'

'No, whenever he was working he was always up and out the door by seven; yesterday was no different. He came home earlier than usual because he was going to Ben's drink.'

'What time was that?'

'Around five o'clock.'

'There was no sign of either Roger's mobile phone or credit cards at the crime scene. Can you give us a list of bank account details so that we can shut them down?'

She started crying again before saying, 'I honestly don't know them, he was always so secretive with his financial affairs.'

Farrows looked up from his notes in surprise. 'You mean to say you don't know any of his financial accounts?'

She dabbed her eyes again and nodded. 'I only have my own account which he credited every week.'

Jennings requested compassionately, 'Of course, we will also need the details of your account Mrs Turnbull.'

She stood up. 'I'll get them for you. I think my handbag is out in the hallway.'

She stood up unsteadily and left the room. Loxley swiftly took the opportunity to contribute some info.

'I did see Jack Foster in The Prince last night, so that part of the story definitely checks out.'

Farrows made a gesture towards the hallway. 'It certainly sounds like she gave him a free rein on the money side.'

Jennings nodded. 'I suppose she was happy as long as he kept feeding the account.' He quickly stopped talking as Lucy came back into the room. She had a plastic bank card in her hand. Farrows took it from her and wrote down the details.

Jennings waited for her to sit down before he asked the million-dollar question. 'What did Roger actually do for a living?'

Again she appeared close to tears as she answered, 'I know it sounds pathetic on my part, but I really don't know. He never ever volunteered any information, and he certainly never gave me any answers when I asked him. He would just say that he did deals. I'm pretty certain that a lot of his business was to do with the property market. It did cause some rows in the early days but in the end I just got tired of asking. I could never have any complaints about the lifestyle he's provided for me. In the end, the arguments didn't seem worth the energy.'

Joe Loxley looked around the room. Softly carpeted and immaculately furnished with ornate mirrors, porcelain figurines and a sixty-inch flat-screen TV, there was no arguing that Roger Turnbull had done well for himself. Was it shrewd financial judgement or ill-gotten gains? He would have liked to have been wrong, but the cloistered mystery and secrecy around his work and his mysterious death strongly suggested it could well be the latter.

Jennings asked, 'Did Roger possess a laptop?'

'There was a time when he did have one in his study, but in more recent years he worked away from home more often, so he had no need for one here.'

'Can we take a look in the study, Mrs Turnbull?'

'Roger cleared it out fairly recently; there's not much in there now, just an empty desk and a chair. I was thinking of converting it into an extra utility room.'

'We'll take a quick look all the same, if you don't mind.'

Lucy stood up and led them all through to the study. She then left them alone and returned to PC Harrison, who had stayed seated in the lounge. The study was pretty much exactly as Lucy had described, just an empty desk and a chair. Jennings had a good look inside the drawers, which were all empty. Just as he had concluded that there was nothing to see, Loxley drew his attention to what looked like the top of a sheet of paper that had somehow lodged in the chair between the cushioned seat and the wooden frame. Jennings carefully extricated the paper and gave it some scrutiny. It was an article about property prices in the New Forest that appeared to have been torn from the local *Daily Echo*. Some of the lines and details in the article appeared to have been highlighted by a marker pen.

Jennings looked at Loxley and gave a brief smile. 'Good spot, Joe, this is exactly why I brought you along. It seems to confirm Mrs Turnbull's claim that he was interested in the property game.' He handed it over for Loxley to read.

Loxley put on his reading glasses and gave it some close examination. The highlighted sections seemed to consist of projected property prices in the less prosperous areas in the New Forest.

He commented, 'It definitely looks like Roger was up for a bit of property speculation.'

Jennings gave it another brief glance. 'Might well be significant, you never know.' He took it from Loxley and handed it over to Ed Farrows, who placed it in a small forensic receptacle.

The three men rejoined Lucy and Sarah Harrison in the lounge and remained standing as Jennings proceeded, 'Do you have any idea where Roger conducted his business when working away from home?'

Lucy blew her nose and looked up with watery eyes. 'He travelled around, but I'm pretty sure in recent times he had an office somewhere in Lymington.'

'Did he have any close friends, or did you ever meet any of his business associates?'

She looked in deep thought. 'He was always well connected. We went to many functions. There were always doctors, lawyers and businessmen with their wives, but I wouldn't describe any of them as close friends. I think he had a few casual golfing friends at the Ferndown club.'

'I want you to think carefully before you answer, Mrs Turnbull. Can you think of anyone who would possibly wish to do your husband harm?'

She was quite definite in her answer. 'I can't think of anybody. He may not have had many close friends, but there were loads of acquaintances. He was generally very well liked due to his generous donations to charity.'

'Are his parents still alive?'

Lucy shook her head. 'No, they've both passed away in the last two years. He does have a brother who lives in Canada. I will have to let him know.'

'PC Harrison is here to help you with that, Mrs Turnbull, if you need her.'

Lucy smiled wanly and nodded her appreciation.

Jennings had noticed a shiny new three-door hatch Mini on the drive when they arrived. He guessed it belonged to Lucy Turnbull and not Roger.

Jennings asked, 'Is Roger's car in the garage, Mrs Turnbull?'

'Yes, he never liked to leave it out in the open when he wasn't using it.'

'Have you got the keys so we can take a look at it?'

She got up and went through to the kitchen where the keys were hanging up on a hook. Having hold of the keys which Roger had only recently held seemed to upset her once more as she handed them over to Ed Farrows.

Jennings asked, 'Have you any relations you can stay with for a few days?'

She spoke through her tears, 'There's my sister who lives in Lyndhurst, that's Ben's mum. She might come and stay with me for a few days.'

Jennings turned to Sarah Harrison. 'Can you see if you can get something sorted, Sarah?'

Harrison stood up. 'I'll get on it, sir.'

Just a few minutes later, Joe Loxley stood nearby in the garage and watched as Ed Farrows and David Jennings gave the gleaming silver-grey Mercedes a good going-over. They had been surprised to find the boot was totally empty, but Farrows' search of the glove compartment had been more fruitful. After removing a logbook, torch and what looked like a box of pills, he then reached into the netted pocket at the back of the driver's seat. He pulled out what appeared to be a mobile phone that was still covered in its plastic wrapping. It did not appear to be Turnbull's normal mobile. He showed it to Jennings, who told him to include it with the other items in his forensic bag.

*

On the short drive back to Loxley's house, David Jennings and Joe Loxley were discussing the case.

'So, you really think that Lucy Turnbull was telling the whole truth regarding Turnbull's affairs? It's a bit of a stretch.'

Loxley sounded definite. 'I know it's hard to believe, but I think I do. She may have had her suspicions, but in my experience it's not the first time I've seen a well-kept partner being kept in the dark by her husband. The one thing we know for sure is that Roger Turnbull is someone who keeps his affairs very close to his chest and has secrets. You don't need me to tell you that those secrets will only be revealed by digging deep into his known associates.'

Jennings nodded. 'We need to get our hands on his business dealings. We might even need to get the fraud squad involved. That new mobile phone in the back of the seat could well be a crucial find and maybe give us some answers.'

Loxley agreed, 'That discovery certainly opens up a few possibilities. Then there's this office tucked away somewhere in Lymington. If you can find out what went on there, you could be more than halfway to solving the murder.'

Jennings sounded a little excited. 'This case is certainly a step up from the usual crime we deal with in these parts, that's for sure. We'll take a look at the camera footage on the M27, see if they picked up any sign of the car that drove James off the road.'

They pulled up outside Loxley's house in Queens Road. The night had drawn in and the lights in the house presented a welcome sight.

Jennings assured Loxley, 'Don't worry, Joe, I'll keep you in the loop now I've given you a taster.'

As Loxley got out of the car, he answered, 'Thanks, David, I'd appreciate that.'

As the car pulled away, Loxley's attention was taken by a distant figure walking swiftly away in the gloom at the end of the street. Once again, he got that uneasy feeling. Was he being paranoid or was he justified in being suspicious?

He took a deep breath. It had been a long day.

THREE
DEEP WATERS

James Cumber was having a restless night. He had woken several times after having a recurring nightmare of cars speeding towards him. The near collision had obviously disturbed him more than he realised and had rekindled old memories and images – memories and images he preferred to forget! After Joe Loxley had returned home that evening, his old partner had given him a brief account of the police visit to Lucy Turnbull, including the discovery of the suspicious phone in Turnbull's car and the secretiveness and mystery surrounding his business dealings. Now lying there restlessly in bed, he was turning it all around in his head. He finally sat up and searched for his mobile to get the time. It was two o'clock in the morning. The night was very warm, and he felt hot and thirsty. He got out of bed and quietly made his way downstairs to the kitchen. His ageing eyes had a little trouble adjusting to the shadowy half-light as he made his way to the sink and poured himself a long glass of water. He gulped it down eagerly until his thirst was quenched. He looked out onto the Loxleys' garden through the window above the sink. It was a still evening and there was nothing stirring in the leaves and bushes that bordered the garden in the gloomy twilight. He could easily have stood there for longer, but it was his intention to get to Ferndown Golf Course in the morning, so he felt he needed to get more sleep. As he turned to go back to bed, his eye caught a movement at the window that ran along the side of the house. It had only been fleeting and he could not be sure. He went to the window and stared out into the darkness. All was still and there was nothing to see. After standing there for a couple of minutes, he decided it was either his eyes playing tricks or his overactive imagination was going into overdrive. He needed some sleep. He slowly made his way back upstairs to the bedroom.

*

It was early Saturday morning at Lyndhurst Police Station and DCI Jennings was standing in front of the whiteboard in the boardroom at Pikes Hill. Listening attentively were DI Ed Farrows, DC Paul Mason, PC Sarah Harrison, PC Matt Packer and Dr Harry Bowyer. David Jennings looked at his small, tightly knit team and knew that they were well under the numbers needed for such a major investigation. He had already spoken to the Area Commander/Chief Superintendent Doug Cobbold, and it sounded promising that there would be some extra resource going forwards. Because of the seriousness and manner of the crime, a DI from the Major Crimes squad in Scotland Yard was also coming down to aid in the investigation. A number of points raised by the inquiries so far occupied the whiteboard but as yet there was not too much to go on.

Jennings took a final swig of his coffee and began proceedings.

'We've identified the victim as Roger Turnbull, a man well regarded in the New Forest community who lived in Ashurst. The fact that he appeared to be stripped of his money cards and there was no sign of his mobile phone has immediately set the alarm bells ringing. The manner of his death suggests it has all the hallmarks of a professional hit, which I think you can confirm, Harry?'

Doc Bowyer stood up. 'No doubt about it. A single shot to the back of the head from a 22-calibre handgun, probably fitted with an integrated silencer. Time of death anything between 10:00pm on Thursday evening and 2:00am in the morning.'

Jennings went on, 'We spoke to his wife, who told us that he left the house that evening at seven o'clock to go for a drink at The Prince in Lyndhurst to celebrate his nephew's twenty-first birthday. It has been confirmed since by eyewitnesses that he was seen in the pub in the early part of that evening. According to his nephew, he left the pub early at around nine o'clock. A reliable witness then saw him around forty-five minutes later getting into a dark sedan near a bus stop in the Southampton Road. Another witness who was driving towards Lyndhurst had to narrowly avoid a collision with a dark-coloured vehicle which was either a Merc or a BMW about fifteen minutes later. According to the witness, the car was being driven very fast and recklessly as it emerged out of the Minstead Road, just a few hundred yards from where the body was found. It seems pretty obvious that it was the same car that picked up Turnbull in the Southampton Road. We thought we might find some CCTV footage of the car on the M27 junction for some number-plate recognition, but unfortunately the cameras have failed to come up with anything. At this point we must assume that the car doubled back through the forest, probably using the Beechwood Road. The big question we're left with is why would an apparently respectable figure like Roger Turnbull end up at the wrong end of a hitman's gun? His wife states that she had no idea what he got up to in his business dealings, though she was pretty sure it had something to do with the property market. She also told us that there is possibly an office tucked away somewhere in Lymington. We simply have to find it.'

Ed Farrows put his hand up. 'We know that Turnbull was given a lift to the pub that night by a fellow called Jack Foster, who we believe works as a local councillor. He could be a good starting point.'

Jennings approved. 'Get on it.' He looked over some further reference points on the whiteboard before asking, 'Anything further on the pills we found in Turnbull's car, Ed?'

'Not had it confirmed by the lab yet, but there is every sign they are amphetamines.'

'So it could be he felt he needed something to keep him alert and up to the mark twenty-four seven, though nothing was flagged up by the pathologist in the official post-mortem.' He turned to Sarah Harrison. 'Get back to Lucy Turnbull, Sarah, and ask if she was ever aware of him using uppers.'

Sarah nodded and wrote down some notes.

Jennings looked towards Paul Mason. 'I believe you have something interesting for us, Paul?'

Mason stood up. 'Yes, sir, we've checked out Lucy Turnbull's Lloyds bank account this morning. It seems it was fed with a cash deposit of around £1000 on a regular basis by Turnbull in Lymington.'

'Interesting, all roads seem to be leading to Lymington. It certainly looks to be the hub of his activity. Anything else, Paul?'

'We've had a good look at the adverts that were highlighted in the newspaper cuttings that were found in Turnbull's study. There's no doubt it seems to highlight properties at the lower end of the market. Hopefully this throws some light on the type of properties he liked to invest in.'

Jennings looked satisfied. 'All sounds good, Paul. I also want you to look into his charity work, see if we can get some idea where his money was coming from.' He turned back to address everyone in the room. 'I think we can all agree from the manner of his sudden and violent death that there's another side to Turnbull which he kept well hidden. This brings us neatly to the new, unused mobile phone found in Turnbull's car. His wife had no idea why it was there. We must ask ourselves, why would a man like Turnbull feel the need for a private pay-as-you-go phone? I think if we get the answer to that one, we're more than halfway there.'

Ed Farrows reasoned, 'A secretive man like Turnbull could have any number of reasons to have a throwaway phone. It's totally in character from what we know of him so far.'

Jennings could see the logic. 'Who knows what he needed it for. For the moment, we'll keep an open mind. In the meantime we've got to put all our efforts into finding that office in Lymington.' He looked at PC Matt Packer. 'Have you got anything to add, Matt?'

'We're still completing the house to house, sir, but so far nobody heard anything on the evening of the shooting. Unfortunately, it's looking like we're going to draw a blank. There was one resident who said he'd been vaguely aware of a vehicle parked off the road as he drove past the murder scene at around ten o'clock that night. The officers did try to pin him down on more detail, but he said it was too dark and he hadn't taken much notice.'

Jennings shook his head. 'That's a shame; little did he know it, but he was probably passing around the time the dirty deed was being done.' He clapped his hands. 'OK, team, get to it. Remember to use your initiative and if you get any leads, be sure to let me know immediately.'

*

'Are you sure we are all secure at the back?' Joe Loxley asked Janet as they were about to exit the house.

Janet reassured him as she handed over the keys. 'I've got it all under control, don't worry.'

It was their usual routine to fit in a stroll to Lyndhurst High Street on a Saturday morning before getting back to receive their Waitrose home delivery service just after midday. James Cumber had already left the house earlier that morning to make his way to Ferndown Golf Club near Bournemouth. Going by his past golfing visits to

Ferndown, that usually meant they would not be seeing him again until the late afternoon. They stepped out of the front door into the hot sunshine. Loxley enjoyed feeling the warmth on his back as he turned to lock the door.

Janet's attention was caught by what looked like a shoebox placed next to a pot plant at the side of the doorway.

'I wasn't expecting any deliveries.'

Just as she went to pick up the box, she heard Loxley's raised voice warning her not to touch it. He warily bent down to pick it up. The box felt light, but it definitely contained something. He slowly pulled off the lid. His nostrils were immediately hit by a rancid stench as he found himself staring at the putrid carcass of a decomposing rat. He rushed to the bin at the side of the house before Janet could get a glimpse.

Janet called after him, 'What was it?'

Loxley returned to her side before speaking. 'I think it's a sick present from our note writer.'

Janet looked at him questioningly.

Loxley realised he had to tell her. 'The box contained a dead rat.'

Janet pulled an expression of disgust. 'Charming. It must have been placed there overnight.'

Loxley felt a mixture of emotions. Certainly anxiety and repugnance, but also a seething anger.

'I swear I'm going to get to the bottom of this.'

Janet could see his rage and instinctively put her arm around him. 'Come on, the High Street can wait, let's go back inside and I'll put on a cuppa.'

Loxley managed to laugh through his tension. 'Where would we be without a cup of tea?'

Janet smiled and gently coaxed him back towards the front door. 'You know it's the cure for all ills; people who were around in World War Two were convinced it was our secret weapon against Hitler's bombs.'

*

'So you've still not heard anything about your promotion to DC?' asked DI Ed Farrows. Farrows and PC Sarah Harrison were making the short drive to Emery Down, about a mile north of Lyndhurst. Though it was a Saturday morning, and the council would normally have been closed, they had been lucky and managed to track down Jack Foster's address from one of his more diligent associates who'd been putting in some overtime at the offices in Beaulieu Road.

Sarah pulled a face. 'I thought I was going to hear something this weekend, but all this business has put it on the backburner.'

Farrows offered some words of encouragement. 'There's no doubt that David Jennings is getting you more involved. For instance, he asked me to take you along today. I reckon you'll be hearing something pretty soon.'

'I hope so. I could really do with the salary increase right now. Everything seems to be getting so expensive.'

Farrows smiled sympathetically. 'You can never have enough money, that's for sure.'

After turning off the A35, they joined a narrow winding road that meandered through the forest before passing over a cattle grid and coming to a stop in front of a large, white, detached house made more vivid by the bright sunlight. It was an old house, but you could see that it had been refurbished and extended to a high specification. They had deliberately not told Jack Foster they were coming, as they wanted an element of surprise. They had taken a chance on him being home. His gleaming white Lexus parked on the driveway suggested they were in luck. They got out of the car and approached the front door. Ed Farrows thought he briefly noticed a face at the upstairs window just before he rang the bell. The two officers looked appreciably around them as they waited at the door. The heat of the day was getting up, but the shaded trees and remoteness of the building seemed to provide a refreshing serenity. The mood was broken a good minute later as the door was answered by a small, plain-looking man with a shock of dark curly hair. He looked a little flustered. Ed Farrows introduced himself and flashed his warrant card.

Foster sounded a little agitated as he led them through to a spacious lounge framed with timber beams painted brilliant white.

'I thought it was my wife returning from shopping in the town. Should you have told me you were coming?'

Farrows apologised, 'Sorry we caught you on the hop, Mr Foster, but we were just passing and hoped we would catch you on the off chance.'

He offered them a seat. 'I take it this is about Roger? I still can't quite take it in.'

Both Farrows and Sarah sat down on a large comfortable sofa. Farrows started the questions as Sarah took out her notebook.

'Roger Turnbull's wife has told us that you gave him a lift to The Prince on Thursday night.'

'That's right, we were celebrating his nephew's birthday.'

'We've heard he left early. Did you leave with him?'

Seeming to regain some composure, Foster sat down on the chair opposite. 'Yes, we both left together. He did not fancy extending the celebrations by going on to Bournemouth afterwards.'

'What time was that?'

'Just after nine I think.'

'Did you leave him outside the pub?'

'No, we went and had a coffee at the Greenwood in the high street.'

'How long were you there?'

'It was about half an hour or so. I would usually give him a lift home on the rare occasions we went to the pub, but he said he'd already got one laid on. I left him outside the Greenwood.'

'How did he seem? Did you get the impression anything was troubling him?'

'Not at all, he seemed in his usual good form.'

'Would you describe him as a good friend?'

Foster's sharp features creased in thought. 'Not really. It's a funny thing, though we always got on well, I never really felt I got to know him totally. Roger liked to keep people at a distance.'

'How long have you actually known him?'

'We go back quite a few years. I think I first met him at the Ferndown Golf Club. Then our paths would regularly cross at charity functions. He was interested in the property business, so occasionally his name would crop up at council meetings. We did very occasionally meet socially for a pint at The Prince. Well, I say "we", but I'm on the wagon so I would normally pick him up and drop him off back home. That was what made Thursday night unusual!'

Ed Farrows leant forwards. 'Do you know where Roger conducted most of his business?'

'I cannot be sure, but I got the impression that he did most of it out of a small office somewhere in Lymington.'

'You've never been there?'

'No, can't say that I have.'

Farrows sounded disappointed. 'So you wouldn't know the address?'

'No, I don't. That's what I mean about Roger: he liked to keep a lot of his affairs to himself.'

'There must be some records of his property transactions at the council offices?'

'I'm sure there must be.'

'Did you ever suspect that he may have taken amphetamines?'

'It never came up in conversation; though now you mention it, I wouldn't be totally surprised. He was restless, always chasing the next deal. It was like oxygen to him.'

Ed Farrows stood up. 'The manner of his death must have come as a big shock to you, Mr Foster.'

'As I said, I don't think it's fully sunk in to be honest.'

Foster got up as Farrows and Sarah rose and made their way to the door.

Farrows informed him, 'We may need to question you further, Mr Foster, but in the meantime, if anything occurs to you that might throw some light on it, be sure to let us know.'

For a brief moment, a questioning look flashed across Foster's brow, but he then nodded and followed them to the door.

As they got back in the car, Farrows glanced across at Jack Foster's expensive vehicle parked on the drive before asking Sarah Harrison for her opinion on Foster.

Sarah thought carefully before she answered. 'He was one of the last to see Turnbull alive and his looks are a bit shifty, but his shock seems genuine enough.'

Farrows started the car. 'Either that or he's one cool customer. Would he have voluntarily come forward if we hadn't dropped a visit today? I'm not so sure. We'll keep a close eye on him. What we do know about Turnbull is that he was one dark horse. So far we haven't even found anyone who knows where his Lymington office is.'

'Going by the timeline when Foster says they parted outside the coffee shop, it could only have been about fifteen minutes or so before Joe Loxley's sighting of Turnbull getting in the black sedan.'

Farrows nodded. 'Turnbull obviously had that liaison already arranged. What we do know is, after getting in the car, the poor bugger never made it home. Very mysterious.'

They joined the A35 and headed back to Pikes Hill.

Back at the house, Jack Foster was still standing at the window where he had watched the police car drive off. He felt distinctly uneasy. The police would surely be digging into Roger's property dealings. Up to now, he had always ensured that nothing could ever lead back to him. He had never asked what Roger actually did with the property information he regularly gave him, though he had always thought the benefits must be purely financial. Now, in view of what had happened, he was not so sure. It had never occurred to him that Roger was maybe involved in darker, more sinister activities. What he did know was that his long association with Roger had proved highly lucrative through the years, particularly in the last year. On that last fateful evening in the Greenwood coffee shop, Roger had mentioned that the rewards might not be so generous going forward. At the same time, Roger had been at pains to assure him that he would continue to make things worth his while. Roger had turned down his offer of a lift that night and was obviously meeting someone before going home. Shockingly, he had ended up in the forest with a bullet in his head. Why? Foster felt a cold shiver go down his spine.

*

James Cumber was having a good day. Everything had gone surprisingly well on the Ferndown Golf Course. Even though it had been hot out there on the course, the air had somehow felt fresher and less stifling than back home in Chigwell. Even his gammy leg had behaved itself. The golf he had produced had reflected that feel-good factor. It was the best he had played for quite some time; one of those days when the club and ball contact feels as sweet as a nut and the greens run true and firm. He was now sitting in the clubhouse bar enjoying a half pint of Moretti with a cheese and pickle sandwich. The clubhouse was beginning to get quite noisy as the players gradually returned from the course, discussing their best shots and giving their bad luck stories. He sat there amused for a while, overhearing some of the conversation and enjoying the ambience. He remembered that he had a meal booked that evening with the Loxleys at Janet's favourite Italian restaurant. He looked at his watch; it was still only mid-afternoon so there was no need to rush. He eventually got up and went to the bar to order a Moretti shandy. While waiting to be served, he was recognised by a club member who remembered him from his previous occasional visits to Ferndown.

The man, somewhere in his fifties, tall with thinning grey hair, came forwards offering his hand.

'It is James, isn't it?'

Cumber instantly recognised the familiar face and shook the man's hand. He even recalled the man's name.

'It's good to see you, Gordon.'

The man nodded, obviously pleased Cumber remembered him.

Cumber continued the charm offensive. 'It's been a while; how are you?'

'Not so bad.' He looked at Cumber's empty glass. 'Here, I'll get this, what you having?'

Cumber put up a token resistance before accepting Gordon's generous offer. A few minutes later, the two men were standing together at the bar with their drinks replenished. They talked golf for a while before Gordon adopted a conspiratorial manner and changed the subject.

'So, James, if I remember correctly, you mentioned you were an ex-policeman?'

Cumber was initially caught by surprise but realised he must have let slip his old profession in previous conversations.

'You have a very good memory, Gordon, I'll say that for you.'

Gordon moved closer and lowered his voice. 'Well then, what do you think about this shooting of Roger Turnbull? The club is still reeling from the shock of it, I can tell you.'

From the previous night's conversation with Joe Loxley, Cumber knew that Turnbull had been known to play golf at Ferndown.

'Was he a fully paid-up member here?'

Gordon looked surprised at the question. 'You must remember him; he sometimes used to join us for a drink.'

Cumber racked his brains until the mist gradually cleared, and he remembered the smooth, good-looking figure that would sometimes join them in the clubhouse conversations.

'Of course, Roger. It just never occurred to me that he was the Roger that was murdered.'

A small, somewhat portly, sandy-haired man came over and joined them. Gordon introduced him to Cumber as Pete, before pursuing the conversation on Turnbull.

'There was always something of a mystery about Roger that I could never quite put my finger on.'

Pete joined in. 'Taciturn Turnbull we used to call him, the man with a thousand secrets. The only thing you could be sure about was that he was absolutely minted.'

Cumber spoke, 'They say he was big on property.'

Pete confirmed, 'Oh yes, he was very successful in property development, he used to run it from a small office in Lymington. I bumped into him once as he was coming out of one of the old houses in New Street just off Lymington High Street. I can remember him being friendly enough, but I somehow got the impression that he was not overly pleased that I had seen him.'

Cumber remembered Joe Loxley mentioning the mystery office in Lymington and the detective in him began to spark.

'He was definitely coming out of a house?'

'No doubt about it, one of the red-brick terrace houses.'

Cumber made a mental note of the street name.

Gordon asked once more, 'So, come on, James, have you got a theory?'

As Cumber moved towards the bar to buy his round, he tapped his nose and gave a knowing smile.

'Not just yet, but I'm working on it.'

*

DI Keith Simpson from the Major Crimes squad in Scotland Yard listened intently as David Jennings brought him up to speed with the investigation into the murder of Roger Turnbull. They were both sitting in the small side partition that passed for an office at Pikes Hill Police Station. Simpson had arrived from London that Saturday afternoon and had wasted no time in getting his first briefing. When Jennings finally came to the end of his update, the DI from Scotland Yard sat there in silence for some time as he perused the case notes. Jennings had heard on the grapevine that Simpson could be a man of few words, but he could not help feeling a restless impatience as the detective finally looked up from the notes and stared straight ahead, lost in thought. Though Jennings outranked him and was still officially in charge of the case, the extra authority that Scotland Yard held seemed to give Simpson an added gravitas.

Simpson finally spoke, 'Turnbull sounds like a jigsaw puzzle with a lot of the pieces missing. You say he's a generous contributor to charities?'

Jennings confirmed, 'Very generous; it's mainly what he was known for.'

Simpson looked unimpressed. 'It's not unusual. It's what rich people with something to hide often do. It gives them a respectable front and makes them look good.'

'He was certainly very well respected in the New Forest community.'

'Well, I strongly suspect that when we scratch under that respectable veneer, we'll find a pile of shit.'

Jennings leant back from the table. 'As things stand, I can't disagree with you.'

Simpson returned to the case notes. 'The unused mobile and violent death suggests he was into something pretty heavy. I see that two of your key witnesses are retired Scotland Yard men, Joe Loxley and James Cumber.'

Jennings smiled. 'Now that was a lucky break.'

Simpson agreed, 'Pretty extraordinary and a fortunate coincidence, I must admit. I knew them both in my early years at the Yard. They were both good men; I had a lot of regard for Joe Loxley in particular.' He stood up from the table. 'Turnbull was obviously up to something when Loxley saw him getting in the car; it's now our job to find out just what that something was.'

Jennings also stood up. 'I've heard you're staying at the Crown Hotel while you're here.'

'That's correct. I've heard good reports.'

'Oh yeah, you can't go wrong there, I strongly recommend the house wines.'

Simpson looked deadpan as he stood up and gave David Jennings a censorious stare.

'Oh no, DCI Jennings, I never drink on an investigation. I always find a clear head is what's needed in this situation. I'll report back in the morning, if that's OK.'

It was to be sometime after Simpson had left the building before David Jennings finally calmed down and stopped cursing the pompous git from Scotland Yard.

*

James Cumber had just polished off his ravioli and was downing his third Peroni as he gave a detailed account of his excellent round of golf earlier in the day. Joe and Janet Loxley shared his obvious delight and did their best to listen attentively to the finer points. They were enjoying a pleasurable evening in Janet's favourite Italian restaurant, which was just a short walk from their house. Janet and Joe were finishing off their spaghetti with seafood as Cumber relived his birdie on the sixteenth hole.

'It's such a great feeling when that ball goes just where you want it too.'

Joe Loxley finished off his second Peroni before asking, 'So, how many times do you have to repeat that performance before your handicap gets officially marked down?'

Cumber laughed ironically. 'Only about ten times. Don't worry, that's just not going to happen. I just make sure I enjoy these rare days when they come along.'

Though a little on the warm side, the ambience in the restaurant was pleasant and lively, with just the correct amount of people and noise. The waiter approached and Joe and Janet ordered a tiramisu, while Cumber settled for a banoffee pie.

Janet took a sip of her Villa Rossi before nudging Joe to mention the unpleasant incident with the shoebox that morning. Without going into too much graphic detail, Loxley recounted the story.

Cumber looked suitably outraged. 'This can't go on, Joe, it's all getting too close for comfort.'

Loxley put his hands out. 'But what can I do? Pikes Hill already has its hands full with the Turnbull case.'

Cumber remembered his nocturnal visit to the kitchen from the night before and his suspicion of a movement outside the window. At the time, he had thought it was his eyes playing tricks but now he was not so sure. He thought it best not to mention it as he did not want to alarm Janet.

'Well, I think David Jennings should be made aware of it at least, Joe.'

Loxley looked across at Janet, who nodded in agreement. He gave in.

'I'll mention it the next time I see him. Talking of which, I bet he was well pleased when you dropped in on him today with your valuable intel.'

After learning of the possible whereabouts of Turnbull's Lymington office from the conversation at the golf club, Cumber had called in to Pikes Hill on his way back to the Loxleys'. He had originally found David Jennings to be in a foul mood when he first arrived, but the DCI noticeably cheered up when he had given the potential street name where Turnbull conducted his business. He had even given Cumber his email contact in case he came up with some other nuggets.

'He was not in the best form when I arrived, to be honest, something about the guy they've sent down from Scotland Yard. I don't think he liked him.'

'I don't suppose he told you his name?'

'No, he didn't give much detail; he was too interested in what I had to say.'

'It was good work on your part, James. I think David needs all the help he can get with this case. It's a crime full of puzzling and surprising uncertainties. Before your valuable input today, I think the only certain thing the police had found out so far was that Turnbull was a sly old fox.'

Cumber looked reflective. 'It looks like he definitely had another side, for all the good it did him. Jennings is sending down a couple of officers to Ferndown tomorrow; he's hoping to dig out some more nuggets from the members while the topic is still hot in the clubhouse.'

Loxley approved, 'You never know.' He then patted Janet's hand after making a decision. 'I'll give David a call tomorrow. I know it's a Sunday but it's a good opportunity to mention our spot of bother, as he did say he was going to keep me in the loop on the Turnbull case.'

Just as a relieved Janet went to answer in the positive, they were interrupted by the desserts arriving and all further conversation on the Turnbull case and the rat in the shoebox was suspended.

FOUR
FLESH ON THE BONES

I t was Sunday morning, and DI Keith Simpson had enjoyed a leisurely breakfast after sleeping well at the Crown Hotel in Lyndhurst. Now making the short drive to Pikes Hill Police Station, all his thoughts and attention were now back on the Roger Turnbull murder case. DCI Jennings had already given him a call at the hotel that morning, informing him of the potential breakthrough regarding the whereabouts of Turnbull's office in Lymington. From all he had learnt so far, it was pretty obvious to him that Turnbull had gotten involved in something that was completely out of his depth. He already had a few theories as to what that something was, but he needed to find out a lot more about Turnbull before he felt he could move the case forwards. That the case was far too big for the regional police to deal with, he had no doubts; Scotland Yard had been right to send him down.

*

DI Ed Farrows was accompanied by PCs Sarah Harrison and Matt Packer as they stood in front of a row of small red-brick houses. David Jennings had told them of James Cumber's visit to Pikes Hill the day before. The information he had given them about the possible location of Turnbull's office in Lymington sounded like it could be a significant breakthrough. They had wasted little time in following up and were now standing in a narrow lane situated just off the high street. Two of the houses they were studying had their front windowsills decorated with a colourful array of well-kept flowers and plants. It was the middle house with all the windows closed that focused their attention. Farrows approached the front door and gave it a push. He found it locked, as he had expected. It was at that point that a woman emerged from one of the adjoining houses.

Farrows took advantage. 'Good morning. Is this house usually empty?'

The woman looked friendly and was eager to please. 'There is a man who occasionally spends time in the house, but he doesn't seem to live there permanently. We are never quite sure what he does there.'

'Can you give us a description?'

'He's on the mature side, but very smart and nice-looking.'

It was the perfect description of Roger Turnbull. Farrows thanked the woman before ordering Matt Packer to break open the front door. Packer went to the police car before returning with a bright-red enforcer ram. After a couple of thumps, there was a loud splintering of wood as the door finally gave way under the assault. Packer stood aside as Farrows led the way into the house. They found themselves in a narrow hallway that led through to a small kitchenette. An electric kettle and teapot stood on the work surface. A couple of tea and coffee mugs hung on a fixed wall bracket. Farrows opened a small cupboard that contained a tea caddy and a half-filled jar of Nescafé Gold Blend. There was no sign of any food.

Farrows turned to Sarah Harrison. 'Not much on offer if you're hungry.'

Harrison agreed, 'It definitely does not look lived in; purely for business from the look of it.'

Farrows nodded. 'That certainly fits in from what we've learnt about Turnbull so far.'

The three officers retraced their steps back to a closed door that led off the passage. They walked into a practically empty room, filled with one solitary sofa chair.

Farrows shrugged. 'There's nothing to see here.'

He led them out of the room towards a small staircase on the opposite side of the passage. At the top of the stairs, there was a bathroom and one other door which Farrows assumed to be the bedroom. The door had a keyhole, and it appeared to be locked. Once more, Matt Packer was employed to do the honours, this time with a couple of thumps from his burly shoulders. Once inside, compared to the rest of the house, the room looked untidily crammed with office materials.

Farrows looked pleased. 'Bingo. This looks to be the place where it all went on.'

There was a desk and PC laptop surrounded by piles of paper with tons of files lined up on the floor.

Farrows surveyed the scene and observed, 'The white-collar crime and fraud squad are going to enjoy going over this lot.'

Sarah Harrison was soon browsing the countless sheets of paper. 'There are plenty of names, mainly building companies and solicitors by the look of it.'

Farrows reached for his mobile. 'Let's give David the good news.'

*

Joe Loxley picked up his landline and rang Pikes Hill Police Station. It was just after lunchtime, and he had just enjoyed one of Janet's grilled-salmon salads. Once again, he was reaping the benefit of Janet being eager to display her culinary skills whenever James Cumber came to stay. After a few rings, he heard the familiar voice of desk sergeant Tom Fallon at the end of the phone.

'Hello, Tom, don't you ever get a day off?'

Fallon recognised Loxley's voice immediately. 'No chance, Joe, as you can imagine, it's all hands to the pump at the moment.'

'Is there any progress to report?'

'The whole crime team are in Lymington at the moment. They are crawling all over Turnbull's office.'

'Hopefully they will find something useful.'

'I heard the discovery all came from a conversation that your old partner had at the golf club.'

'That's right, you can always do with a bit of luck.' Loxley remembered Cumber mentioning the new DI from Scotland Yard. 'I've heard you've got someone down from London.'

Loxley detected a slight hesitation before Fallon answered, 'Yes, I don't think David is too impressed to be honest, says he seems a little bit up his own arse.'

Loxley laughed. 'What's his name?'

'DI Keith Simpson.'

Loxley gave a gasp of recognition. 'I know him; he was a fast-rising star at about the time I retired. He could be a bit of a cold fish, but he was excellent at his job.'

'You will just have to convince David; good luck with that.'

Loxley changed the subject. 'I'm still getting a bit of harassment, Tom. Yesterday morning I had the express delivery of a dead rat in a box.'

'Lovely. Sounds like whoever it is, he's upping the ante.'

'Unfortunately, Tom, I think you're right. I know you're all under the cosh at the moment, but I would appreciate if you could escalate it upstairs at some stage.'

'No worries, Joe, I'm sure David would want to know.'

'Thanks, Tom. David did mention he was going to keep me posted regarding the Turnbull case, so I'll probably hear from him at some stage.'

'I'll give him a gentle reminder.'

'Thanks, Tom.'

Loxley had no sooner put the landline down when it rang. Loxley picked it up and answered. There was no reply, but Loxley detected a slight breathing and faint background noise that told him there was someone at the end of the line.

Loxley asked who was calling but his question was met with the same slightly sinister silence.

Loxley felt his voice rise slightly. 'I know someone's there; what do you want?'

The phone cut off abruptly and Loxley quickly rang 1471 but, not surprisingly, the caller had withheld their number. He rejoined Janet and James, who were lounging in a shady spot in the garden. Janet immediately noticed Loxley's pensive expression and asked what was up.

Loxley sat down beside them. 'I'm not sure. Just had a call on the landline but nothing was said, and they hung up after a minute.'

James Cumber tried to be upbeat, though he didn't sound convinced. 'It could just be a coincidence.'

Loxley shook his head. 'I don't think so. Anyway, I've put all this nonsense in the hands of Pikes Hill now.' Loxley picked up what remained of his San Miguel. 'By the way, James, it looks like they've hit the jackpot with the house in Lymington. I should imagine you are a very popular guy with DCI Jennings at the moment.'

Cumber looked pleased at the thought. 'You never know, he might even recruit me in his team to help crack the case.'

*

It was late afternoon in the open-plan office at Pikes Hill and even though it was a Sunday, the place was absolutely buzzing with activity. The investigation into the murder of Roger Turnbull was now in full swing. In just a short space of time, all weekend leave had been cancelled, budgets had been allocated, and men on the ground had been assigned. All the intricacies of a major inquiry were now falling into place. Area Commander Doug Cobbold had been true to his word in following up on his promises. David Jennings had also been assured that experts and specialists would all be available to him if and when needed. They had found plenty to get stuck into at Turnbull's Lymington office. The designated space put aside for the investigation area was now crammed with boxes of papers and files collected from the murder victim's office. When they had finally departed from Lymington, they had left behind two CSIs to go over the house with a fine-tooth comb in search of fingerprints and trace evidence.

David Jennings was standing in the middle of the hubbub. 'With all what we have here, there should not be any excuse not to have a comprehensive picture of Turnbull's business affairs by next week. Check every name and company that he dealt with. Where is Turnbull's PC, Ed?'

'It's with the IT geek team as we speak; they will be working on it twenty-four seven,' Farrows answered.

Sarah Harrison and Matt Packer were already carefully sifting through the boxes with the aid of extra uniformed officers who had been drafted in from the Devon and Cornwall Police.

Jennings turned to DC Mason. 'I want you to make sure, Paul, that every name fished out of those boxes is filed, cross-checked and followed up. We've got the resource; be sure to use it.'

It looked a daunting task, but Paul Mason was up for it. 'Yes, sir, we're on it.'

Standing slightly to the side and looking to contribute was the man brought in from Scotland Yard, Keith

Simpson. He turned to David Jennings with a sheet of paper in his hand.

'DC Mason has made a good start on Turnbull's charity activity and given me a list. I think it will be a good idea to dig a little deeper; you can find out a lot about a man by his civic contacts. In the meantime, if it's alright with you, I'd like to have another word with his wife and get some history. Something just might crawl out of the woodwork.'

David Jennings had already surmised that Simpson was no team player, but if he wanted to go off and do some solitary sleuthing, he had his blessing.

'If you think it might help, be my guest.'

'I think it might. We'll compare notes tomorrow at the progress review meeting.' With that, Simpson gave a curt nod and walked away.

Jennings watched him leave with a slightly puzzled expression. His new Scotland Yard compatriot certainly had his own way of doing things.

*

By late evening, Pikes Hill had fallen a lot quieter. It was still occupied by a small group of officers still sifting through what remained of Turnbull's paperwork, but most of the investigation team had either left for something to eat or gone home. David Jennings sat back from his PC and rubbed his eyes. They had already gleaned a lot of information from the paperwork gathered at Roger Turnbull's office in Lymington, more than enough to start putting serious meat on the bones as regards his business activities. The list of names and contacts they had unearthed ensured that the progress review meeting scheduled for Monday morning was going to be an informative one. After all the noisy activity throughout the day, the office now felt eerily silent, with only the occasional raised voice echoing through the empty corridors. He heard a laugh coming from the vicinity of Desk Sergeant Tom Fallon. Not for the first time, he wondered if Tom ever went home or even if he wanted to. He became vaguely aware of a familiar voice joining in the conversation with Fallon. It was Joe Loxley. Jennings left his desk to greet Loxley in the public reception area.

'Hi, Joe, what brings you here at this time of night?'

Loxley looked a little apologetic. He had left his visit to the station as late as possible, as he knew they were in the middle of a full-scale murder investigation.

'I was just informing Tom about a little local hostility.'

Tom Fallon removed the two threatening notes from the envelopes and handed them over to Jennings.

'They've been checked for dabs but no luck, sir.'

Jennings took them over to the desk and gave them a quick scan. 'How long has this been going on, Joe?'

'The first one was delivered just over a couple of weeks ago. I've had a couple of silent phone calls on my landline today from two anonymous numbers. The showstopper was yesterday morning when I woke up to a dead rat in a box on the doorstep. It looked like it was dumped there overnight.'

Jennings shook his head. 'It definitely looks like someone out there doesn't like you, Joe. Can you think of anyone off the top of your head?'

Loxley gave a wry grin. 'When I look back on my career, I've probably left a lot of time for grudges to grow and fester.'

'Your trouble, Joe, is that you were too bloody good at your job. On a serious note, I'm not going to ignore it and risk something unpleasant happening. I've got some extra resource at the moment so I can spare a uniform to patrol the area around your place overnight.'

'That's really good of you, David, it's much appreciated. It will make Janet feel so much better, I'm sure.'

Jennings patted him on the shoulder. 'In view of what you gave the service, Joe, it's the least we can do.'

Feeling a little embarrassed, Loxley changed the subject. 'Did you find anything useful in Lymington?'

'There's plenty to get our teeth into, that's for sure. Your man Cumber is still doing the business, even when he's out enjoying a game of golf.'

Loxley laughed. 'I trained him well.' He remembered Cumber's comments about Jennings not being too impressed with the DI from Scotland Yard. 'I've heard they've sent down Keith Simpson from London?'

Jennings face clouded. 'You know him?'

'I remember him as a young DS; always very keen to impress, but not the easiest personality, as I recall.'

Jennings scoffed. 'Well, you'll be pleased to know he hasn't changed much. I certainly don't warm to him.'

'He was always a bit of a lone wolf, always more interested in theories than people, but I do remember him getting some excellent results.'

'He went off on his own today, wanted another word with Lucy Turnbull.'

'If I were you, I'd give him a bit of slack. He was always a bit unconventional, so I wouldn't take it too personal if I was you.'

Jennings pulled a face. 'I'll try to take your advice, but I can't help feeling he looks down on us regionals. He spoke well of you though, which could be useful. Might need you to keep him in line; he'll probably listen to you.'

Loxley smiled. 'I'm sure you can handle him, David. He could well prove to be a valuable asset on this particular case.'

Jennings appreciated the reassurance, though he didn't feel totally convinced. 'Time will tell, I guess.' He looked at the clock. 'Fancy a quick pint in The Rabbit before it closes?'

Loxley hesitated. The White Rabbit pub was just a short distance from the police station. James Cumber was back home with Janet, but he didn't want to take liberties.

He heard himself saying, 'Oh go on then, but we'll have to make it a swift one.'

Jennings looked pleased. 'Good man.' He turned to Tom Fallon at the desk. 'I take it you will be eventually going home tonight, Tom?'

Fallon grinned and looked at his watch. 'Don't worry, sir, I will be getting relieved of my duties in just about ten minutes thirty seconds.'

'Glad to hear it. See you tomorrow.'

Jennings and Loxley left the police station together.

*

It was just over an hour later when Loxley finally left The Rabbit public house for the short drive back home. David

Jennings had given him a brief update on what they had found out so far as regards Turnbull's property business, without going into too much detail. Having been casually acquainted with Turnbull over many years, the sudden and violent manner of his death still did not sit right. In truth, he still felt quite shocked by the episode. He pulled into Queen's Road and caught a glimpse of his neighbour Phil Shaw in his headlights. He was giving a late-night walk to his cairn terrier, Chalky. Shaw stopped and watched Loxley pull on to his drive.

Loxley got out of the car. 'Giving Chalky a late-night stretch, Phil?'

'Got no choice with this fella; he's the boss.'

Loxley bent down and gave the dog a ruffle. 'How's it going?'

'Oh you know, the usual. Ninety-nine per cent of the time I feel anxious; the other one per cent I'm just worried.'

Loxley smiled. 'You'll have to get some medication for that, Phil, worrying's no good for you.'

'I can't help it; we live in worrying times.'

'You should take a leaf out of Chalky's book. He seems happy enough.'

'Funny you should say that, as he seemed to take a dislike to your big boxwood plant earlier. I couldn't get him to shut up. He seems alright with it now.'

'When was this?'

'When we came out, about twenty minutes ago.'

Loxley walked over to the plant to check it out. 'You say he kept barking?'

'In the end I had to drag him away. Obviously saw

something that spooked him. Could have been a fox skulking, I suppose.'

Loxley turned on his mobile and bent down to look at the base of the plant in the light. There was no doubt that the dry ground was disturbed, and was that a faint indentation of a footprint? A disturbing thought entered his mind. Could his tormenter have been crouching behind the plant in order to keep out of sight?

'You didn't see anyone around?'

'No one at all; that was what made it strange.'

Loxley immediately thought of Janet in the house and walked swiftly towards the front door after hurriedly wishing his neighbour goodnight. He felt a discernible sense of relief when he entered the house and heard Janet call out from the lounge.

'About time you made an appearance. I could do with the company.'

He entered the lounge to see James Cumber dozing contentedly in the chair.

Loxley laughed and gave Janet a quick kiss before saying, 'It's your fault; you shouldn't feed him so much. Sorry I'm a bit late. Jennings forced me to have a pint with him.'

Janet smiled indulgently. 'I bet you put up such a struggle. I'll warm your dinner up in the oven; should be ready in about twenty minutes.'

Loxley looked towards the snoozing figure in the chair. 'I'm surprised he left anything for me.'

Janet laughed as she got up and entered the kitchen. 'It was touch and go.'

Loxley followed her. 'Fancy a coffee?'

James Cumber suddenly stirred in the chair. 'Only if there's one going.'

Loxley shouted back from the kitchen, 'I wasn't asking you, fathead.'

Cumber straightened up. 'Charming.'

As Loxley stood at the sink filling the kettle, he decided not to mention the incident with Phil Shaw and his dog. After all, his original suspicions could well be wrong. He would take another look in the morning when the light was better.

*

It was early Monday morning and David Jennings was once again standing in front of the whiteboard at Pikes Hill. Standing alongside him was DI Keith Simpson and Ed Farrows. The room was crowded with the investigation team eagerly awaiting the latest information gleaned from the discoveries at Turnbull's office in Lymington.

Jennings put down his cup of coffee before picking up a whiteboard presentation stick and pointing to a board now filled with information on Roger Turnbull.

'I'm glad to say that we've now filled in a few gaps regarding the business activities of the murder victim. From what we discovered yesterday, it's fair to say that he appeared to be a very successful property developer. His building company is called Burgeon Construction, and it appears to specialise in buying up land for development and doing up old properties before selling them on.'

DC Mason put his hand up. 'Did he run the business with anyone else?'

'From what we know so far, it appears he only had employees not partners.'

'Anything at this stage to suggest he was a bit dodgy?'

'Nothing obvious so far, though we all know that there can be a thin line in that business. What we do know is that he operated on a large scale right across the New Forest area, from offices to affordable housing. We found several names that crop up quite regularly in his paperwork. They range from solicitors and architects to quantity surveyors and planning consultants. I suggest we interview these people as they have obviously played a big part in his success through the years. It should all help in finding out more about the type of man he was and what made him tick.'

There was a low murmuring amongst the gathered officers as DI Keith Simpson made it known to David Jennings that he wanted to add something before stepping forwards. He surveyed the room with a steady gaze.

'I've also done a bit of digging regarding Turnbull's history and charity contributions. It seems that back in the eighties, when he was an estate agent in his twenties, he did very well out of the government's Right to Buy scheme. He did this by simply buying up cheap council houses from long-term tenants who were tempted by his offers before smartening them up and selling for big profits. From that point on, he never looked back, and he was probably already well on the way to being a millionaire by the time he met his wife Lucy in the early nineties. After living in Dulwich for a few years, they moved down to the New Forest in 1999. As I said, I've also had a good look into his charity work. I have to hand it to him, he had everything covered: young people, old people, animals, even the Bournemouth Lifeguards. To all intents and purposes, he was a thoroughly good egg, but we all know that thoroughly good eggs don't usually end up dead in a ditch with a bullet in the head. I suggest we should leave no stone unturned in drilling down into his property dealings. To sum up, I smell one big dead rat!'

The room had been hanging on to every word from the man from Scotland Yard and there was a noticeable silence before David Jennings gave a muttered "thanks" and resumed the review.

'The IT team are still working on the PC found at the office and we should have something in the next couple of days. However, amongst the paperwork we did manage to identify what looks like his main business account. We've notified the bank concerned and cancelled his platinum credit card. In the meantime, I will circulate the names of the people we need to talk to.' He sounded enthusiastic. 'Let's get to it.'

Keith Simpson ushered him to one side as the crowd of investigative officers dispersed.

'I was thinking I might go and have a chat with Joe Loxley and James Cumber at some stage, if that's OK?'

'No problem; I'm sure Joe will be pleased to see you. I'll give you his address. He did remember you.'

Simpson remained deadpan but Jennings could see that he was secretly pleased.

'I'm flattered. I just want to go over their version of events on Thursday once more.'

Jennings handed him Joe Loxley's address. 'Have you got any theories so far?'

Simpson gave a sardonic laugh. 'I think it's pretty obvious Turnbull's a wrong 'un. The covert way he led his life, the unused mobile found in his car, the cash deposits in his wife's account, not least the manner of his death. He could have been involved in any number of shady dealings, but my mind is still open as to what they might be.'

'Yes, for the moment we can only speculate, but hopefully we'll find something more concrete in the next couple of days. What was your feeling about his wife?'

Simpson thought back to his meeting with Lucy Turnbull. 'Apart from her looking genuinely lost and distraught, I thought she was telling the truth. It looks like she made a conscious decision to turn a blind eye to how he made his money and resigned herself to being kept in the dark.'

'She certainly didn't want for anything; that probably helped.'

Simpson nodded and looked at his watch. 'Better get on. I want to check out a few more details on some of these names.' He picked up a bulky folder and left the office.

David Jennings watched him go. In spite of himself, he had to admit that Simpson's address to the room had been impressive, both in content and authority. He remembered Joe Loxley saying he might be an asset; maybe he had just given a glimpse of why he was worth that comment!

*

'There's definitely been some disturbance here.' James Cumber was crouched down examining the ground around the boxwood plant at the front of Joe Loxley's house. They had just returned from the High Street in Lyndhurst after escorting Janet Loxley to the charity shop where she worked. Loxley had updated Cumber on the incident the night before with Phil Shaw's dog on the walk back to the house.

Loxley confirmed, 'If you look closely, you can just about make out the outline of a footprint.'

Cumber traced the outline of the footprint in the dry earth surrounding the plant with his finger.

'Whoever it was must have been up to something when Phil and his dog came along. The question is what that something was.'

Loxley glanced around the front garden area. 'That's what worries me.'

Cumber thought back to his experience in the early hours of Saturday morning in the kitchen. He had dismissed it at the time as a trick of the light, but was it possible that he had caught a glimpse of someone who had been lurking furtively in Loxley's garden? He stood up and walked to the side of the house before coming to an abrupt halt as he was confronted by a large message which had been sprayed on the side of the house in bright-red paint.

'I think you'd better take a look at this, Joe.'

Loxley came around the side of the house and stood staring at the stark message glinting brightly in the mid-morning sunshine. It read:

YOU KILLED MY DAD

As Loxley stood momentarily transfixed, his career in the force flashed before him like a videotape. So many faces and names that would have had cause to resent him, so many cases that could have caused families to harbour a deep hatred in a twisted criminal mind.

Cumber was the first to speak. 'Doesn't exactly narrow it down, does it?'

Loxley stood looking pensive. 'I'm pretty sure it wasn't there yesterday. Our friend behind the bush either came back or he had already completed his piece of street art when Phil and his dog were walking past.'

Cumber put a comforting arm around his friend's shoulders. 'It's looking like you're really going to need that extra resource David Jennings promised.'

Loxley shook his head ruefully. 'I'm getting to the stage where it can't come soon enough, to be honest.' He took another look at the wall. 'In the meantime, it looks like I'll have to get in touch with the nearest graffiti removal service.'

*

Ed Farrows and Sarah Harrison pulled up in front of a well-proportioned Georgian house just outside Brockenhurst, its brickwork glowing impressively in the hot midday sunshine. Along with the rest of the murder team, they had been allocated a list of architects, planning consultants, solicitors and contractors, the common denominator being that they all appeared to have figured prominently in Roger Turnbull's property dealings through the years.

Sarah took a good look at the house from the car window. 'Now that's definitely a house I could easily aspire to.'

Farrows laughed. 'Perhaps the owner will be open to offers.'

Sarah pulled a face. 'At a stretch, I might just be able to afford the garage.'

'I take it you've still not had your promotion confirmed yet?'

'Not even a hint of it. Everyone seems too busy. Do you think it's got to the stage yet where I should have a word with David?'

Farrows shook his head. 'Believe me, there's really no need. This is purely off the record, you understand, but it's official. I've seen the papers going through. You've got it.'

Though Sarah had felt reasonably confident about her elevation, she still felt a huge rush of excitement and relief at the confirmation. She found it hard to keep the grin from her face.

'You are being serious?'

Farrows looked offended. 'You think I would joke about a thing like that? Just remember to act surprised when you hear it officially.' He looked towards the house. 'Now, let's see what Mr Ferguson has to say.'

Still feeling excited with the news, Sarah made a conscious effort to compose herself. She felt a slight tremble in her hands as she scanned through the names on the sheet and read aloud from the paper in front of her.

'Adrian Ferguson. Says here that he is a planning consultant who, from the evidence discovered in the admin, appears to go back a long way with Turnbull.'

Farrows moved to get out of the car. 'Sounds like the ideal candidate to possibly fill in a few gaps.'

Farrows gave the hefty knocker on the front door a good bang. They were eventually confronted by a large man, both in height and girth. He was wearing a tartan unbuttoned waistcoat over a checked shirt with loose-fitting trousers that could be described as baggy.

After showing his ID, Farrows enquired, 'Adrian Ferguson?'

The man nodded and stood aside to let them in. 'I take it this is about Roger?'

Ed Farrows confirmed, 'I'm afraid it is.'

The two officers followed Ferguson's shuffling figure down a long hallway.

They were shown into a large sitting room that smelt heavily of wood and polish. After Ferguson gestured for them both to sit down on a leather sofa, the big man, somewhat defensively, remained standing.

Farrows started his questioning sympathetically. 'His murder must have come as a big shock to you. I know you knew him a long time.'

'The best part of twenty years, pretty much since he moved down to the New Forest.' Ferguson seemed to sway slightly as if the realisation of Turnbull's death had hit him afresh. He steadied himself on the back of the chair. 'I can't believe anyone would have wanted him dead; he was a good man. You would only have to look at his charity work to see that.'

'How closely did you work with him?'

Ferguson looked momentarily surprised at the question. 'Extremely closely, we must have co-operated on at least a hundred property developments through the years. Burgeon Construction was far and away my biggest employer.'

'What did you do for him exactly?'

'He would occasionally employ me on short-term contracts, usually to make applications to the council for any properties he'd either purchased or identified for development.' He glanced towards the kitchen. 'I've just made some coffee; would you both like some?'

Farrows could smell the coffee and was tempted. He looked at Sarah, who nodded her encouragement to accept the offer.

'That's very kind of you. Black for me, please.'

Ferguson went into the kitchen and came back carrying three steaming mugs and a milk jug on a tray. After handing them over, he sat down in an armchair directly opposite.

Farrows took a quick sip before asking, 'Would you describe him as a good employer?'

'I would say he was one of the best I've had to deal with. He was always spot on with the detail and one step ahead with what was going on. Not least, he was a very generous employer. I can have no complaints.'

'Would you describe Roger as a friend?'

Ferguson took some time to answer. 'Well, he was in a way; becoming one, at least. Putting aside the fact I'm not the most sociable myself, even I would have to say that he was a difficult man to get to know well.'

'So we keep hearing. How would you describe his character?'

'He was always focused, but I got the impression he could be easily bored, always looking for the next venture.'

'Do you think that constant urge for the next deal could have led him to get out of his depth?'

Ferguson looked down at his feet and took a deep

breath, seemingly deep in thought. 'I suppose we can all get complacent with the people we have to deal with in the property game. It's not difficult to imagine that the buzz Roger seemed to get from deals could have led him into trouble.'

Sarah Harrison put down her coffee and wrote down a few notes.

Farrows was detecting a consistent characteristic. It was not the first time they'd heard about Turnbull's restless nature, his apparent need to be wheeling and dealing. It was becoming a constant theme when talking to his associates.

Sarah stopped scribbling and took time to look around the sitting room. It was furnished heavily with lots of dark wood and thick rugs. It struck her that though it all looked comfortable, there was something missing. She realised that it lacked the feminine touch.

She felt confident enough to ask, 'Do you live alone, Mr Ferguson?'

For a moment, he seemed surprised by the question. 'Oh yes, I've always been happy enough on my own.'

Sarah's curiosity caused her to follow up. 'I think you would have to be, Mr Ferguson, it's a big house for one person.'

Ferguson hesitated before he answered, as if he had never thought about it before. 'I suppose it is. I see it as my sanctuary when I'm not working; it was passed down from my parents. I'm very lucky in that I don't often feel the need for company; I guess you just get used to it.'

Farrows took up the questioning. 'When did you last see Roger?'

'He came to visit me a few weeks ago.'

'Was that unusual?'

'Yes, most of our contact was normally on neutral territory or on the mobile.'

'How did he seem?'

Ferguson appeared to think hard before answering. 'Even more hyper than usual, as I remember. He was very excited about some properties in the Hythe area. That was him, always chasing the next project.' He suddenly looked at his watch and stood up abruptly. 'I don't want to appear rude but if that's all, Inspector, I'm expecting a work call very soon. You can always feel free to come back to me if you think I can help in any way.'

Farrows answered, 'Thanks very much for the coffee and your time, Mr Ferguson.'

The two police officers rose from the sofa, and he escorted them to the front door.

Sarah Harrison gave a reflective glance back at the house as they drove away.

'Lovely house, but was I wrong in detecting something a bit sad about Mr Ferguson?'

Farrows agreed, 'I make you right. Just goes to show money isn't everything. A lovely big house but I don't sense too much happiness.'

'He seemed a bit of a contradiction. Is it possible for such an apparently gentle soul to exist in the property game?'

Farrows smiled. 'Now you're sounding just a little too cynical. I like to think the property business is not totally filled with crooks and shysters. At the same time, I see where you're coming from. The fact is, Ferguson was a long-time associate with what looks like a very dodgy property developer.'

'Do you really believe there can be any other kind?'

Farrows gave a chuckle. 'That's just what we're trying to find out.'

Back in the house, Adrian Ferguson sat down heavily on his sofa. He felt a deep despair begin to creep over him. The sudden death of his long-time associate had hit him hard. A small solitary tear began to slowly trickle down his cheek.

FIVE

MENACE AFORETHOUGHT

It was Monday afternoon, and Joe Loxley was spending some time in his study going through some of his memorabilia from his career in the force. The spray-painted message on the side of the house had disturbed him more than he had cared to admit to James and Janet. James Cumber had taken a photo of the message with his iPhone and attached it to an email before sending it to David Jennings at Pikes Hill. Fortunately, the graffiti removal company had been very accommodating and had arrived soon after lunchtime. He and James had watched them for a while before going back inside to get some relief from the hot midday sun. Previously over lunch they had discussed the meaning of the message and had agreed that it could well be a clue of sorts but had hardly narrowed it down. Janet had suggested that it might be a good idea if he took another look at his historic cases. Though he had entered his study with the best of intentions, he was finding it difficult to focus on the job in hand, as each case brought back recollections and side-tracked him into nostalgic reminiscences. He picked up a tattered old notebook with a pencil stored in the spine. It was his original notebook kept from his first days on the beat. He looked at the notes of some of his first arrests. Somehow, it seemed like it was only yesterday, but at the same time, felt like a different world and a different life. He remembered it being a time when he had begun to feel happiness in his life for the very first time. He pulled open the bottom drawer of the desk and rummaged through its contents. He pulled out a pair of handcuffs, a souvenir from his very first arrest of a hardened criminal. He remembered the man putting up a hell of a fight before he had finally managed to fit the bracelets on him. He recalled the satisfaction he had felt at the time; he was still proud of that one! He pulled out a further assortment of items: a duty belt, bulletproof vest and handgun holster. The final item in the drawer was a baton. He slapped it into his hand; it still felt solid. He figured the way things were going it might well prove useful. He placed it to one side before returning the other mementos to the drawer.

He heard a ring on the doorbell. Thinking it was the graffiti boys coming for their money after finishing the job, he left the study to answer the door. Entering the hallway, he saw that James Cumber had beaten him to it. Almost immediately, he recognised the face of the man introducing himself to James; it was Keith Simpson. Definitely more weathered and fleshier in the features than he remembered, it was undoubtedly Simpson, nonetheless.

Loxley held out his hand. 'DI Keith Simpson from Scotland Yard, I believe.'

Simpson looked pleased that Loxley remembered him. 'I hope you don't mind me giving you a call unexpectedly, Mr Loxley, but I expect you've heard I've been brought down on the Roger Turnbull case.'

Loxley showed him into the lounge. 'No problem, Keith. I'm sure that David Jennings is grateful that he is getting some expertise from the Yard.' Loxley showed him a seat before he and Cumber took a couple of chairs opposite. 'By the way, you can call me Joe.' Loxley nodded his head towards Cumber. 'This is my old accomplice James Cumber, by the way.'

Simpson glanced towards Cumber with obvious recognition. 'I guessed it was. I was hoping that I would catch the two of you.'

Janet popped her head in the room. 'Is everyone up for coffee?'

Loxley caught Simpson's appreciative nod. 'That would be great, pet.' He looked back at Simpson as Janet exited the room. 'That was my wife Janet, by the way.'

Simpson seemed to nod his approval.

Loxley leant forwards in his chair. 'Now, how can we help?'

Simpson pulled out a small notebook and started going through his written notes. 'The night you saw Roger Turnbull getting in the car, did he seem to get in willingly?'

Loxley thought back to that evening. 'I first caught a glimpse of him at the bus stop before the car came along. He seemed to be trying his best to keep out of sight.'

'You would say that he was acting suspiciously?'

Loxley was definite. 'No doubt about it. When the car pulled up, I remember there being a brief conversation before the rear passenger door opened and Turnbull slowly got in.'

'So it looked like there was someone sitting in the back who seemed to invite him in?'

'That was certainly what it looked like.'

Simpson turned to James Cumber. 'I just wanted to confirm with you, James, that the car you almost collided with showed no sign of stopping after the incident.'

Cumber laughed softly. 'Completely the opposite; it was obvious they were very keen to get away from something. It looked at the time that they were racing for all they were worth to get to the M27—'

Simpson interrupted, 'Except they never made it; nothing showed up on the M27 CCTV cameras.'

Loxley suggested, 'Looks like they could well have double backed towards Lyndhurst on the Beechwood Road.'

There was a brief silent pause as Simpson wrote some entries in his notebook.

Janet entered with a tray of coffee as Simpson put his notebook away. The man from Scotland Yard looked appreciative as he took his first sip before asking Loxley his next question.

'From all that you know of Turnbull, Joe, could you say with your old policeman's hat on that you felt you could trust him?'

Loxley thought long and hard before answering. 'Not surprisingly, I have repeatedly been asking myself that question. I think most people who knew him would say that they found him friendly and polite enough, but it was all on the surface. I don't think he had many friends simply because he wasn't interested in having any.'

Simpson commented, 'Interesting. Would you say he was basically a loner that was capable of using people for his own ends?'

Loxley didn't hesitate for too long before he answered, 'I would say that, on balance, very probably.'

They were interrupted by the sound of the doorbell. Loxley got up.

'That will be the graffiti boys after their money.'

As Loxley left the room, Simpson questioned Cumber. 'I noticed the men working outside; has there been a little trouble?'

Cumber glanced across at Janet before answering, 'Just a little. Joe has been getting some anonymous threats and harassment. Pikes Hill has been made aware of it.'

Simpson looked interested. 'Someone local?'

Janet answered, 'As far as we can make out. Joe has been looking into his historic cases just in case it's someone harbouring a long-term grudge.'

Cumber showed Simpson the image of the graffiti he had taken on his iPhone.

Simpson studied it before looking up. 'This all sounds very familiar. About a year ago there was a similar case with another retired superintendent. What was his name… Kent, Kemp?'

Cumber sat bolt upright on the end of his chair. 'You don't mean our old boss Bill Kemp?'

'Yes, that's the name, lived somewhere in the Cotswolds.'

Joe Loxley came back into the room. Janet was quick to inform him. 'It seems that Bill Kemp may have been getting the same treatment as you, Joe.'

Loxley sat down. 'When was this?'

Simpson expanded, 'All in the last year or so. As I understand it, the family were investigating it with Scotland Yard right up until the old fella died.'

Loxley felt the now familiar pang of guilt pass over him. He really wished he had been there more often for his old friend in his last years, even more so if he was being tormented and menaced by some nutcase.

'It's got to be more than just coincidence?' Cumber sounded pretty certain.

Simpson attempted to recall the details. 'I know the son got quite heavily involved in the investigation along with the old man. Going over all his historic cases and working with the Yard.'

'Do you know the nature of the threats?' Loxley asked.

'All the usual stuff, as I understood it: threatening letters, unsavoury parcels, unexplained noises in the night.'

Loxley reflected, 'Sounds pretty much the same treatment I've been receiving.' He looked across at Cumber. 'Sounds well worth a dig, don't you think, James?'

Cumber nodded. 'We both know his son, young Mark. I think we should get in touch.'

Simpson agreed, 'It wouldn't do any harm to compare notes at least; what you got to lose?' He finished his cup of coffee and stood up. He turned to Janet. 'Much appreciate the coffee, Mrs Loxley; I find I can't get enough fluids in this heat.'

Janet smiled. 'No problem. We're just not used to these temperatures in this country.'

Simpson agreed, 'It's certainly not showing any signs of relenting, that's for sure.' He moved towards the door.

Both Loxley and Cumber rose from their seats and followed him to the front door. Simpson turned as he stepped out into the sunshine.

'Much appreciate your assistance. It was good to meet up again after all these years.'

Loxley answered, 'Likewise, and thanks once again for the info on Bill Kemp.'

'Hope you get some joy with that. In the meantime, I'm sure that you will be kept abreast with any developments with the murder case.'

Loxley smiled. 'Much appreciated.'

Both Loxley and Cumber watched him drive away. Cumber was the first to speak as he closed the front door.

'He seems a good sort; don't know what David Jennings is complaining about.'

Loxley smiled. 'Don't run away with the idea that he treats us the same as DCI Jennings. I think he is one of those men where you have to earn his respect. I think we should take it as a compliment that he feels we've earned it.'

Cumber laughed. 'Are you going to tell David that?'

Loxley laughed. 'No, I think that's one theory we should keep to ourselves for a while, don't you?'

*

Jack Foster was feeling increasingly anxious as he glanced in his rear mirror. When he had arrived at the council offices that morning, he had noticed a wine-red Hyundai parked across the road from the entrance. It had particularly brought his attention because it appeared to be occupied by two men who seemed to be staring at him as he got out of his car. After a few seconds, the two men had driven off in the direction of Lyndhurst. He remembered thinking at the time that it seemed a little odd. He had thought no more of the encounter until now. He was sure that there had been no sign of the red Hyundai when he had left the office, but now there it was in his slipstream, seemingly following him home. He had been feeling on edge ever since Roger's murder. His wife had even remarked on his obvious anxiety. He looked in his rear mirror once more. The two men were still there on his tail, sinister and menacing. He could feel the panic rising inside him. Who were these people? Undercover police or something even worse? What the hell had Roger been getting into? He made a conscious effort to keep calm and try to rationalise the situation. Sure, he had given Roger advance information on properties coming up for purchase, information he knew full well he should have kept to himself. His career would be sure to be ruined if it ever came out. He knew he had given Roger the advantage in obtaining these properties and there was no doubt he himself had benefited personally, with Roger often showing his appreciation with his more than generous financial rewards. He was not the first councillor to indulge in such unethical practices and he would certainly not be the last. But this was something completely different. The manner of Roger's brutal murder suggested that he had been into something far more serious. At this stage in his homeward journey, he would normally turn off the A35 to head in the direction of his home, but something told him that, in the circumstances, that would probably not be a wise move. He felt the perspiration dripping from his forehead and his heart was beating hard as he looped the car back towards Lyndhurst. Sure enough, the red Hyundai doggedly followed. Feeling progressively more desperate and frightened, he made several more turns, but each time the following car relentlessly mirrored his manoeuvres. His torment intensified when his car was forced to a halt by traffic lights and the red Hyundai glided up on the outside and stopped alongside. Foster was grateful that there were other vehicles stopped in the queue, and he was not alone with the two men. He felt compelled to keep looking straight ahead but he was aware that the men were looking across at him. Struggling to control his rapid breathing, he slowly turned his head to see the two men staring right at him. They were both wearing shades and he did not recognise them. The two men did not gesture or say anything, but he detected a menacing grin playing around the mouth of the man seated in the passenger seat closest to him. To Jack Foster, it seemed an age before the lights finally turned green and his ordeal ended with the Hyundai speeding off ahead of him. Letting out a huge sigh of relief, Foster turned off the main road and stopped the car. He immediately draped himself over the steering wheel, taking in deep breaths. He noticed his shirt was clinging uncomfortably to his skin and he realised the whole terrifying encounter had left him saturated in his own sweat.

*

David Jennings closed the door and rolled up his sleeves as he joined Ed Farrows and Keith Simpson in the small side office at Pikes Hill. It was early Monday evening, and the police station was still buzzing with activity. Jennings had called the meeting with his senior officers in order to collate some information and see if there were any fresh leads.

He sat down opposite the two men and asked hopefully, 'Have we made any progress, gents?'

Ed Farrows gave a grimace. 'Sadly not too much so far. The geeks have just finished with Turnbull's PC and though he looks to have been a tough negotiator who drove a hard bargain, the fraud squad say they haven't found anything that doesn't look above board.'

Jennings could not help voicing his disappointment. 'Well, that's a bummer; I was fully expecting them to find something. I hoped to spare Lucy Turnbull the stress of a thorough search of her house, but it looks like now we've got no choice.' He looked across to the man from Scotland Yard. 'Does the lack of criminality on his PC surprise you, DI Simpson?'

'Not really, it all seems very much in character from what we know of Turnbull so far. It's this apparent respectable front that allows him to get involved in the more shady dealings. It's for us to break through that front, because, believe me, one way or the other this man was into something pretty heavy.'

Having frequently associated with Roger Turnbull for several years, Jennings still found it hard to be totally convinced that Roger had been involved in something so seriously criminal that it had led to his callous execution.

'You don't think we could be scaling this up to something bigger than what it actually is? After all, making the odd enemy is unavoidable in any business. It's a competitive world out there and there's plenty of greed.'

Simpson looked unimpressed. 'I've already taken a look into his property purchases and I've hardly the touched the sides. The man has practically bought, developed and sold half the properties in the New Forest over the last ten years. The secrecy around his dealings is just not normal; he must have had another reason other than pure speculation. I know corruption when I see it. The whole thing stinks.'

Jennings asked, 'So you're suggesting he may have been working with someone inside the council?'

Simpson gave a soft chuckle. 'You sound surprised. Councillors and developers have been known to flaunt the rules ever since I can remember. I've dealt in the odd case when a councillor was either bought or even blackmailed. At best, it's not been unknown for the council to look the other way. It would be a good idea to send an investigative team into the council offices to go through every one of Turnbull's property dealings with a fine-tooth comb. Believe me, having seen the volume of his property purchases, it's a big job.'

Jennings nodded. 'I'll get a big team on it.' He picked up a sheet of paper and looked through a list of names. He asked Ed Farrows, 'What impression did you get from the councillor, Jack Foster?'

Farrows creased his brow in recall. 'Well, if he knew more than he was saying about the murder, he did a pretty good job of covering it up. There was still something about him though.'

Simpson looked up, interested. 'This was the man who gave a lift to Turnbull the night he was murdered?'

Farrows replied, 'Yes. I wouldn't say there was anything obvious, but I wasn't totally convinced by him. At the same time, I wouldn't want to give you the wrong impression.'

Simpson gave Farrows a steady stare. 'I can assure you that I never permit myself to get false impressions from anything anyone tells me. I form my own judgements. If you can give me his address, I think he might well be worth another visit.'

Farrows fumbled in his folder and handed Simpson a sheet. 'Be my guest.'

Once again, the term "pompous prick" came to mind as Jennings listened to the man from Scotland Yard, but he took a deep breath, kept his head down and looked over his notes.

'We've still got a lot of his associates to interview; hopefully something else will crawl out of the woodwork.'

Ed Farrows commented, 'The planning consultant, Ferguson, was a strange one.'

Jennings looked up. 'Strange in what way, exactly?'

'Not what I expected, all on his own in a big house. He was pleasant and helpful enough, but he seemed more than a bit down in the mouth.'

'Because of Turnbull's death?'

Farrows pulled a face. 'Difficult to tell, but I will say one thing. Going by the houses of Turnbull's associates so far, they all seem to be doing very well for themselves, if that means anything.'

Jennings nodded. 'All this apparent wealth could have

a bearing but remember there are very few poor people in the property game.'

Farrows picked up his list and stood up. 'I'll carry on interviewing these associates. I take it that Sarah Harrison is with me again tomorrow?'

The mention of PC Harrison reminded Jennings that he must have a talk with her at some time about her promotion.

'Yes, for now. I would have given you Matt Packer, but I've temporarily taken him off the team for night patrol at Joe Loxley's place, see if he can throw some light on Joe Loxley's tormentor.'

'No problem.'

After Farrows had left the room, David Jennings turned to Simpson and asked him how he had got on at Joe Loxley's.

'It was worthwhile going over a few points. It was good to see him.'

'Yes, he's definitely one of the good guys. Did he tell you about the idiot who sprayed some artwork on the side of his house?'

'Yes, he told me about the harassment and threats he's been getting lately. I told him it sounded very similar to something a retired senior officer was getting last year. It turns out that this senior officer is his old retired boss. The old boy had used his connections and got the Yard involved in the investigation right up until the last year of his life.'

David Jennings leant forwards. 'That sounds like there could well be a link. Did they get anywhere?'

'They were still doing the digging when the old man

passed on. I don't think they bothered to put in the resource after that.'

Jennings looked disappointed. 'I bet there could well be a connection in the shared case history.'

Simpson nodded his agreement. 'Sounds more than likely. Anyway, he and his old sidekick Cumber are going to follow it up with the son.'

Jennings could not help shaking his head and giving a slight chuckle. 'What with them both being involved in the Turnbull case, they must be feeling like it's the old days. Let's hope it leads to something. I wouldn't put it past them to crack both cases.' He picked up the Turnbull murder notes and stood up from the desk. 'In the meantime, DI Simpson, let's see if we can give them some help with this one.'

*

Joe Loxley had come in from the garden, leaving James Cumber dozing peacefully on the sun lounger. The early evening was pleasantly warm and still. He popped his head in the lounge: Janet was watching an episode of *Dragon's Den*. He went into the hallway and searched through his phone book. He eventually found Mark Kemp's number. The conversation with DI Simpson earlier in the day had been an interesting one. He thought back to Bill Kemp's funeral and remembered Mark mentioning that the last year of Bill's life had been a stressful one. At the time he had thought he was referring to Bill's grief at losing his wife Ann and his deteriorating physical health, but from what he now knew, there had obviously been more to it. The ringing tone purred softly for a few seconds before Mark picked up.

'Hello, Mark, it's Joe Loxley. How are you?'

Mark sounded surprised. 'Hello, Joe. I'm doing OK. What can I do for you?'

'It's about your dad, to be honest. I hear he was getting a bit of harassment in his last year.'

'More than a bit, it was quite heavy stuff.'

'The thing is, and at this stage I don't really know whether there's a connection, I've been recently getting the same treatment.'

'I'm sorry to hear that, Joe.'

'I hear that Bill got Scotland Yard involved.'

'Yeah, at one stage he had a small team working on it. Dad got quite obsessed about it. He started looking at his old cases; it really got to him.'

'Did he have any theories?'

'He had a few favourites, but they didn't lead to anything solid. He built up a folder as long as your arm.'

'I don't suppose you've still got it?'

'As a matter of fact, I've just got it back from the Yard. They had another retired cop working on it. You probably know him; Dad called him "Bloodhound", but his name was Steve.'

'Steve Harmer. I might have guessed he'd want to keep his hand in. Did he get anywhere?'

'He was looking into a theory that Dad had thought the most likely. He said it was his last case before he retired, a serial killer that also involved a family from South London.'

'The Marcus Varney case?'

'That's the one. Steve Harmer said he may have found a possible lead, but now that Dad's gone the Yard don't see much point in pursuing it.'

'I was also on that high-profile case, and I do remember a dodgy criminal family being implicated leading to a wrongful arrest. I suppose there's a real possibility the case could be the link between your dad's harasser and mine.'

'You can have the folder if you like. It's also got Steve Harmer's contact number in there.'

'I would like that very much, Mark; just got to get it off you. You're in London, aren't you?'

'Greenwich.'

'Let me have a think. Thanks for your time, Mark. I'll get back to you.'

Loxley put the phone down. There was more than just a chance that Bill could have been onto something. He went to the drawer in his study and pulled out his stack of old case notes. He thumbed back to the year 1986. There it was: the Oxford Trinity case involving Falklands hero and serial murderer Marcus Varney. He sat down at his desk and painstakingly went through the notes.

*

It was late afternoon, and Adrian Ferguson was still sitting on the sofa in his dressing gown. After waking up that morning, he had laid in his bed with no motivation or interest. There had seemed no point in getting up. It must have been sometime around midday before he had eventually forced himself to get out of bed. Try as he might, he could not get the death of Roger Turnbull out of his mind. He had always known that there had been a reckless streak in Roger, a part of him that craved excitement. That intangible element of danger had always been one of the characteristics he had found most attractive about him. But the manner of his brutal end now suggested his old associate had sailed far too close to the wind this time. He had always felt an affection and admiration for Roger, but now, with the finality of his passing, he realised his devotion and feeling of loss went so much deeper. He stood up and walked towards the window. The sun was shining bright and the trees were in full leafy bloom, but when he looked out onto the forest, he saw only an immense black abyss stretching out despairingly before him. He'd had this feeling before. He recognised the symptoms. A big black cloud was descending.

*

'Well, if you're sure you don't mind, James?'

'It really is no problem. If I go by train, I will be there and back in a few hours. I'm sure it'll be worth it; there's more than a good chance Bill was onto something.'

James Cumber was sitting in the lounge with Joe and Janet Loxley drinking an evening coffee. They were discussing the practicalities of getting down to London sometime in the week to pick up Bill Kemp's folder from his son Mark. Loxley had filled him in on the telephone conversation he'd had earlier with Bill Kemp's son. They had both gone through the notes once more on the Marcus Varney case. Cumber had become more and more impressed with the theory that Bill had been working on.

The fact that his old boss had brought in both Scotland Yard and their old compatriot Bloodhound Steve Harmer made him even more convinced.

Cumber went on, 'The train comes in at Waterloo and I can meet Mark somewhere on the Southbank. I might even be able to fit in a lunch with Kelsey.'

Janet nodded approvingly. 'Sounds like a plan.'

Joe Loxley didn't like the thought of James having to interrupt his stay, but he had to admit it would prove both helpful and useful. He would have gone to London himself, but though he wouldn't tell her to her face, he didn't feel comfortable leaving Janet on her own for too long while this disturbing harassment was going on. Somewhat reluctantly, he conceded.

'Well, it would solve the problem.'

Cumber was warming to his theme. 'That settles it. We've just got to agree on a suitable day with Mark.'

They were interrupted by a ring on the doorbell. Joe Loxley instinctively went to the window to see who was at the door. It was David Jennings and PC Packer. Loxley went to the door and let them into the hallway.

Jennings was in a businesslike mood and refused to intrude any further into the house. He gave Loxley a very brief summary of where they were with the Turnbull case before introducing Matt Packer.

'This is PC Packer, Joe, he'll be keeping a low-key evening surveillance around your house for a few days. Hopefully he will get lucky and catch the bastard if he tries to exhibit more artwork on your house.'

Loxley shook his head. 'It does make you wonder what this joker might do next.'

'That's what he wants, Joe, to keep you in a permanent state of anxiety. Keith Simpson told me your old boss had been getting the same shit.'

'That's right. I rang his son tonight and he told us Bill had put an investigative folder together before he died. He identified one historic case in particular that we had both worked on.'

'It sounds like it could well be worth getting your hands on that folder.'

'Funny you should say that; we've just been talking about it. James is going up to London this week to pick it up.'

'He doesn't have to do that, Joe; I'll see if I can get someone to pick it up for you. But as you can imagine, it's all hands on deck at the moment.'

Loxley put his hands up. 'I fully understand; it's really not a problem. James is going to go up by train and fit in a lunch with his daughter.'

'Well, if you're sure, let's hope it's all worth it. I'll get Pikes Hill to cover the tickets.'

Loxley went to protest but Jennings brushed his objections aside. 'It's an on-going investigation, Joe, we're only carrying on where Scotland Yard left off.'

'That's very kind of you. I'm sure James will appreciate it.'

Jennings fished in his jacket pocket and handed Loxley what looked like a spray can.

'Here, take this, Joe, could be a bit of useful reassurance for Janet. Hopefully she won't have call to use it.'

Loxley looked at it doubtfully. 'Is it legal?'

'All above board, Joe, works like a pepper spray, squirts

a red gel that stains for a few days; could buy Janet a few precious seconds if the worst came to the worst.'

Loxley put it on the hallway desk. 'I really appreciate all that you're doing for us.'

Jennings smiled. 'I always like to think we look after our own, Joe.'

Loxley changed the subject. 'How have you been getting on with Simpson?'

Jennings pulled a face. 'Well, let's just say he's an interesting character and leave it at that.'

Loxley laughed. 'He's a pussycat; I'm sure you can handle him.'

Jennings looked far from convinced. 'I think the jury's still out on that one.'

After the two policemen had left, Loxley picked up the self-defence spray and studied the writing on the canister. It read, *Startle and Stain.*

At that precise moment, he really hoped the time would never come when Janet would ever have to test the theory.

*

Matt Packer yawned once more and blinked his eyes. He would have to get used to this all-night shift. He was parked discreetly in an unmarked car at the end of the road, giving himself a good view of Joe Loxley's house. For what seemed the umpteenth time, he glanced at his watch: it was three thirty in the morning. He had hoped by now to have seen some action, but the shift had been tediously boring. Once more he felt his eyelids begin to drop. Unable to resist, he slowly rested his head on the steering wheel and closed his eyes; he was asleep within seconds. He awoke with a start about twenty minutes later. Angry with himself for falling asleep, he hurriedly poured out a coffee from his flask and took a big gulp. He looked in the direction of Loxley's house. He was relieved to see that everything looked as it should be. David Jennings would have his guts for garters if he'd missed anything. Feeling refreshed after his short nap and concentrated shot of caffeine, he settled down for the rest of the shift. Unbeknown to Packer, in that unscheduled twenty-minute nap, a vehicle had slowly glided up alongside him. The driver of the vehicle had paused momentarily to take a look, before gently accelerating away to the end of the road and turning right.

SIX
DOUBLE JEOPARDY

It was early Tuesday morning and David Jennings could not remember the last time he had seen the CID room at Pikes Hill looking so full. Despite the cost-cutting and uncertainties of recent times, Chief Superintendent Cobbold had obviously pulled all the right levers in getting Head Office to release a sizable chunk of the budget to solve the Turnbull case. Because there were not enough chairs, officers were sitting on desks and leaning against walls. There was the usual buzz of excitement in the room that always accompanied a high-profile murder case. Jennings had a big expectant audience as he opened the morning's briefing.

'I need not remind you that New Forest villages like Minstead are quiet, peaceful communities. It's our job to make sure that violent incidents like this do not make people feel unsafe. One way to ensure that is with a visible presence, meaning we are going to put more patrol cars and officers on the roads.' He turned to the whiteboard and pointed to the numerous names that were listed. 'All of these known Turnbull associates are being put through the database to see if there are any criminal links or previous form. In the meantime, we'll carry on with the interviews and see if we can pull any worms from the woodwork. Don't be afraid to go back to these people if you are not sure or your instincts tell you something doesn't sit right. We have the manpower available, and we'll talk to every one of them until we're satisfied, no matter how long it takes.' There was a stirring of restless anticipation as Jennings went on. 'Disappointingly, the IT team in the fraud squad could not find anything incriminating on Turnbull's laptop, so we had to do a thorough search of Turnbull's house.' He looked directly at DC Mason, who had led the team that conducted the search. 'How did you get on, Paul?'

Mason stood up. 'We went through the house with a fine-tooth comb, but apart from some personal effects and an expensive wardrobe of clothes, there was surprisingly very little connected to Turnbull considering he actually lived there.'

Jennings looked a little crestfallen. 'What, nothing at all? Come on, Paul, you must be able to give me something.'

Mason held up a small forensic bag. 'Well, the one bit of good news is we didn't come away totally empty-handed.'

Jennings perked up, 'I knew you wouldn't let me down, Paul, give us the detail.'

'We found this small bunch of keys tucked away in the garage. Mrs Turnbull said she had no idea what doors they related to and that it was the first time she'd seen them. We suspect they could well belong to some of his properties.'

'There was nothing to tell you that she was being economical with the truth?'

Mason shrugged. 'No reason to think she wasn't being straight.'

David Jennings gave it some thought. 'If those keys are in any way connected to some of Turnbull's properties, then it's going to take some time to match those keys to the houses, but we have a big team led by DI Simpson and we should get there in the end. The team have been going through his property transactions over the last few years, covering both the paperwork we found at his office and his historic council transactions. It might just be worth checking the keys for dabs, might throw someone up in the system. It's a long shot but you never know.'

Ed Farrows stood up and moved to Jennings' side. 'A possible lead has opened up after I had an interesting chat with one of the names on the list. An architect called Joe Bigbury, who has done a lot of work for Turnbull through the years. He could not throw any light on his murder, but he did say he'd heard that Roger had recently had a serious dispute with another property developer called Sandringham Construction, who operates out of Christchurch. Seems they fell out over some land awaiting development. According to Bigbury, it all got pretty nasty. He also mentioned that Turnbull's behaviour had become a bit peculiar lately. Remember, Bigbury had known Turnbull for a long time, so for him to notice any change could be significant. Might be something or nothing, but it could lead to a useful line of inquiry.'

Jennings nodded approvingly and decided to wrap up the review on that promising note. He pointed back to the names on the whiteboard.

'In the meantime, we need to eliminate some more of these people from our inquiries, so let's get on with it.'

*

The hot sun dappled the forest floor as Loxley removed his sun cap and brushed a hand through his silver-grey hair before taking a long swig from his water bottle. Both Cumber and Loxley had once again been enjoying their morning walk in the New Forest. They were now seated in their familiar spot where a couple of old fallen trunks provided a good shady area to take a welcome and cooling break. Because of the uncertainty and anxiety created by their anonymous tormenter, Loxley had thought it best to take a week off from his job at the Beaulieu Motor Museum. They had left Janet back at the house having a coffee morning with a couple of friends from her Pilates club. Earlier that morning, Loxley had rung Mark Kemp once again to arrange for James Cumber to meet him around twelve o'clock the following day on the Southbank near Southwark Bridge. The two retired policemen could not wait to see what their old boss had collated in his folder. As was usually the case, the calm surroundings of the forest had put Joe Loxley in a reflective mood. He was talking about the treasured time he had spent with Janet since he had moved to the New Forest.

'The life we've enjoyed since we moved down here is very precious to us. The last fifteen years or so have probably been the best we've ever had together. It's that more than anything that makes this recent aggravation such a pain in the arse. I hardly need to tell you how difficult it was to find quality time together when we were active in the force.'

Cumber thought back to his own failed marriage and nodded ruefully. 'Tell me about it.'

Loxley had a faraway look in his eyes. 'I had enough misery when I was a kid; I really don't need it again at this time of life.'

Cumber had known for many years that Loxley had endured an unhappy childhood, but he had never gone into detail. The opportunity to find out more had never really presented itself, but sitting here now in the tranquillity of the forest, he sensed that his friend might just be in the mood to unload.

'You can tell me to mind my own business, Joe, but you have never told me the full story of your childhood. Is it that painful?'

Loxley stared at the ground. 'To tell you the truth, James, I never wanted to talk about it, but I find that advancing age really does have a mellowing effect; it gives you a new perspective.' He gathered his thoughts before continuing. 'There really is not too much to tell. My father was an American Marine. I was a classic product of the silk-stocking, chocolate and chewing-gum culture in the war. My mum was English; she succumbed to his charms, and I was born. I'm not even sure whether my dad even knew about me. I never did find out. The bottom line is he went back home, and my mum didn't want me. As a result, I pretty much spent the first fifteen years of my life in an orphanage.'

Cumber gave out a low sigh. 'I'm really sorry to hear that, Joe.'

Loxley still remembered that first taste of loneliness; sour and depressing. He went on, 'It's not a great feeling to realise you're not wanted when you're young, but kids are resilient; I knew no different. What I do know is that I was never happy. I realised early on that I was pretty much on my own, but I also felt there was something inside me that was missing, an empty feeling deep inside that I could never quite make out. It was only when I joined the force and met Janet that I found out the answer. That feeling of being happy, feeling valued, wanted... and, yes, loved, was something I had never known up to that point. I remember it filling a massive void in me at the time. It's only now, looking back, that I realise that was the point when my life really began.'

What it was like to have never known your parents was something Cumber could not even contemplate. He thought back to his own happy childhood. He had only ever known the security of loving parents who were devotedly in his corner, who always unstintingly had his back. It was true that, unlike Loxley, a lot of his own adult personal life had been shit, but at that moment he felt a deep sorrow for his old friend.

'I can't even begin to imagine what that must have felt like as a child, Joe.'

Loxley stood up and gave a long sigh. 'It was what it was, James, the good news is I struck lucky in the end.'

They were sharply interrupted by the sound of sun-scorched tree bark being trodden underfoot. The sound had come from the trees behind them and Loxley had first thought it was the forest ponies. Then he caught a brief glimpse of someone passing furtively through the trees, not once but twice, maybe three times.

'It looks like we might just have some company, James.'

Cumber stood up and stared into the trees. 'You definitely saw someone?'

Loxley was positive. 'No doubt about it.' Suddenly feeling uncomfortably vulnerable, he wished he'd thought to bring his old police baton out with him.

Cumber shouted loudly in the direction of the thick undergrowth, 'Hello, can we be of assistance?'

His question was met with a stark silence. As if for security, the two ex-policemen gravitated towards each other. They stood there silently together for some time before they detected the faint sound of retreating steps somewhere deep in the forest.

Cumber dismissed the incident, 'It's probably someone's idea of having a laugh.'

Loxley was not quite so sure. He looked at his watch. He had an uneasy feeling that he could not quite explain.

'I think it's about time we got back, James.'

*

Janet could not help smiling to herself. Her two friends had just left the house after their coffee morning and she was still thinking back to some of the more amusing topics in the conversation. There had been plenty of laughs and it had done her the world of good to have a good chat and forget about the recent menacing harassment, even for just a couple of hours. She picked up the coffee cups and took them to the sink. Joe and James probably wouldn't be back for an hour, so she had a chance to do a bit of housework.

It could only have been the merest blur of movement in her peripheral vision that made her suddenly turn towards the patio windows. It was then that she saw him: a man standing in the garden looking in. He stared at her expressionless for a brief moment; then he was gone. A shadow passed across the window at the side of the house. It had all happened in the blink of an eye, but she had seen him. Janet felt her heart thumping hard as she ran towards the patio doors to make sure they were double-locked. Had the man tried to get in? She had no way of knowing for sure. She distractedly remembered her mobile phone was in the bedroom upstairs. Her legs felt heavy as she made her way to the landline in the hallway, a stressful knot of nausea building in her stomach. Before she could pick up the phone to ring Joe, she made an involuntary jump as the doorbell rang loudly. She stood there transfixed, unable to move, her breathing increasingly rapid, her head throbbing. The doorbell rung once more, increasing her apprehension, the reverberating chimes seeming to fill the house with noise. She took some deep breaths and picked up the self-defence spray that was standing by the phone. She entered the lounge and slowly edged towards the window at the front of the house. She slowly pulled the curtain back a few inches and strained to see who was at the door. The small gap she had created made it difficult to see who was there. A noise followed by a shout came from the direction of the front door. Her release of tension and sense of relief was palpable as she heard the familiar voice of her neighbour Phil Shaw shouting through the letterbox.

*

'I had just left the house for my lunchtime constitutional with Chalky when he started barking loudly as we drew level with Joe's house.' Phil Shaw turned towards Joe Loxley. 'It was pretty much as he did the other night, Joe.'

Phil was giving a statement to Matt Packer in the lounge of the Loxley's house. Loxley and Cumber had got back from their walk to find Phil standing on the doorstop comforting Janet, who looked badly shaken. Loxley had felt the rage rising within him as he heard the story of what had happened. They had immediately rung Pikes Hill and PC Matt Packer had arrived within the hour.

Phil Shaw went on, 'It was when I was trying to quieten Chalky that a man appeared from the side of the house and rushed past me with barely a glance. I watched him walk quickly to the end of the road before he got into the passenger seat of a white van. It then sped off and turned right into the Southampton Road. I knew straight away from the look of him that he was dodgy. He'd obviously been up to no good. I'd seen Joe and James going out for a walk earlier, so I knew there was a good chance of Janet still being in the house at that time, so I went and rang the doorbell.'

Janet spoke with feeling, 'I've never been so glad to hear your voice, Phil.'

Phil laughed. 'That'd be a first.'

Joe Loxley sounded grateful, 'I don't know who to thank more, you or Chalky.'

Phil looked pleased with himself. 'I'm quite prepared to share the glory.'

Matt Packer was busy writing it all down in his notebook. 'Can you give us a good description of the man, Mr Shaw?'

Phil Shaw nodded. 'He was tallish and skinny, fair-haired, scruffy. He didn't look a healthy specimen, to be honest.'

'What was he wearing?'

'Tatty jeans and a grimy-looking T-shirt, bit like a builder.'

'And you're sure the white van turned right into the Southampton Road?'

Phil had no doubt. 'One hundred per cent.'

'Thanks very much for that, Mr Shaw.' Matt Packer turned to Janet, who was looking a little drawn and pale. Joe Loxley was sitting on the wing of the chair where she sat, a comforting arm around her shoulder.

'You say you saw him staring at you through the patio door at the back of the house.'

Though obviously shaken up by the whole experience, Janet had a determined expression.

'Yes, but only for a split second. I could see he was fairly tall but that's about it.'

'And you say the patio door was locked?'

'Fortunately, yes.' She looked at Joe. 'We thought it would be a sensible to lock it whenever I was on my own.'

James Cumber interjected and directed his comment to Matt Packer. 'With Phil's physical description, the white van and the knowledge that there are two of them, it gives you a good chance of tracking them.'

Packer nodded. 'It definitely gives us something to get our teeth into.' He walked over to the patio doors and examined them. He asked Phil Shaw, 'Did you notice whether he had gloves on?'

Phil Shaw gave the question some thought. 'Now you mention it, I think he did. They looked soiled, like plasterer's gloves.'

Packer added this information to his notes.

Joe Loxley stood up. 'There must be a good chance of some CCTV footage on the Southampton Road.'

Packer shut his notebook and smiled. 'You can be sure we'll get onto it.'

After Packer and Phil Shaw had left, Joe Loxley turned to James and Janet. 'I don't know about you two, but I think a stiff drink is in order.'

Janet was the first to answer, 'Make sure mine's a double.'

Loxley had a thought. 'You don't think that goon in the forest playing silly buggers this morning was the other fella? If he was parked nearby, he would have had more than enough time to get back and pick up his mate.'

Cumber thought back to the strange episode in the forest. 'It looks possible; he could have been making sure he knew where we were while the other one came here to frighten Janet.'

Loxley looked across at Janet and felt his fists clench at the thought. Where was that drink?

They spent the rest of the afternoon sitting in the garden and going over the incident. Despite Phil Shaw's valuable info, they all agreed that James should still keep his rendezvous with Mark Kemp in London the next day and pick up Bill's folder.

*

Ed Farrows and Sarah Harrison entered the smart offices of Sandringham Construction just on the outskirts of Christchurch. They had already researched the company and established that a Paul Maybank was the head poncho. They flashed their warrant cards and asked the young male receptionist if Maybank was available. After making a quick call, he ushered them through to a luxuriously furnished reception room.

They were invited to sit down on a plush leather sofa and offered a coffee. They accepted the offer and looked appreciably around them.

Farrows could not help commenting, 'Looks like Mr Maybank appears to be doing something right.'

Sarah Harrison nodded her head in agreement. 'Yet further confirmation that the property game is definitely where the money is.'

They were kept waiting sometime and had almost finished their coffees before Paul Maybank finally came out of his office to greet them. The man standing in front of them was about thirty, tall and tanned with an easy smile that showed off his gleaming white teeth.

'Sorry to have kept you waiting. Come straight through.' He invited them to take a seat and sat down behind his desk. 'Now, how can I help?'

Farrows went straight to the point. 'We are investigating the murder of Roger Turnbull.'

Maybank's face momentarily clouded. 'I guessed that might be the case.'

'Did you know him well?'

'I certainly had dealings with him. Through the years we've co-owned some land developments.'

Farrows went in for the kill. 'I heard you had a recent disagreement with him.'

Maybank looked a little defensive. 'Oh, you heard about that. Word certainly gets out.'

'Is it true?'

'We'd agreed to share a land purchase in the Fawley area. Nothing was formal and Roger certainly didn't do handshakes, but the next thing I knew he had gone ahead on his own and snapped it up.'

'Has he ever done anything like that before?'

'No, never. As I say, we had always worked amicably together in the past. I was livid and let him know it.'

'How did he take that?'

'He didn't bat an eyelid. I told him I had always thought there was room for both of us in the New Forest.'

'He didn't agree?'

'He just smiled and said it was a cut-throat business. I remember him being so cold about it. I told him there and then that he'd put the kybosh on any future deals between us.'

'Did he get angry?'

Maybank laughed. 'The opposite; he looked like he just didn't care at all.'

'Were you surprised at the manner of his death?'

Maybank gave the question some thought. 'The manner of it maybe. But his untimely end? To be honest, no, he had changed big time in the last year.'

'Changed in what way exactly?'

'He seemed to be getting more edgy, as if he was craving

some new excitement. You had the feeling he could get into trouble. I washed my hands of him.'

'This land he did the dirty on you, do you have the details?'

Maybank opened a drawer and pulled out a sheaf of papers. He quickly sorted through them and pulled out a sheet and handed it over.

'That's the one. We were going to flatten it and put up some affordable housing.'

Farrows scanned the sheet. 'Do you think that's still what he intended to do?'

Maybank shrugged his shoulders. 'Who knows?'

Ed Farrows stood up. 'Thanks for your time, Mr Maybank, you've been most helpful.'

The property developer flashed a winning smile. 'Anything I can do to help.'

On the drive back to Pikes Hill, Sarah Harrison could not help voicing her admiration.

'Good-looking and rich, I think I've just met my dream man.'

Farrows laughed. 'Yes, but would you be happy, Sarah?'

Sarah pulled a disconsolate expression. 'Fat chance I'll ever get to find out, but I'd be open to putting it to the test.'

'Believe me, Sarah, you can do much better than him. It's the info he gave on Turnbull that I found most attractive about him. My advice to you would be to focus on that. We'll check out this development address, see if it was in his Lymington office documentation.'

'Once again, we heard the familiar theme about Turnbull's craving for excitement.'

'It certainly keeps coming up. Do you know what I think?'

'I'm sure you're going to tell me.'

'For all his wealth, it really does sound like Roger Turnbull was just plain bored.'

*

'So you've got no idea where Mr Foster has gone?'

Councillor Simon Loveday tried to contain his agitation. The policeman's manner was not the friendliest and he resented the small army of police staff that had invaded the office and interfered with the daily routine.

'He didn't say, just phoned in this morning and said he had a few days owing and he and his wife were going to take advantage of the sunshine.'

DI Simpson swore under his breath. He was at the New Forest District Council offices on the Beaulieu Road with his investigative team. They were working through Roger Turnbull's historic property transactions. He had thought it would be a good opportunity to follow up on Ed Farrows' initial interview with Turnbull's friend Councillor Jack Foster. He had been one of the last to see Turnbull alive and Farrows had mentioned that though there was nothing obvious, he wasn't totally convinced Foster was telling him everything. Since that encounter, the fact that Foster had apparently decided to disappear for a few days could be significant; but then again, he could have been genuinely upset by Turnbull's death and understandably felt he needed a few days off.

'How long has Jack Foster worked here?'

'He goes back years; he was here long before I started.'

'So he's highly valued by the council?'

'Very much so, a lot of the people here see him as the guru.'

'How do you get on with him?'

Simpson thought he noticed a slight moment of hesitation before the councillor spoke.

'May I ask why are you asking these questions?'

'Mr Shaw was one of the last to see Roger Turnbull alive.'

Simon Loveday looked surprised. 'Oh, I didn't realise; he never said. To be honest, Jack can be a bit cantankerous at times and go his own way, but on the whole we have a good working relationship.'

'Did he give you any idea what day he will be back?'

'I got the impression sometime next Monday.'

'Thanks for your time, Mr Loveday, that should be all for now.'

Keith Simpson decided there and then to take a drive over to Foster's house just in case. There was always the chance that he was not being totally honest and was still holed up there. He informed his team of investigators of his intention and left the council office.

*

It was late afternoon when Ed Farrows drove into a neglected derelict area just outside Fawley. He was accompanied by Sarah Harrison and DC Paul Mason. After returning from the Sandringham offices in Christchurch, Farrows and Harrison had wasted no time in going through Turnbull's paperwork and PC data to see if there was any reference to the Fawley land development that had caused so much discord. Much to their surprise, they had found no reference relating to the purchase in any of the data connected to Burgeon Construction. They had informed David Jennings of this surprising development, and he had suggested they should drive down to Fawley and take a look. Paul Mason thought it would be a good idea to tag along with the bunch of keys discovered in Turnbull's garage. They had just been returned by forensics. Unfortunately, they had drawn a blank, Roger Turnbull's dabs being the only prints found.

They parked up and looked out at the deserted-looking wasteland. There were a few outbuildings scattered around, and a large pile of rubble dominated the central area.

Farrows was the first to comment, 'I'd love to know what Turnbull had planned for this place.'

Sarah Harrison answered, 'The guy at Sandringham had suggested flattening it and building some cheap housing.'

'It wouldn't be surprising if Turnbull may have had other plans.'

Sitting in the rear of the car, Paul Mason remarked, 'Well, whatever he had planned, it doesn't look like he'd made much of a start on it.'

They got out of the car and walked towards one of the buildings. It looked like an old garage that had not been used for years and was already starting to crumble. There were a couple of other structures that looked much the same, but Sarah Harrison's attention had been caught by a newer, more solid-looking building. It was still a shabby-looking dwelling but compared to the others it looked a little more habitable. She called over to Farrows and Mason and drew their attention to it. Unlike the other buildings, this one had both a lock and a padlock fitted on the door and steel shutters were drawn down over the windows. Paul Mason started going through the various-shaped keys found at Turnbull's house to see if any of them fitted. He spent quite a few minutes trying and discarding before he suddenly looked up with a triumphant grin.

'Bingo.'

He then went back to the car and returned with a pair of cutters. After shearing through the padlock, they were soon looking into the gloomy exterior of what looked like an abandoned office.

Ed Farrows gave a low whistle. 'Now, what do we have here?'

Sarah Harrison pulled a torch from her tunic and illuminated a small desk and chair with a coffee cup still containing some remnants of its sticky and congealed remains. A small scalpel and what looked like sealing wax with small bottles of different types of ink lay on the table. There were also traces of previously cut photographs sprinkled around the floor. Paul Mason slipped on some forensic gloves and pulled open the desk drawer. He felt a slight intake of breath when he saw what was inside. It was a mini laptop.

'I think we had better get David Jennings, DI Keith Simpson and a full forensics team here right away.'

*

Keith Simpson was standing outside Jack Foster's house. After ringing the doorbell several times, he had been greeted with total silence. Disappointingly, it really did look like the councillor had chosen to go away for a few days at very short notice. Why he had done so at this time could be entirely innocent, but his well-honed instincts somehow kept telling him differently. He looked around him. The house was completely surrounded by the New Forest trees and totally secluded. It felt eerily quiet, as if the trees had eyes and were silently staring at him. He felt himself jump slightly when his mobile sprang loudly into life.

'Hello, sir, this is Desk Sergeant Tom Fallon at Pikes Hill.'

'Yes, Sergeant?'

'If you're not too far away, DCI Jennings wants you back at Pikes Hill immediately. Seems there's been a significant find at a lock-up near Fawley; he needs your expertise.'

'Tell him I'm about fifteen minutes away.'

After giving the house one more cursory glance, he got back in his car and drove away.

As the car disappeared up the meandering single track road that led away from Jack Foster's house, a man stepped out from the trees. Though his manner appeared casual, there was something about his body language that suggested something more sinister. The man's eyes narrowed as he stared at the house for some time before eventually reaching into his pocket for his mobile.

*

An hour later, in Fawley, Jennings and Simpson were discussing the significance of the find whilst watching the forensics team in their white overalls doing their stuff.

David Jennings was sounding a little incredulous. 'So you're telling me that Roger could have somehow been involved in some sort of people trafficking?'

Keith Simpson nodded. 'Worse than that, we're probably talking about the illegal entry of criminals. My guess at this stage is Eastern European drug gangs.'

'How the hell did Roger let himself get involved in that?'

'These gangs find a way of getting people immersed in their web and once you're in, you can't get out. In Roger Turnbull's case, it was probably through his property portfolio. Plenty of opportunity for money laundering. Believe me, this is serious stuff.'

Jennings glanced towards the small office where all the forensic activity was going on.

'So what exactly was going on here then?'

'In a nutshell, I would guess document modification, creating new identities and false backgrounds with fake papers and false work references, even passports; it all plays a critical part in a criminal's existence. It's a very special skill: a good documents man is priceless to these criminal gangs.'

'Surely you're not suggesting that Roger Turnbull was that man?'

'I've no idea if he had the sufficient skillset. Though a lot of what I've seen so far suggests he could be reckless, I've heard from some people who dealt with him who thought he was a very intelligent man.'

Jennings thought back to the highly respected man he knew. 'He was certainly pretty sharp, but believe me, if you knew him as I did, you would find all this criminal activity hard to swallow.'

'Nothing surprises me, David. Either way, if he wasn't capable of faking papers, he was certainly working with someone who was. What puzzles me is this office still looks like it's been recently active. These gangs are usually very good at covering their tracks. If, as it's beginning to look like, Turnbull was on the wrong end of a gang execution, this place has been left remarkably untidy and incriminating. You would have expected it to have been cleaned up in the likelihood we might eventually come snooping.'

'So you're saying we may have caught them on the hop?'

Simpson reflected, 'Knowing the way they normally work, someone's slipped up, that's for sure.'

A forensic examiner walked past with the mini laptop in a plastic bag.

David Jennings pointed towards the bag. 'From all that you've said, I'm looking forward to seeing what the techies might discover in that PC.'

'We don't know for certain yet that it belonged to Turnbull, but hopefully the fact it was left here could be a massive own goal on the gang's part.' Keith Simpson expanded on his theory, 'I was pretty much convinced from the beginning that Turnbull's death was gang-related, but I made the decision to approach it with an open mind. From what we've seen today, we can now get the Homicide and Major Crimes Unit totally involved with the National

Drugs Intelligence Unit to compare their criminal data. Believe me, the tentacles from this sort of operation spread far and wide.'

'It definitely looks like we've got something to work on, which reminds me, I'd better get back to prepare the ground at Pikes Hill.'

Simpson asked, 'Historically, do you get much of a drug problem in the New Forest?'

'There are always drugs, of course, but as a rule it's normally pretty low level.'

'I think it will also be a good idea to get in touch with the local regional drug squad, see if they've recently noticed an upturn in activity.'

Jennings nodded. 'Makes sense.' He gave a slight nod of approval to the man from Scotland Yard. 'Much appreciate your expertise on this one, DI Simpson.'

For a split second, a slight smile played around Simpson's lips. 'It's what I'm here for.'

Though he was trying to remain calm on the service, David Jennings' adrenaline was flowing big time as he walked back to his car. In his time in the force, he could not remember a case when he had felt so pumped.

*

Jack Foster was sitting under a parasol at the front of the Highcliffe Hotel in Bournemouth. On the table in front of him was a bottle of his favourite, Famous Grouse Whiskey, with a bucket of ice. The late-afternoon sunshine felt pleasantly warm with a slight cooling breeze coming off the sea. After the disturbing episode with the two men in the car the day before, he'd felt he just had to get away and fast. He needed time to think, to try to make sense of it all. That Roger had gotten himself into something pretty horrific was obvious; the question was what the hell it was, and how much he himself was implicated. Fortunately, his wife Sandra had readily agreed to the idea of a short-term break. She had noticed he had not been himself since the murder of Roger Turnbull. In truth, she had been quite surprised by just how much Turnbull's death had affected her husband. She agreed that a few days away on the sunny coastline would do him the world of good.

Slowly, the combination of the whiskey, the sea view and the warm sunshine went some way to calming his anxiety, if only temporarily. Sandra had just gone back to the room to shower and get ready for dinner. He took another swig of his whiskey and closed his eyes behind his sunglasses and drifted. He was brought back into consciousness some minutes later by the sound of a footfall swiftly followed by a chair being pulled around the table. He thought at first it was one of the hotel staff come to clear the table. It was then he heard a voice with a strong accent.

'You can run, Mr Foster, but you can't hide.'

Foster opened his eyes. He immediately recognised the smile of one of the men he'd seen in the car the previous day. He sat up with a jolt.

The man gave him a steady stare. 'We know everything about you, Mr Foster. We know what you do and, more importantly, what you did for Roger Turnbull.'

Foster took off his glasses to get a good look at the man sitting in front of him. His head was shaved and shiny, his neck as thick as a rugby prop forward, emblazoned by a large tattoo displaying a two-headed serpent. Behind his head, the blue azure of where the English Channel met the Atlantic Ocean, twinkling and sparkling in the bright warm sunshine.

Foster finally managed to splutter out a question. 'What do you want from me?'

'Simple, we just want to be sure that you are on our side. That when we eventually get a replacement for the unfortunate Mr Turnbull, you will continue to provide the service we require.'

Struggling to rationalise the implications of what the man had told him, Foster could not think of anything to say.

The man's expression hardened. 'I hope you are not thinking of going to the police. That would be very foolish of you. I can assure you that if you did decide to go that way, we would hunt you down like a dog. There would be no hiding place, neither for you nor your wife.' He stood up from the table. 'Have no doubt, Mr Foster, we will be watching you.' He smiled once more. 'We will be in touch.' He then walked away swiftly and was gone.

Jack Foster sat there in a daze for some minutes. Had that really just happened? Was it a bad dream? It was only when he reached for his glass that his violently trembling hand told him it had all been so terrifyingly real.

SEVEN

A SHAFT OF LIGHT

It was Wednesday morning at Pikes Hill and David Jennings was once again seated in the small partitioned side office, accompanied by Ed Farrows, Paul Mason and Keith Simpson. They were discussing the significance of the breakthrough discovery of one of Turnbull's development sites in Fawley the day before.

David Jennings was talking. 'I've spoken to the County HQ Drugs Squad, and they've confirmed a recent rise in Class A drug use in the New Forest area. Now we still don't know for sure whether that has got anything to do with the lock-up we found yesterday. We hope to find that out when forensic come back with their reports and the geeks get inside the mini laptop that was discovered.'

Keith Simpson sounded more certain, 'I've already had a brief conversation with the drug squad in London and they've already come up with some useful info.'

Jennings leant forwards. 'I'm all ears.'

'It seems that a well-known drug criminal was found

dead a couple of weeks ago in Haslemere. His name was Charlie Sayer, and they think his execution was significant as regards Eastern European drug gangs moving in and taking over. These gangs are intent on taking over the county lines in the major towns, and believe me, those lines spread right out to the rural areas. Don't be left in any doubt that we are dealing with people who are ruthless with anyone who gets in their way.'

It was Ed Farrows who asked the obvious question. 'I assume you're including rural places like the New Forest in that analysis?'

Simpson nodded. 'Believe me, there's no limits on their territories. My theory is that it's likely that Charlie Sayer was targeted by one of these gangs and he had no choice but to work alongside them before they decided it was the time to get rid of him. It's the normal pattern; once he had helped them establish the lines and trap houses in new areas, they had no further need for him. That's when they take over completely.'

Jennings was still taking it all in. 'So you think it's a pretty sure thing that one of these gangs is now operating in the New Forest?'

'It's showing all the signs.'

'But where does Roger Turnbull come in exactly?'

'That's what we have to find out for sure, but it's looking like anything from money laundering through his properties, to using them as a base for falsifying identity documents and sale and storage of stuff like cocaine. One thing for certain, he couldn't have been doing it on his own.'

Jennings whistled softly. 'Well, hopefully some more

names will creep out of the woodwork in the next twenty-four hours—'

Ed Farrows interrupted, 'The council have confirmed that Adrian Ferguson submitted the planning application for the Fawley land development. He was obviously working for Turnbull, so I think we should pay him another visit, see how much he knew.'

Jennings nodded. 'Sounds like a good place to start.'

DI Simpson went on. 'The guy, Foster, who works on the council and was matey with Turnbull has disappeared for a few days. He's supposed to be back at the offices on Monday. I think we should bring him in for questioning as soon as he gets back. As regards the potential for money laundering, I think it will also be worth taking a much closer look at any accountants and solicitors that crop up on Turnbull's transaction history.'

Jennings looked reflective. He was still struggling with the idea that Roger Turnbull had become entangled so deeply with European drug gangs.

'Well, it looks like we have several interesting lines of inquiry.'

Keith Simpson frowned. 'The one thing about this case that does not quite add up is the state of the lock-up we discovered yesterday. As I said before, the gangs of which we're talking would normally make a much better job of covering their tracks.'

'Perhaps we caught them on the hop with our Fawley raid?'

Simpson pursed his lips thoughtfully. 'It's a possibility. It will be interesting to see exactly what the IT team discover on that mini laptop.'

'With any luck, we should find out tomorrow.' Jennings stood up and turned to Paul Mason. 'How many names left on your list, Paul?'

Mason scanned his list. 'We're slowly getting there, sir. There are a couple of contractors, a surveyor and a solicitor.' He looked across to Ed Farrows. 'Many left on yours, Ed?'

Ed Farrows looked at his sheet. 'Pretty much all through, but in view of what we discovered yesterday and what DI Simpson has said here this morning, I think a few of the legal men could be well worth a revisit.'

Jennings looked satisfied. 'Sounds sensible. Let's leave no stone unturned, no matter how much shit we find underneath.'

*

James Cumber was enjoying the novelty of travelling first class to London by train from Bournemouth. DI Jennings had insisted on paying for his return ticket and he was quite relaxed about enjoying his generosity. He had ordered a ham and pickle sandwich and was now washing it down with a cool glass of Moretti as he stared out of the window. The Hampshire countryside was looking a picture in the bright sunshine, with the sun glinting off obscure reservoirs and vividly highlighting the architecture of the occasional church tower. When he thought back to the previous week and his nightmare journey to Lyndhurst, he wondered why he didn't travel this way more often. An attractive and smartly dressed lady of middle age was sitting across the aisle from him. Throughout the journey, he had noticed she would occasionally give him a slight smile whenever they happened to catch each other's eye. He could not help feeling slightly flattered. Though the good looks he had enjoyed in his youth were now somewhat weathered by age and experience, he liked to think that with his tanned, even features and closely cropped greying hair he still cut a presentable figure. Enjoying the feeling of the warm sun on his face, he closed his eyes and drifted off into a pleasant dream where he was on a golf course somewhere in Spain. He was still in this peaceful state when the train finally rolled into Waterloo Station. The smart lady opposite smiled gratefully as Cumber politely let her go before him as they exited the train. On another occasion when he might have had more time, he might well have been tempted to strike up a conversation and see where it led, but he reminded himself he had important business to attend to. With the vague feeling that he just might have missed out on an opportunity, he exited the train and merged with the thronging rush of humanity on the platform. Coming after his peaceful sedate journey, suddenly emerging into the noise and bustle of a London train station came as a stimulating shock to the senses. He passed through the numerous barriers before exiting the station and turning left towards the River Thames.

The sun shone brightly and hot on Queen's Walk as he turned eastwards and made his way past the structures that housed the National Film Theatre and the London Television Centre. He could not help feeling a little excited. Not only did it feel like the old days, being involved in solving a crime, but he was also looking forward to meeting up afterwards with that rare bright jewel in his personal life, his daughter Kelsey. As he neared Southwark Bridge, he recognised Mark Kemp immediately, as he was the spitting image of his dad when Bill was younger. Cumber also noticed he was carrying a sizable blue folder.

They greeted each other warmly and made their way to a convenient seat that overlooked the Thames. As Cumber looked across at the City of London, he was reminded once again of how the new construction of countless high-rise buildings since the millennium had much changed the face of the square mile as he remembered it.

Mark Kemp gave a good natured grin. 'So the old partnership that my dad used to talk about so admiringly could possibly be making a comeback?'

Cumber pointed to his leg and answered, 'It's a nice thought, Mark, but unfortunately it's never going to happen. Besides, Joe wouldn't be interested; he loves his retirement. That's why nailing this tormentor is so important to him.'

'It was much the same with Dad; it really got to him. I fully believe the stress of it knocked a couple of years off him.' Mark handed over the folder. 'It's all in there; he worked on it night and day for a good few months with the Yard and Steve Harmer. Steve's number is also in there. From what Joe said on the phone, it sounds very likely it could be the same fella.'

Cumber looked at the bulky folder. 'Bill certainly had a good man on his side if Steve Harmer was on the case. It wasn't often the old Bloodhound didn't get to the bottom of it. You say your dad was zoning in on the Varney case in 1986?'

'My dad remained pretty convinced, even though pretty much all of the Tyler brothers are no longer with us.'

'What made him so sure?'

'It was something the writer let slip in one of the threatening notes, some nonsense to do with the university masons looking after him in his retirement. Remember, it was Dad's last case before he called it a day.' Mark pointed to the folder. 'It's all in there.'

Cumber thought back to those far-off days in the mid-eighties. 'We all worked on the case at the time. I think your dad would've have seen it as confirmation of his suspicions now that Joe is getting the same treatment.'

'I know Steve Harmer has some new information that he considers significant, but he didn't go into detail. I could have followed it up and made a fuss, but after Dad passed away I just wanted to move on.'

Cumber tapped the folder. 'Don't worry, Mark, this is not only for Joe; we'll also sort it out for Bill. Your old dad was a top man; it's the least we can do.'

*

Sarah Harrison sounded a little deflated. 'I don't think I'm going to hear anything about the promotion until this Turnbull business is closed.'

Ed Farrows replied, 'You're probably right. David will get around to it at some stage. At the moment he's like a kid with a new toy; he can't think of anything else but this case.'

Sarah pulled a face. 'I hope he doesn't forget about me, or, even worse, change his mind.'

Farrows smiled at her reassuringly. 'Not a chance. Stop worrying, you're a shoo-in.'

They were driving towards Brockenhurst. After what had been discussed at the morning meeting, they were both making a return visit to the planning consultant Adrian Ferguson. He had been heavily involved in the planning application for the Fawley development. How much else he knew was still open to question. What they did know was that he had worked closely with Turnbull for many years, so they needed some answers. Pulling up in front of his house, the large Georgian structure looked just as impressive as on their first visit.

Sarah Harrison looked on admiringly as she thought back to their previous interview.

'I wonder if Mr Ferguson will be a little more upbeat this time – cannot understand how anyone who lives here could be anything other than euphoric.'

'He did seem a solitary soul; perhaps we just caught him on a bad day. One of his regular associates had just been brutally murdered, after all.'

Sarah mused, 'In view of the shit we suspect Turnbull might have been swimming in, I still find it difficult to imagine a man like Ferguson being involved. He seemed so decent and gentle.'

Farrows wagged a finger. 'First rule of policing: you can't go by appearances. Let's see if we can make a dent in that favourable first impression.'

They got out of the car and approached the house. As before, the house seemed quiet, as if there was no one inside. After knocking on the door, they waited for several minutes.

Farrows stood back from the house and looked up at the windows; they were all closed.

'That's a shame; it looks like we've missed him.'

It was Sarah Harrison that first detected the faint throbbing sound of an idling engine.

'Can you hear that?'

Farrows picked up on the sound and nodded. It seemed to be coming from around the corner of the house in the garage area. The two officers walked round the side of the house to investigate. The garage door was locked but the sound was definitely coming from within. There was a distinct, unmistakable whiff of petrol fumes hanging in the air. Farrows and Harrison looked at each other in silent confirmation; sadly, it was an all too familiar scenario they had confronted many times before. Ed Farrows was on to the emergency services immediately.

*

James Cumber had arranged to meet Kelsey at the southern end of the Millenium Bridge. Even though there were throngs of people walking across the bridge, he caught sight of his daughter long before she got to him. Seeing his beautiful daughter walking towards him in a bright summer dress with the iconic dome of St Paul's as a backdrop, he was once again filled with that familiar sense of pride. A radiant smile lit up her face when she saw him. Giving Cumber a big hug, she stood back and looked at him approvingly.

'You're looking trim.'

Cumber could not help feeling pleased at the compliment. 'I do my best.'

She put her arm through his as they headed eastwards along the Thames towards The Anchor pub in Southwark.

*

Ed Farrows and Sarah Harrison wasted no time in approaching one of the crime scene officers as soon as he emerged from the garage. Though the forensic work still had some way to go, they were keen to hear his initial findings.

Farrows asked, 'Have you found anything so far to suggest it's not a suicide?'

The SOCO shook his head. 'It's all looking pretty straightforward.'

Farrows exchanged glances with Sarah Harrison before asking, 'So we can definitely say there's no trace of foul play?'

The officer sounded pretty sure, 'Something could still turn up, but I would say it's looking like an open and shut case of suicide.'

Farrows' creased his brow in thought. When the emergency services had arrived and eventually forced open the garage doors, they had found the dead body of Adrian Ferguson slumped in the driver's seat of his car. With what had happened to Roger Turnbull, Farrows' immediate suspicions that Ferguson's death might not be as appeared seemed well founded. But now with the SOCO's initial findings appearing to rule out any criminality, he tried to make sense of its significance. Did the planning consultant's apparent suicide mean that he had been somehow implicated in Turnbull's death; an obvious case of Ferguson jumping before he was pushed? Surely it could not just be a coincidence. It had to be connected in some way. Ferguson's laptop and mobile phone had already been bagged and taken away. This would only be the start. Adrian Ferguson's professional and personal life would have to be put under the microscope and given the utmost scrutiny.

*

Cumber took a deep swallow of a foaming pint of London Pride. Kelsey had done well to find a seat in the crowded bar. The pub was obviously a popular lunch spot for both office workers and the many tourists. They had both settled for the ham, egg and chips and were busy getting stuck in. Kelsey had chosen a small glass of the house white to accompany her food.

Kelsey looked up from her plate and nodded towards Bill Kemp's folder. 'That looks important; what's in there?'

Cumber smiled. 'You wouldn't believe what's been happening down there in the sleepy New Forest.'

'Oh, I think I could. I heard something on the news about a murder.'

'I can't say too much at the moment, but what would you say if I told you Joe and I are vital witnesses in the case?'

Kelsey took a sip of her wine and shook her head. 'Once a copper, always a copper; you just can't help yourself.'

'Joe and Janet have also been getting a bit of menacing harassment. Hopefully what's in that folder will help nip it in the bud.'

Kelsey looked curious. 'All very intriguing. I'll be around for a couple more weeks so you will have to tell me the outcome when you get back.'

Cumber pushed his empty plate away and took another swig of his beer. 'How're you getting on at the flat; have I got anything left in the freezer?'

Kelsey laughed. 'I'm working my way through it. Actually, I'm quite enjoying the peace and quiet. I've even found the time to rediscover my old reading habit. I didn't realise you had so many books.'

Cumber gave his dodgy leg a stretch. 'I think you forget I've been a long time retired. Which books have taken your eye?'

'I must admit, I have a weakness for a good crime story; I must get it from you.'

'There are plenty of those on the shelves; fill your boots. By the way, Janet Loxley said some nice things about your acting.'

Kelsey gave a dismissive grin. 'She's just being nice. I've no illusions there. I hit my marks, remember to say my lines and take the money. Meryl Streep can rest easy.'

Cumber looked a bit disappointed with her response. 'You're too modest; you should be prouder of yourself. Surely it must still be nice to hear.'

Kelsey gave a slight shrug and took another sip of her wine.

Cumber went on, 'Well I for one agree with Janet: I think you're very good and I'm very proud of you.'

Kelsey looked momentarily touched. 'That's very sweet, Dad, but you could be just a teeny bit biased.'

'Your mum should feel proud too. Is she still doing OK?'

Kelsey hesitated and her expression clouded over. 'She's fallen off the wagon again. I've got her back under the doctor.'

Cumber shook his head sorrowfully. There was no doubt that Susan had given him a few miserable years at the time of the breakup, but he also remembered some of the happier times. Time had moved on and he wished her no ill will.

'I'm sorry to hear that.'

Kelsey's expression looked a little desperate. 'I really hope she's not going to be a hopeless case like Jamie.'

Cumber felt a pang at the mention of his wayward son and remained silent. Kelsey broke the sombre silence by getting onto her favourite subject.

'Have you met any nice ladies?'

Cumber's eyes rose up into his head. 'You're like a broken record. When are you going to accept that ship has probably sailed?'

Kelsey giggled mischievously. 'There must be some old boot out there ready to take you on.'

'Thanks a million. Anyway, when are you going to settle down and stop gallivanting?'

'I've told you before, I don't like long-term commitments; they hold you back. Men can be so clingy.'

'You won't always be beautiful, you know.'

'Now you sound like Mum.'

'Perhaps you should listen to her; she knows that truth more than most.'

Kelsey looked out of the pub window and gazed wistfully across the Thames at the much-changed skyline of the City of London.

'I guess I will just have to cross that bridge when I come to it.'

*

Jack Foster looked deep in thought as he barely touched his minute steak. He was sitting in the restaurant of the Highcliffe Hotel with his wife Sandra. The menacing visit he'd received from the tattooed man the day before had shaken him up badly. At first, he had been confused. What did it all mean? But after having all day to think, it now seemed blazingly obvious that the off-the-record property information he had been giving Roger Turnbull all this time had been used for far more sinister reasons than he could ever have imagined. The realisation that the gravy train he had enjoyed for so long had come to an end had slowly manifested itself throughout the day. He had come to a decision. It was going to mean the disgrace of a jail sentence and the end of his career. He really had no choice; the alternative was unthinkable. He looked across the table at his wife. Sandra was staring at him, concern creased across her face. He felt a huge sadness envelop him. He would have to tell her everything before calling Pikes Hill Police Station in the morning.

*

The evening was closing in at Pikes Hill and David Jennings was once more in his office with Ed Farrows, DI Keith

Simpson and DC Paul Mason. They were discussing the latest developments in the Turnbull case. Ed Farrows was giving the information on the Adrian Ferguson suicide.

'To all intents and purposes it looks like a genuine suicide. We've delved into his medical records, and it seems he's had a long history of depression. It could be that the murder of Roger Turnbull pushed him over the edge.'

Not for the first time, Keith Simpson sounded a cynical note. 'All the same, we cannot totally rule out he knew more than he was letting on.'

Farrows replied, 'It's possible, but having spoken to him, my gut feeling tells me that Turnbull more than likely kept him in the dark.'

Jennings commented, 'It could be that unless something obvious comes out of his business history, we may never know for sure.'

Simpson cut in sharply, 'What we do know is that he was involved in a lot of Turnbull's dodgy dealings, including the Fawley development.'

Jennings turned to Paul Mason. 'I hear you've got something interesting for us, Paul.'

Paul Mason had been waiting patiently. 'Yes, sir. There is a solicitor whose name appears frequently in the Burgeon Construction documentation called Brandon Lyons. It seems he recently took an office in Lyndhurst High Street after originally operating from Lymington. We found his office closed for business today. One of his customers happened to come along while we were there and told us that it had been shut since the end of last week.'

Both Jennings and Simpson were all attention.

David Jennings made the obvious observation, 'So, pretty much since Turnbull's execution.'

Mason nodded. 'He has a posh flat in the Evening Hill area of Sandbanks. When we paid it a visit this afternoon, there was no one in. A neighbour said he'd not been around for a few days.'

Jennings speculated, 'There's a slight chance it's an innocent coincidence but it could be highly significant. He must have some staff who worked with him at his office, be worth finding out if his disappearance caught them by surprise.'

Mason nodded. 'I'll get on it.'

Keith Simpson looked down at his notes. 'I've followed up with the regional drug squad and they have given me some names of pushers that operate in the area. I think this could be a fruitful line of inquiry as no one in the drug world likes outsiders pushing in. I'm quite open to doing a little snooping; people might just be prepared to squeak.'

David Jennings approved but felt he should give the man from Scotland Yard a warning.

'I know you like to work alone, DI Simpson, but go careful, we don't want any solo heroics. I would prefer you to be accompanied by officers in the drug squad; don't forget there's plenty of backup available if you need it.'

Simpson reassured him, 'Don't worry, I'm well aware of my limitations. I'm working with one of the squad's top men, seems he has a few informants.'

'All sounds very promising.' Jennings turned to the others. 'It looks like it's been a productive day, gents, plenty to get our teeth into. Hopefully the IT team will bring something extra to the party tomorrow.'

*

James Cumber had returned from his trip to London in the late afternoon, just in time to enjoy one of Janet Loxley's delicious tomato pasta dishes. The three of them were now sitting in the lounge discussing the contents of Bill Kemp's folder. Joe Loxley was going through the threatening notes that had been sent to his old boss. The messages were practically a carbon copy of the messages he'd received, a combination of abuse and sinister threats. Once again, the author of the notes threw in an accusation that Bill Kemp had somehow been responsible for the death of his dad. However, there were two extra notes that might have convinced Bill it had something to do with the Varney case in 1986. One of them was a sketch of what looked like a snake with the words "Varsity Viper". The other seemed to accuse him of being associated with the Freemasons, some rubbish about the university lodge protecting their own. It was all nonsense, of course. He had known Bill for many years and on the odd occasion he ever remembered him mentioning the masons, it had hardly been in the most complimentary terms, to say the least. As for Bill Kemp ever going to university, it was rubbish; he knew for a fact that he had been educated at a grammar school somewhere in South London. He handed over the notes to James Cumber.

'What do you think of that?'

'If Bill focused on the university stuff about the masons and the viper varsity reference, you can see why Bill might have thought it had something to do with the Varney case. According to these notes, Tony Tyler is the only one still alive from the original brothers.'

Loxley thought back to the case. 'I remember them being a sizable band of brothers. The Tyler tribe were just one of the many dodgy families that lived in South London at that time. All of them criminal to the core and twice as nasty.'

The details of the case were coming back to Cumber through the misty haze of time. 'They were a wild bunch. I can remember the night we wrongly arrested the Tyler brother we thought was responsible for the first murder.'

Loxley filled in the gaps, 'His name was Danny. That was the night you rescued poor old Brian Parrish from a serious going-over.'

Cumber looked sad at the memory. 'As it was, he had to spend a night in the hospital.'

'As usual, you were a top copper that night, James.'

'I only wished I could have done the same for him ten years later when we were mowed down by the car.'

'That was a tragedy, James, you couldn't have done any more. Christ, you were a whisker away from being killed yourself.'

'You know how it is, Joe. There are still times when I can't help rerunning the events of that night through my mind, each time hoping for a different outcome. Of course, the reality is Brian Parrish is no longer with us, and it ended my career with the pain in my leg reminding me every day.'

Loxley glanced across at Janet as he felt a pang of compassion for his old mate.

'We're only too aware that you've had to deal with that reality ever since, James.'

Janet Loxley reached over and gave Cumber a

comforting pat on the arm. 'We know things have not been easy for you, James, but you have handled it better than most.'

Cumber gave a sad smile. 'I like to think so. If I have managed, then it's only because I'm blessed with having two good friends like you.' There was a brief silence before he added with a grin, 'Plus the golf, of course.'

Janet laughed. 'Don't forget the golf.' She stood up. 'Cup of coffee all round I think.'

Loxley picked up the folder. 'Good idea. Now, let's get back to Bill's paperwork. I wouldn't want him looking down and accusing us of slacking.'

Joe Loxley started going through Bill's notes on the original case. The Varney serial murders had been a difficult high-profile case of ill-fated coincidence. At the time of the first murder, young Danny Tyler had been in the wrong place at the wrong time, leading to his false accusation and arrest. When the second murder was carried out, Danny was locked up in police custody. From that point on, the investigation shifted swiftly to the collegiate word of Oxford and the pursuit of Marcus Varney. Loxley remembered the national embarrassment for Scotland Yard at the time weighing heavily on Bill Kemp, who was at the head of the investigation. There was no doubt that it contributed to him taking his early pension soon after. Bill had scribbled some notes on Danny Tyler provided by Scotland Yard. James looked over Loxley's shoulder as they read. The notes made grim reading. It seemed that Danny had gone on to live a relatively short life fuelled with drugs and filled with spells in prison for theft and violent crime. He had been found dead in an alley in Walworth, renowned as a street refuge for addicts and alcoholics.

Cumber gave a soft sigh. 'Not exactly a life well lived, I think we can agree.'

'Some people can't be helped, I guess.' Loxley continued reading Bill Kemp's notes. 'Looks like Bill and Steve Harmer were trying to establish whether any of the brothers had children. Looks like he drew a blank with Danny, but there were a few offspring from the other brothers. Looks like Scotland Yard traced them, but they were all eliminated from the inquiries.'

Cumber reached over and picked up a sheet of paper displaying Steve Harmer's name and telephone number.

'I think it's about time we rang Steve Harmer to find out the significant development Mark mentioned. Perhaps you should ring the old Bloodhound tonight.'

Janet entered the lounge with the coffees and handed them out. 'That sounds like a good idea, Joe; surely the sooner we know his news, the better.'

Loxley looked at the time. It was still early evening. There was a good chance that Steve would be around and as eager as ever to reveal his findings. He took a gulp of his coffee.

'Now seems as good a time as any.'

Five minutes later, Loxley was ringing the number of his old Scotland Yard compatriot. The familiar voice of Steve Harmer answered the phone.

'Hello?'

'Hello, Steve, it's your old boss Joe Loxley.'

'Christ, there's a blast from the past. How are you?'

'I'm doing OK. You and the wife good?'

'We're ticking over. I'm still keeping my hand in with Scotland Yard.'

'So I've heard.'

'They know I get a bit bored, so they occasionally throw a few things my way to get my teeth into. I think I'm benefiting from the lack of resource in the force these days.'

Loxley laughed. 'It's good to know that someone's getting a benefit.'

'Did you get to Bill's funeral? Unfortunately I couldn't make it.'

'Yes, I did. It went as well as could be expected.'

'So you're enjoying life in the New Forest? I heard there was a nasty murder down there recently.'

'Yes, you won't believe it, but James Cumber is down here on a visit and we've both ended up vital witnesses in the case. Can't say too much at the moment but you're welcome to come down for a visit sometime when it's over and I'll tell you all about it.'

'That sounds interesting. Thanks for the offer, Joe, I will take you up on that.'

'You're more than welcome. Anyway, the reason I've rung you is my idyllic existence down here has been recently disturbed.'

'Oh, what's up?'

'I understand you were doing some work for Bill in his last year.'

'That's right. He was getting some harassment which we thought might be related to an old case. We got Scotland Yard involved for a spell.'

'Well, I'm now getting exactly the same treatment.'

'In view of what I found out, that kind of makes sense, so I'm not surprised. Bill was convinced it had something to do with the Varney case back in 1986 and I was inclined to agree with him. Now you're also getting the same aggro, it seems even more certain that we were on the right track.'

'James is helping me, and he went up to London yesterday to pick up a folder from Bill's son Mark.'

Harmer was enjoying this. 'Christ, it's just like the old days. Bill spent a lot of time on that folder; there's some useful stuff in there.'

'We've just been going through it. I see from Bill's notes that he got the Yard to look into the Tyler brothers' children, but it looks like they drew a blank.'

'That's right, but there's been an interesting discovery since then. Recently, the surviving brother Tony volunteered a piece of useful information regarding Danny.'

'I'm all ears.'

'It seems that Danny had an illegitimate son called Terry.'

'Is he in the system?'

'Scotland Yard didn't have anyone called Terry Tyler on file, so I managed to persuade them to use the HOLMES computer to run a DNA comparison report and they managed to find a match with Danny Tyler.'

'It's amazing what they can do nowadays.'

'It's a guy called Terry Evans. He's got a history of drug crime both as a user and a pusher.'

'Sounds like a chip off the old block.'

'Because this news came out some time after Bill died, his son Mark didn't think it worth pursuing.'

'Got a physical description?'

'All I know is he's somewhere in his early thirties and is a lot taller than his dad Danny.'

'That wouldn't be difficult. As I'm sure you remember, it was one of the unhelpful coincidences that both Danny and Marcus Varney were such a pair of short arses that caused a lot of the problems. I take it that this son is a bit of a drifter?'

'He had no fixed address and the Yard is far too stretched to bother looking for him if Mark isn't interested.'

'So there's a fair chance he could be down here in the New Forest?'

'As you know, Joe, I'm not a betting man, but even I would be tempted to put a wager on it.'

'I'm really grateful, Steve. We'll see what we can find out from this end. Don't forget my invitation; it would be great to see you.'

'I'll have a word with Linda and give you a few dates. Give James my regards and good luck.'

'Will do and thanks.' Loxley put the phone down. He'd scribbled down the name that Steve had given him. He felt emboldened by the knowledge. If Steve was correct, and his old Scotland Yard colleague wasn't often wrong, the tormentor who was causing them so much stress was no longer nameless!

EIGHT

PLAYING WITH FIRE

Desk Sergeant Tom Fallon quickly signed off some more paperwork before picking up another phone call. The Thursday morning in Pikes Hill had been a busy one, with investigative officers buzzing about with their written reports and well-meaning members of the public still ringing in and offering information on the Turnbull case. It had now been a week since the murder. Fallon found it interesting that they now seemed to be getting more calls from amateur sleuths than at the time of the murder. As was invariably the case in these investigations, most of the info was pure conjecture and guesswork, but every call had to be logged and followed up just in case there was a valuable nugget amongst the theories.

'Pikes Hill Station.'

There was some hesitation at the end of the phone before he heard a voice.

'This is Councillor Jack Foster and I'm ringing in connection with the Roger Turnbull case.'

Fallon thought he could detect someone crying softly in the background. 'What have you got for us, Mr Foster?'

Again there was a hesitation before Foster answered. 'I'm staying at the Highcliffe Hotel with my wife in Bournemouth.' There was another pause. 'Basically, I think we are in danger, and I want you to come and get us. I've got a confession to make.'

Fallon could detect the obvious distress. 'We can arrange for that, Mr Foster. I'll get it organised for someone to pick you up in the reception of the hotel, if that's alright?'

'We'll be waiting.'

Jack Foster put his mobile back in his pocket. He looked across at his sobbing wife and sighed deeply. He'd had to come clean with her, but it had not made things any easier. How do you tell your wife of thirty years that you are not the man she thinks you are? That you are in reality a corrupt fraud with no ethics enjoying riding the gravy train alongside Roger Turnbull with no moral conscience whatsoever. Now came the reckoning: career-ending disgrace and a prison sentence. Looking at his wife standing there so obviously distressed and devastated, he felt at that moment it was the least he deserved.

*

DI Keith Simpson turned left off the A337 into the Avenue Road in Lymington on his way to the police station. That morning, he had made an early start. He was keen to pursue his inquiries into the underground drug world that he suspected was spreading its dark, far-reaching malevolence into the idyllic setting of the New Forest. He had arranged to meet a DS John Craddock at Lymington Police Station. He was one of the regional drug officers known to have a good network of informants. He parked up in the grounds of the Lymington Town Hall where the police station was based and entered a large three-storey building. DS Craddock was waiting to meet him at the reception desk and the drug officer wasted little time in leading Simpson upstairs to a small, uncluttered office furnished with just a desk, a small side table and two chairs.

Keith Simpson took a seat and studied the man in front of him. Craddock was a big man whose genial expression and craggy facial features gave a favourable first impression of rugged integrity.

Craddock got straight to the point. 'I've been bringing myself up to speed on what you have so far on the Turnbull case. Though so far there is nothing concrete to connect him, I think there's more than enough here to suggest that he may well have been getting a slice of the action.'

Simpson nodded. 'That was my feeling. I've heard that recent drug activity in the New Forest seems to have gone up a grade.'

'No doubt about it. We're in danger of losing control, to be honest; the money and manpower needed to combat it is just not there. We've recently suspected that new drug gangs have been operating in the area, but if, as you suggest, it's Eastern European gangs moving in from the urban areas, then that really is a different league. There have been a couple of occasions in the last month when we thought we were closing in on them, but so far they've always seemed to be one step ahead.' He looked down once more on the notes in front of him and shook his head. 'Why an apparently well-respected man like Turnbull should have got involved beats me.'

They were interrupted by a fresh-faced officer poking his head around the door.

'Sorry to interrupt. Can I interest anyone in a piece of cake?'

DS Craddock looked appreciative. 'You bet; cut me off a big slice.'

The young officer entered the office wearing a wide grin and carrying a large cake. Craddock turned to Keith Simpson in explanation.

'This is DS Nick Stainrod. He's celebrating his thirtieth birthday.' Craddock gestured towards Simpson. 'This is DI Keith Simpson from Scotland Yard.'

Stainrod looked impressed. 'Can I offer you any cake, sir?'

Simpson politely declined. 'I'm watching the waistline, but many happy returns anyway.'

Stainrod put the cake down on a side table and cut Craddock a generous portion with a paper knife.

Simpson turned his attention back to DS Craddock. 'From all we've learnt about Turnbull so far, I'm getting the impression he seemed to have a sense of entitlement and invulnerability that he felt put him above the law. Given that perception, it would not be difficult to imagine that he saw himself sitting at the top table as a major player.'

Craddock shook his head. 'If that's the case then he was seriously deluded. You don't need me to tell you that he was never going to be a match for these people. If he was involved, it looks likely they were also using his property transactions for money laundering, turning dirty money into clean.'

'It could be more than that. Going by what we found at his Fawley development, it looks like he may well have been actively involved in the criminal activity on the ground.'

Craddock was again perusing the Turnbull notes in front of him and studying the findings at Fawley.

'In my experience, a skilful documents man is a vital part of any criminal gang's operation. For as long as they are useful to them, they are very highly valued. Did Turnbull have the skillset to have been that man?'

'Forensic are on the case as we speak. As it stands, we simply can't rule it out.'

Craddock turned his attention back to DS Stainrod, who was still in the room meticulously cutting the cake into regular uniform slices.

'You still here, Nick? The office will be wondering where you've got to.'

'I like to be fair. I don't want to be accused of favouritism.'

Craddock laughed. 'Well, if you want any reassuring, you're definitely the most popular man in the office today.'

'People keep telling me you're only thirty once, so why not?' Stainrod replied.

'That's very true.' Craddock took a large bite of his cake as they watched Stainrod complete his cake slicing before leaving the office with a cheerful wave.

Simpson commented, 'Seems a bright spark.'

Craddock grinned. 'He's certainly that. He's only been

working with the Hampshire drug squad for the last year after recently getting hitched with his wife Cathy and transferring down here from the Met. In the short time he's been here, he's made quite the impression and is already highly thought of.'

Simpson sounded a philosophical note. 'It looks like the Met's loss is the drug squad's gain.'

'To tell you the truth, DI Simpson, we are grateful for all the talent and help we can get.' After swiftly finishing off the cake, Craddock stood up. 'I think it's about time I introduced you to my man on the ground. With a little incentive, I might even be able to get him to throw some light on this Turnbull business.'

Simpson looked pleased. 'That's what I came here for.'

The two men left the building and made their way to Craddock's car.

*

You could have heard a pin drop in the interview room at Pikes Hill. David Jennings and Ed Farrows sat opposite Jack Foster and his legal representative. They had picked up Foster and his wife from the Highcliffe Hotel in Bournemouth after his morning phone call. Farrows could not help noticing the difference in Foster after their first meeting. His hands were shaking, and his legs and arms were constantly moving as he sat in the chair. He could almost smell his fear. David Jennings switched on the recording and began.

'So, Mr Foster, you have something to confess in connection with the Roger Turnbull case?'

Foster's eyes were darting everywhere as he took a deep breath and answered, 'For the last seven years or so, I've been giving Roger Turnbull unofficial information. This was regarding properties that were coming up for development in order for him to snap them up on the cheap before they were common knowledge.'

'I take it you were getting lucrative unofficial financial rewards in this arrangement.'

Foster paused for a second or two before answering, 'Yes, I was.'

'So why are you confessing now?'

'I've very strong reason to believe that my life is in grave danger, and I include my wife in that.'

'Care to expand?'

'Since Roger's death, I have been stalked by two men who I believe were involved in his murder.'

'And they're threatening to do the same to you?'

'Yesterday, in Bournemouth, one of them approached me at the front of the hotel and left me in no doubt that if I wasn't prepared to continue the arrangement I'd had with Roger, I would meet with the same fate.'

'Was your wife present?'

'No, he'd obviously waited till I was on my own, but he made it obvious the threat also included my wife.'

Ed Farrows came in with a question. 'Do you know why Roger Turnbull was shot?'

Foster raised his arms in bewilderment. 'I've honestly no idea.'

'Come on, Mr Foster, you don't really expect us to believe that, do you?'

Foster looked a little desperate. 'It's true. All I know is

that the financial rewards for the info I'd given him had been much more lucrative in the last year.'

'So you didn't think to ask him why?'

'I did ask him more than once, but Roger was a very secretive person. I certainly had no idea that he was getting into anything that could be construed as dangerous.'

'I want you to think very carefully before you answer this next question. On that last evening you saw him, can you remember anything that was said that might have suggested something was changing?'

There was a long silence before Foster answered. 'He did say that the money would be taking a drop going forwards. I've thought about it long and hard since, but I honestly can't say for certain if that revelation had anything to do with his death.'

David Jennings asked, 'Can you give us a good description of this man that threatened you?'

Jack Foster thought back to the sinister smile of the man who had effectively ruined his life.

'He spoke with an accent – probably Eastern European – tall, shaven head, with a large tattoo of a snake on his neck. I'd seen him previously when he was with another man. They followed me in their car, a wine-red Hyundai.'

While Ed Farrows wrote down the details, Foster went on with more than a hint of despair.

'You will give me and my wife protection, won't you?'

Jennings was quick to reassure him, 'Mr Foster, you won't be going anywhere for the time being. You will first be charged with abuse of position for personal gain. If we do find out in the course of our inquiries that you knew more than you're saying here, then you'll be going down for a very long time. In the meantime, we'll make the security arrangements for your wife.'

Jack Foster silently nodded his gratitude, the relief on his face obvious.

After Foster and his brief left the room, Ed Farrows turned to David Jennings.

'Do you believe he has told us everything?'

'It's difficult to tell for sure, but on balance I'm inclined to believe him. Unlike the reckless Turnbull, I just don't see him having the nerve to knowingly get involved with drug gangs.'

Farrows looked at the description he'd written down. 'I'll get this circulated to the investigative team; can't be too many like him hanging around in the New Forest.'

Jennings agreed, 'He certainly looks and sounds like a nasty piece of work. In fact, the archetypal drug-gang villain. Probably a good idea to keep this description in house for the moment, we don't want to panic the gang into doing a runner just yet.'

Farrows questioned, 'Even if Foster is telling the truth, I find it hard to believe that Roger Turnbull has been working totally alone in this drug activity.'

'What are you suggesting, a conspiracy?'

'It's got all the signs.'

Jennings looked encouraged. 'Well, you know what they say. Every conspiracy has a network, and every network has a weak link.'

On that optimistic note, the two officers left the interview room.

*

DS Craddock stopped the car on the edge of a derelict waste ground just outside New Milton. It was surrounded by what looked like long-abandoned allotment sheds. Keith Simpson got out of the car and surveyed the desolate landscape. The heat of the day was already rising sharply and through a slight haze he noticed some strategically placed CCTV cameras.

Craddock read his thoughts and gave him some detail. 'This whole area was given over to vegetable growing for many years, before it became an unhappy hunting ground for all sorts of users in recent years. It's only in the last year that we've managed to clean it up. With the cameras, we now ensure it's a strict no-go zone for anything drug-related.'

Simpson wondered whether the land had also been on Roger Turnbull's radar for future development.

'We're still going through Turnbull's property dealings; wouldn't be surprised if he'd had his eye on this land.'

Craddock shook his head. 'No chance of that. We're working very closely with the council on this one. It's earmarked to be a large sports centre for the local schools and communities.'

Simpson nodded approvingly. 'It's only right that something good should come out of it, I suppose.' He caught sight of a battered old Ford parked across the way and was reminded of why they were there. 'Where's our man?'

Craddock gave a slight smile. 'Follow me.'

They walked along the row of old allotment sheds before Craddock stopped in front of one with an old tin bucket that had been deliberately placed outside. Craddock turned to Keith Simpson and pointed to the shed.

'He's in there.'

Craddock tapped on the door, and it was opened by a man who Simpson guessed to be much younger than he looked.

Craddock spoke first. 'Hello, Alfie, is there room for two more?'

Alfie Jenkins looked anxiously at Keith Simpson as he let them enter the shed.

Craddock reassured him, 'No need to worry, Alfie. This is DI Simpson from Scotland Yard.'

Keith Simpson studied the man in the gloom of the interior. Jenkins had a few days' growth of gingery stubble and a silver stud in his nose. His eyes had a watery washed-out look which added to his generally undernourished appearance. He was dressed in faded and grubby jeans and a red, well-worn T-shirt. The aroma inside the hot stuffy shed could be described as earthy at best.

Craddock cut to the chase. 'We're here because of the recent shooting in Minstead.'

Jenkins immediately looked defensive. 'Why would you think I know anything about that?'

Craddock was undeterred. 'We have every reason to think it was drug-related.'

Jenkins still looked anxious but, more importantly, he suddenly looked interested.

'Maybe it was.'

What played out next was obviously a much-repeated routine in which Craddock pulled out a bulky envelope from his jacket and pushed it into Jenkins' clutching fingers.

'OK, Alfie, give us what you've got.'

Jenkins took a little time to answer, as if he was weighing up the balance between risk and reward. Eventually, he made up his mind.

'About six months ago, there were rumours an Eastern European gang had moved in on a share with Charlie Sayer's county lines. It all seemed to be going smoothly when suddenly there was a changeover at the top. Charlie used to be the big man, top of the tree. Then, all of a sudden, he wasn't.'

Keith Simpson cut in. 'Did you know Charlie Sayer had been executed?'

Alfie Jenkins did not look totally surprised. 'There were rumours going about, but then there always is.'

Simpson went on, 'That's what we're dealing with here, Alfie, gangs that are in a completely different league from any you have known before.'

DS Craddock decided to push a little harder. 'That's why we need to clear them out before they get too big a hold. The New Forest really doesn't need these gangsters. We need all the help you can give us.' Craddock looked pointedly at the wad of notes nestling in Jenkins' hand. 'It would obviously mean plenty more from where that came from.'

For a few long seconds, Jenkins seemed to be wrestling with his thoughts before speaking again.

'The man who was shot near Minstead, I think I've seen him a couple of times. I think he was the man who provided the trap houses. Stinking rich.'

It fell to Keith Simpson to ask the key question. 'Is there anything that you know that could prove helpful in nailing this gang?'

Jenkins hesitated once more before finally answering. 'All I've heard is that there is someone called "K" who's pulling the strings in this area.'

Craddock showed his appreciation. 'Good man. Believe me, Alfie, you're doing us all a great public service.'

An anxious-looking Alfie Jenkins did not seem to fully share their enthusiasm as he furtively left them at the entrance to the shed before hurriedly driving off in his battered Ford.

Someway along the road that led away from the abandoned allotment area, he would not have been aware that a lapiz-blue VW Golf slipped stealthily into his slipstream.

*

'Touch wood, it's all been pretty quiet since the incident with Janet on Tuesday. Hopefully my neighbour and his dog have scared him off.' It was approaching midday and Joe Loxley was on the phone to Desk Sergeant Tom Fallon at Pikes Hill. He was answering Fallon's enquiry about the harassment.

'Hope that's the case, Joe; you can really do without this shit. I heard that PC Packer is on the case with the CCTV, something about a white van.'

'I'm waiting to hear.' Loxley changed the subject. 'How's the Turnbull case progressing?'

Fallon's voice noticeably dropped. 'Well, I'm only getting bits and pieces, but I heard they got a big breakthrough yesterday. Seems they made a discovery in the Fawley area, something to do with some undeveloped land.'

'Sounds interesting.'

Fallon lowered his voice. 'I can also tell you something else. I took a call from Jack Foster this morning asking to be picked up at the Highcliffe Hotel in Bournemouth. He sounded pretty terrified.'

Loxley felt a slight stir of excitement. 'What happened when he came in?'

'He was brought in with his wife and taken straight to the interview room.'

'Is he still there?'

'He's in the cell. I heard he was so scared he was practically begging to be arrested and imprisoned. His wife's got the official security blanket so it must be pretty serious.'

'It sounds pretty obvious he's got the same people after him who done for Turnbull,' remarked Loxley.

'That would more than probably explain it.'

Loxley reminded himself of why he had rung Pikes Hill in the first place. 'I did ring for a favour, Tom.'

'Fire away, Joe.'

'It's to do with my tormentor. James went into London yesterday to follow up on a possible lead. The bottom line is we've got a name which could be very interesting.'

'Do you want to give it to me, Joe?'

'His name is Terry Evans. He's on file so would appreciate if you can give me everything on him, including an image if you've got it.'

'No problem, Joe, leave it with me.'

After putting the phone down, Loxley rejoined Janet in the lounge. She was sitting on the sofa with her feet up as she read a TV magazine. The soft Gaelic melodies of The

Corrs hummed gently in the background. They had the house to themselves for the afternoon as James had once again taken himself off to the golf course.

Janet looked up. 'Any CCTV news on the white van?'

Loxley sat down and shook his head. 'Not yet, though it sounds like the Turnbull investigation is picking up a pace. His friend Jack Foster has been arrested.'

Janet pulled herself up to a sitting position. Though she had never met Jack Foster, she knew his wife Sandra from her Pilates classes.

'What the hell for?'

Loxley gave it some thought. 'Well, for starters, he worked for the council. That could have been very useful for a property developer like Roger Turnbull.'

Janet looked shocked. 'Surely you're not suggesting he was corrupt.'

'It would not surprise me, to be honest. He was a shifty-looking character.'

'Poor Sandra.'

'She's under strict police protection, so it must be heavy stuff.'

Janet thought of the little chatty woman at the classes who always seemed so cheerful.

'She must be at the end of her tether, poor woman.'

'At least she should be safe,' Loxley reassured her. His mind turned to Cumber knocking a small white ball around eighteen holes in Ferndown. 'We can give James the latest scoop when he gets back from driving himself mad on the golf course.'

With a start, Janet suddenly stood up and walked swiftly towards the landline.

'You've reminded me: I've got to book a table for tonight at Pergola's.'

*

James Cumber's Audi moved smoothly through the gears on the A35 road back to Lyndhurst from Ferndown. Though his golf had not reached the heights of the previous week, he'd played enough shots of sufficient quality to compensate for the occasional hook and slice. After finishing his round, he'd only spent a short time in the clubhouse as he was conscious that Janet Loxley was booking another meal at her favourite Italian that evening. Once more he'd bumped into Roger Turnbull's old golfing mates Gordon and Pete. As he'd expected, they had been very eager to talk about the investigation into Turnbull's murder. He liked to think that he had managed to field their questions without giving too much away. Just before he left the clubhouse, Pete had mentioned that one of Turnbull's occasional golfing partners, who they only knew as Chris, had not been seen at the club since the murder. He had made a mental note of the name. He decided he would drop in briefly at Pikes Hill to give them the info. Making sure he would not be late for the meal that evening, he pushed the accelerator pedal down a little harder in anticipation.

*

There was an excited murmuring of anticipation as the meeting room filled up with the investigating team after everyone had been unexpectedly called back to Pikes Hill for a briefing. All gathered were wondering whether there had been an arrest or a significant breakthrough. David Jennings let them down gently as he informed them that there was still some way to go with the investigation. Sensing a slight feeling of anticlimax in the room, Jennings enjoyed what he had to say next.

'However, there has been a recent dramatic development.' He felt the excited atmosphere in the room rise once more. 'The councillor who gave a lift to Roger Turnbull on the evening of his murder, Jack Foster, handed himself in this morning. It seems he was profiting from Roger Turnbull's property dealings, and he is now under arrest for abusing his position for personal gain. But that's only half of it. We had to collect him and his wife at a hotel in Bournemouth, as he seemed to be genuinely in fear for his life. He's stated that he and his wife are being threatened by an Eastern European gang who he thinks were definitely involved in the murder of Roger Turnbull.' Jennings pointed to a police identikit image of a face on the whiteboard behind him. 'This likeness has been circulated out to Hampshire Constabulary but is not yet ready for public consumption. It is based on a description given to us by Foster of a man he says approached him in Bournemouth yesterday. Needless to say, we're taking these threats very seriously and as a result we've also put his wife Sandra Foster under strict security. Foster's adamant that he had no idea of the extent of Turnbull's criminality and at the moment, on balance, I'm inclined to believe him. I just can't see him knowingly getting involved with drug gangs. For that's what we appear to be dealing with from what we know so far. Now, if we believe that Foster is telling the truth, then there is surely somebody else out there who was in this with Turnbull and if we keep digging, I'm confident we'll soon find out who they are.' He looked expectantly at Ed Farrows. 'Now, I believe you've just had the forensic report back from the lockup at Fawley, Ed?'

Ed Farrows stood up. 'There is no doubt that the place was used for the creation and modifying of fake documents; anything from false passports, freight bills and false work references. It's pretty apparent that whoever it was left in a hurry because an operation like this would normally have been cleaned up afterwards. As a result, the forensic team found a number of DNA samples, one of which, significantly, was Roger Turnbull's. Unfortunately, none of the others found at the scene were on file. The unidentified DNA sample that was most prominent was that found on the ink bottles and small scalpel; it seems obvious that this must be our documents man. The mini laptop that was found at the site is still being worked on by the techies and we should hear something later this evening.'

Jennings was a tad disappointed with the findings but tried not to sound too deflated. 'The sooner we hear back from the geeks in IT, the better. But this at least confirms that Turnbull was in it up to his neck.' He looked at Paul Mason. 'Have we heard anything on our missing solicitor, Paul?'

'We tracked down two of Brandon Lyons' admin clerks who said he surprised them by mentioning on Friday night that he was going abroad for a weekend break. They both expected him to be back at work on Monday, so they're completely mystified. We've been doing a bit of digging into Lyons' history and, interestingly, a few years back he was linked with some possible money laundering but at the time nothing was proven. In the meantime, we're keeping a close watch on Brandon's flat in Sandbanks.'

Jennings made a decision, 'It looks like he has also done a runner. Hopefully his disappearance is nothing more sinister than that at this stage. If he's not back by Saturday, we'll have to put a search out on him. In the meantime, see if you can find out anything about his personal life – any close relatives, men or lady friends.' Jennings turned back to the sea of faces. 'It's pretty obvious there's a lot of fear in this case. We have a bent councillor and his wife under police protection, a planning consultant who committed suicide and a solicitor who's disappeared, the common denominator being they had all worked regularly with Roger Turnbull over the last few years in his property deals.' He turned to Keith Simpson. 'I believe you found out something significant this morning, DI Simpson?'

The man from Scotland Yard stood up and positioned himself alongside David Jennings.

'I had an interesting chat this morning with a drug informant and, believe me, fear doesn't cover it; terrified would be a better word. The informant strongly suggested that an Eastern European drug gang have moved in on the area. It seems a well-known London drug criminal, Charlie Sayer, was the main man who controlled the county lines that stretched out to this area. I believe it's no coincidence that he was recently found executed in Surrey, much in the manner of Roger Turnbull. Crucial to this investigation, the informant also identified Turnbull as the man who has been providing the properties in the New Forest to peddle the drugs. In view of what Jack Foster has told us about the threats he's received, it wouldn't surprise me if this missing solicitor, Brandon Lyons, has also been getting the same treatment.'

Along with all the other people in the room, David Jennings was still coming to terms with the confirmation that Roger Turnbull really had been at the forefront in the drug operation. So much so that Roger had eventually found himself totally out of his league, resulting in his brutal and tragic death.

Jennings enquired, 'Could the informant give any further intel on the Eastern European gang?'

Simpson gave a slight smile that suggested there was a bit of him that was enjoying the attention.

'There's one little titbit that I have the National Drugs Intelligence Unit working on as we speak.' Simpson paused once more as he looked at the expectant faces. He pointed to the facial image on the whiteboard. 'It seems the gang have a major player who goes by the title of "K". Now, whoever this "K" may be – and he could well be the man who threatened Jack Foster in Bournemouth – there's little doubt that he and his cronies seem to be the main drivers in this reign of terror.'

Jennings couldn't disguise his admiration. 'Excellent work, DI Simpson. I like to think you were not totally alone when you spoke to this snitch?'

Simpson allowed himself a slight chuckle. 'Rest assured, I was in good company with a representative of the regional drug squad. It seems the squad have already had a couple of near misses in nailing this gang, but, unfortunately, so far they seem to have been just behind the curve.'

'So the gang have been lucky?'

Simpson spoke knowingly, 'In my experience with these gangs, luck rarely comes into it. They like to control everything, including everyone who could prove useful to them.'

Not for the first time, David Jennings felt he could not quite fathom the man from Scotland Yard, but he remembered Joe Loxley's praise for Simpson's police work and in that moment he had to agree.

'Are you suggesting they might have people on the inside?'

There was no hesitation in Simpson's voice: 'I'm saying that we can't rule anything out. In my experience, these people are dead inside with no conscience. They feed off greed and fear.'

Jennings looked back at the crowd of faces that filled the room. 'From all that we've heard here, I think we now know the nature of the beast we're dealing with. I'm fully expecting that we should know a lot more when the techies come back with the mini laptop. It's been a busy week for everyone, and I want it known that I'm much appreciative of all your efforts. It's time to take a breather because it looks like the next week could be every bit as busy.'

There was a short spontaneous burst of half-hearted applause and self-congratulation before the crowd slowly began to disperse and the large meeting room emptied.

*

Brandon Lyons stepped back from the curtain, his heart once more beating fast and hard, his relief palpable. The noise at the front door of his brother's house had only been the postman. It had been like this ever since he'd heard the horrific news of Roger Turnbull's death. A morbid fear of a knock at the door, or, even worse, the sound of breaking glass in the dead of night. These people could not be reasoned with. Roger's execution had proved that. Sooner or later, they would be coming for him; he was in far too deep. The murder of Charlie Sayer had been a game changer. The moment when the rules of the game he'd found so lucrative changed forever.

He went back to the sofa and drew another cigarette from his pack of Marlboro Red King. His brother and his wife had been surprised when he'd appeared on their doorstep and asked to stay for a few days. His brother Michael knew it must be serious. His elder sibling had known him long enough to know that there was probably a criminal element involved. Tactfully, Michael had asked no questions of his brother; he knew his dodgy history all too well and really did not want to know any more. His sister-in-law Tania had looked at him quizzically from time to time but had thought it best to hold her council for now. She knew when someone was in trouble and Brandon Lyons looked like a man with the weight of the world on his shoulders.

Brandon Lyons took a long drag on his cigarette. Michael and Tania were both out at work and the house felt ominously quiet. He knew they would not appreciate him smoking in the house, so he made a mental note to make the cigarette his last before they got home. How could he even begin to explain to them that he was so afraid, so fearful to even contemplate unlocking the back door? He knew there was a limit to their hospitality, and he could not carry on like this; he would need to have a plan. The trouble was that sitting there with his hands shaking and his brain scrambled, he felt himself incapable of logical thought. One thing he knew for sure, he daren't go back to his flat in Sandbanks or his solicitor's office in Lyndhurst. No doubt his staff would by now be asking questions; he only wished he was in a position to be able to give them some answers.

He picked up his mobile phone and pressed redial once more. After purring for fifteen seconds, the line clicked onto answerphone. He threw the phone down in exasperation. Where the hell was Chris?

*

James Cumber laughed good-naturedly. 'Hallo, hallo, one man and his dog.' He was returning from an evening at the nearby Italian restaurant with Joe and Janet Loxley. They had enjoyed a convivial evening and were enjoying the short stroll back to the Loxleys' house in Queens Road. The air was pleasantly warm, and the sky twinkled with thousands of stars. They had turned into the road to find Phil Shaw with his dog Chalky. Phil was standing quite still, whilst staring up intently into the night sky.

Joe Loxley was always pleased to catch a word with his long-term neighbour and drinking partner.

'Hello, Phil. All quiet on the Western Front, I hope?'

Phil Shaw was momentarily caught by surprise but soon found his voice. 'Well, Chalky's not started barking at your box plant so I think we can take that as a good sign. I take it you've been to the Italian?'

Janet answered, 'Right first time.'

'I think you must have shares in that place, Janet.'

Janet laughed. 'It's the restaurant that keeps on giving. It never lets you down.'

James Cumber stood up from fussing Chalky and looked back up at the sky. 'Doing a bit of stargazing, Phil?'

They all followed Phil's gaze as he looked up into the sky once more. 'It's a spectacular sight, isn't it? You know, not enough people take the time to look up at the sky on nights like this. It's very humbling. It gives a proper perspective on life. Politicians and dictators fight wars and ordinary people can get upset about such small things, but they should all occasionally look up at those millions of solar systems and be humbled at their own insignificance.'

Loxley chuckled. 'Wow, you are quite the philosopher tonight, Phil. You know, for an old unrepentant cynic, you can be a wise old codger.'

'It comes with age. What's the point of travelling all these years if you can't gain a bit of wisdom on the journey?'

Janet agreed, 'Well said, Phil.'

They were interrupted by the sound of a car door shutting and the sight of PC Matt Packer approaching from the other end of the street. He was still carrying out his evening patrol duties around the environs of the Loxleys' house.

Loxley asked him, 'Anything to report, Matt?'

Packer reassured him, 'Absolutely nothing to report so far, Mr Loxley. I make that about the third incident-free night this week.'

Loxley answered, 'Of course, they could still just be

lying low and waiting for another suitable opportunity to create some mischief.'

Packer looked at him reassuringly. 'Somehow I doubt it. I've just heard some good news from HQ on the CCTV footage. The white van was caught on camera two times, once heading towards Brockenhurst and the other down in the New Milton area. They look like they might have the plate recognition so should hear something tomorrow.'

Loxley could not disguise his delight. 'With any luck, it looks as if the net may finally be closing in on the bastards.'

Cumber added, 'It will be interesting to see if Terry Evans proves to be the culprit.'

Loxley sounded pretty definite, 'I feel it in my bones that he's our man.'

Cumber smiled. 'Well, that's got to be the clincher; the old Loxley instincts are not often wrong.'

Loxley laughed. 'Let's hope they've not withered with age.'

*

A few miles south-west of Lyndhurst, a tall, fair-haired youth lay back on a bed in a grubby back room. He was feeling hot, restless and agitated, his mind fixated on real or imagined grievances. It was always the same when the effects of the drugs wore off; a raw, despairing feeling of victimhood in which there had to be something or someone responsible. Lying there sweating on the bed, that focal point of his resentment came starkly and clearly into focus once more; it was the tall, elderly figure of Joe Loxley.

NINE

THE NET CLOSES

It was early Friday morning at Pikes Hill and David Jennings was sitting in his office accompanied by senior members of his investigation team, Keith Simpson, Ed Farrows and Paul Mason. Empty coffee cups littered the table as they busied themselves mulling over the info gleaned from the mini laptop found at the lock-up in Fawley. The computer forensic analysts had presented it first thing and they had done a good job in extracting the files and emails.

Jennings was cross-checking the bunch of properties listed that had not originally appeared on Turnbull's PC found at his office in Lymington. Significantly, the bulk of them seemed to have been acquired in more recent years. There was a note of excitement in his voice.

'I take it our councillor Jack Foster would have been pivotal in tipping Turnbull the wink for these transactions?'

Keith Simpson nodded. 'No doubt about it. It gave Turnbull the jump on everyone in obtaining the properties.

I still remain to be totally convinced that Foster knew nothing about what was going on further down the line.'

Jennings looked at Ed Farrows. 'Get these addresses out to the teams straight away, Ed; I want them all checked out by tomorrow at the latest.'

Farrows nodded. 'I think we can already make a good guess at what we might find.'

Simpson agreed, 'It's a good bet that the vast majority of those properties have been lined up or have connections to drug crime in one way or the other.'

Jennings asked him, 'Have we got anything more on our Eastern European?'

Simpson shook his head. 'Nothing as yet. I've sent the identikit image to the national drug squad, see if that throws anything up. I've also got them looking into the possible significance of the letter "K".'

Jennings nodded his approval. 'Have you found anything suspicious to back up the suggestion the gang could be getting intel from insider sources?'

'Nothing obvious so far, though I will go back to Lymington and have another chat with the officer at the regional drug squad.'

'You don't need me to tell you to be subtle, Keith; we don't want to be stirring up a hornet's nest for no reason.'

Di Simpson gave him a look suggesting the instruction was unnecessary but remained silent.

Paul Mason looked up from studying the laptop emails. 'I'm seeing that the missing solicitor Brandon Lyons was involved in the bulk of these deals. It's definitely looking like he was taking a ride on Turnbull's gravy train.'

Jennings leant forwards. 'His disappearance is beginning to look more significant by the minute. Did you get anything on his family relations, Paul?'

'So far we've found out that he split with his wife a couple of years ago and he has a brother called Michael.'

'Find out their addresses and pay them a visit.' A sudden thought occurred to him. 'You say the staff in his high-street office had a key?'

Mason was ahead of the game. 'Yes, we've already checked it out. No sign of him inside, dead or alive. Wherever he's gone, he took his laptop with him. We also checked the weekend departure listings from Bournemouth Airport. No mention of a Brandon Lyons.'

Jennings frowned. 'If we don't get anything useful from his relations, we'll have to get into his flat in Sandbanks. Are there any other names on the files that crop up on a frequent basis?'

'There is one name that looks very interesting, a Chris Barlow. He seems to have been communicating with Turnbull constantly. Definitely worth trawling through the email content, could be very revealing, I reckon.'

David Jennings let out a shout. 'Wasn't Chris the name that James Cumber left with the desk sergeant last night? He was a golf mate of Turnbull's who hasn't been seen at the Ferndown club since the murder. There's a slim chance it could be a coincidence but somehow I doubt it. Get a team on it, Paul, looks like we've got plenty to get stuck into.' He glanced at his watch. 'I think it's a good time to report into Chief Super Cobbold and give him an update.'

*

Joe Loxley could not help noticing how surprisingly quiet it was as he entered the public reception area at Pikes Hill. It was late morning, and he had come into the station after Desk Sergeant Tom Fallon had phoned and requested he come in. Loxley had a good idea what it was all about, so he had wasted no time in getting there.

'Seems very serene in here today, Tom?'

Tom Fallon looked up. 'That's because they've practically got the whole investigation team on the road checking out Roger Turnbull's properties.'

'I'm still processing the thought that people like Turnbull and Foster were getting involved with criminal gangs. I take it we're definitely talking drugs?'

Tom Fallon nodded and dropped his voice. 'From what I'm hearing, that's the nub of it. It sounds like they got themselves in too deep with some seriously heavy Eastern European outfit.'

Some officers entered the reception hall and Fallon straightened up and handed Loxley a large envelope.

'It's all in there, Joe, an image of Terry Evans and his police record plus the owner of the white van. The number plate has gone out to all patrols, should only be a matter of time.'

'Can't say how grateful I am to you and all the boys, Tom, especially when they've got this other stuff going on.'

Fallon put his hand up and grinned. 'Don't mention it, Joe, it's the least we can do for one of our top tecs.'

Loxley gave a slightly embarrassed laugh. 'You might have had a different opinion if you'd worked with me.'

Fallon smiled and replied, 'Somehow I doubt it.' He went on, 'Matt Packer is still running with your case, so he'll be reporting in to me with any developments. I'll let you know as soon as.'

'Much appreciated, Tom. I owe you a pint if you ever manage to get some free time.'

Fallon pulled a face. 'Free time? What's that?'

*

Ed Farrows and Sarah Harrison got out of the car and approached a building that could best be described as bordering on the derelict. It was situated on the New Milton perimeters and was the fourth of Turnbull's empty properties they had visited that morning. The others had been in various stages of neglect and development, but this one in particular looked like it had been a long time since it had been cared for. The brickwork was starting to crumble and crack and there were weeds growing out of the roof slates. Amazingly, there were traces of dirty net curtains still hanging in the windows.

Farrows gave a slight chuckle and turned to Harrison. 'I reckon you could pick this house up at a snip, Sarah, first rung of the ladder and all that.'

Sarah gave him a disdainful look. 'Very funny; for a minute I thought you were serious.'

Farrows approached the front door. 'I wonder what Turnbull had planned for this place?'

'From the state of it, whatever it was, it must have been very much in the planning stage.'

Farrows gave the door a firm push. After some initial resistance, the door gave way and opened. He stepped in and could not help emitting a triumphant whoop at what he saw. The room in front of him was a chaotic mess of empty beer bottles and rotting food. Stained mattresses lay on a floor that was littered with used needles and grubby clothing. On what looked like a bedside table, there were thin powdery traces of Class A drugs and wrappers. A large knife had been stuck into the table and protruded menacingly from its heavily marked surface.

Farrows turned to Sarah Harrison. 'We've hit the jackpot here, Sarah, a twenty-four-carat trap house if ever I saw one.'

Sarah trod carefully through the debris and picked up a crushed food carton with her gloved hand.

'It looks like the cuckoo has flown but only recently, judging by the date on this container.'

Ed Farrows nodded. 'They appear to be one step ahead but we're not far behind.' He reached inside his pocket for his mobile. 'Let's get the forensic team over here pronto.'

*

Phil Shaw studied the police photo of Terry Evans very carefully. Joe Loxley had wasted little time in calling his neighbour over to the house after returning from Pikes Hill. Both Loxley and James Cumber waited patiently for the neighbour's judgement. Phil finally looked up.

'He looks younger in the photo but I'm sure it's him.'

Loxley looked pleased as he took back the photo. 'Right answer, Phil.' He turned to Cumber. 'I think this pretty much confirms that Bill Kemp was barking up the correct tree.'

Phil asked, 'Does that mean I get a reward?'

Loxley laughed. 'Sorry, Phil, but there will be an extra pint in it for you, I'm sure.'

'Oh, that's alright then, I've never been one to chase the money. It's why I never do the lottery; suddenly winning big money messes with the mind. You've only got to read about the tragedies that befall the winners. Give me a pint of Old Speckled Hen any day.'

Cumber laughed. 'Is that your thought for the day, Phil? I reckon you should put all your homespun wisdoms in a book; it would be a bestseller.'

Phil kept a straight face. 'You're not wrong. It's bound to be top of the sales list. I would give all the proceeds to a charity of my choice.'

Loxley suggested, 'I've heard the Cherries could do with a cash injection.' Loxley was referring to Phil's favourite football club AFC Bournemouth.

Phil's face brightened. 'Now there's an idea.'

After Phil had left the house, Loxley and Cumber settled down in Loxley's study to scrutinise the contents of the envelope provided by Pikes Hill. Not only were there details of Terry Evans's criminal history but also a name, image and details of the owner of the white van that had picked up Evans at the end of the street. The name was Trevor Whitelock, a New Forest local who had a long history of drug abuse and petty crime. Like Terry Evans, he'd served several prison sentences in his short and troubled life.

Loxley commented, 'Looking at their lifelines, they look like peas in a pod apart from the fact that Terry Evans is a Londoner. From what we know here, it looks like Whitelock has rarely strayed far from the confines of Hampshire.'

Cumber reflected, 'I wonder how he ended up being in collusion with Terry Evans in this harassment caper.'

Loxley sounded certain in his answer, 'The common denominator in all of this is the sordid world of drugs.'

Cumber nodded. 'Of course it is. Drug crime stretches its tentacles far and wide.'

Loxley looked back over the notes on Trevor Whitelock. 'It says here he has no fixed abode but Tom Fallon at Pikes Hill sounded pretty confident they'll soon pick him up on the van reg.'

The tuneful melody of Elton John's "Sacrifice" emanating faintly from the lounge reminded Loxley that Janet was in the house and would be expecting an afternoon cuppa any time. He got up from the desk still looking at the images of the two men.

'Only a matter of time, I hope, before we have reason for celebration.'

*

Keith Simpson was sitting at his allocated desk in Pikes Hill when the phone rang. He had been studying the reports he had been sent from the National Drug Intelligence Unit. He was determined to delve deeper into the workings of the Eastern European drug trade in order to try and unearth the mysterious "K".

He answered the phone, 'DI Simpson.'

'Hello, Keith, it's Brian Phelps.'

Simpson had known Brian Phelps ever since he had been in the force. They had risen through the ranks together before Brian had transferred to the national drugs squad.

They had kept in close touch and Simpson could think of no better contact when it came to a drug investigation.

'Hello, Brian, what have you got for me?'

'We've gone through the likenesses to the image you sent us, and it's thrown up a few possibilities.'

'Don't suppose there are any names beginning with the letter "K", by any chance?'

'No, not exactly, but there is one who might just qualify.'

Simpson was interested. 'Go on.'

'He goes by the name of Serge Ostrog, and we know he's been in and out of the country for the last two years. The likeness is very strong.'

'That's interesting but what makes you think he's our man?'

'Here's the thing, he's sometimes known as Ivan Kriska.'

'Have you got anything on his whereabouts at the moment?'

'Nothing at all; he appears to have totally fallen off the radar.'

Simpson felt a surge of excitement. 'I like it. Can you send me over some detail?'

Phelps pressed his sent button. 'It's already on its way.'

'You're a top man.'

Phelps laughed. 'It's often been said but modesty forbids.'

'Many thanks, Brian.' Keith Simpson was already studying the sent data as he ended the call.

*

Paul Mason and a team of uniformed officers were making their way in convoy towards a Ringwood address. Their destination was the home of Brandon Lyons' brother, Michael. An earlier phone call from a neighbour in Sandbanks had injected a greater sense of urgency in finding the missing solicitor. A Miss Talbot had reported seeing two suspicious men looking through the window of his flat when she had come home late the previous evening. At first she thought it might be the police, but there was something about the menacing body language that suggested differently. Mason and his team had already paid a visit to Brandon Lyons' ex-wife in Weymouth, which had proved fruitless. She had told them that she had not seen him for several weeks, before grudgingly giving them permission to conduct a quick search of her home, which seemed to confirm her story. The convoy had wasted little time in heading back to the Hampshire address of Brandon Lyons' sibling. They finally pulled up in front of a detached house in a typical suburban street. It was situated on one of the newer estates built on the edge of Ringwood. Accompanied by a couple of uniformed officers, Mason approached the front of the house. A twitching curtain in one of the neighbour's houses confirmed that their arrival in the quiet street had not gone totally unnoticed.

Inside the house, Brandon Lyons took another long drag on his Marlboro Red King. Left alone once more in his brother's house, the afternoon had seemed to stretch out interminably. For the umpteenth time, he glanced anxiously at the ticking clock on the wall. At least his brother would be home from work soon. He stubbed out the cigarette and went to the kitchen to bin the evidence.

Not that he was fooling anyone; non-smokers like Michael and his wife Tania were all too finely tuned to the smell of tobacco smoke. Like so many things he tried to hide from his brother, it was often noticed but mostly went unsaid. It was when he went to fill the kettle that the doorbell rang. For a second or two, he froze on the spot, his heart instantly going into overdrive, the now familiar feeling of panic and dread. He steeled himself and edged slowly into the lounge before peering through the window. He caught a glimpse of DC Paul Mason and two uniformed officers standing at the door. Feeling the air rush out of him in relief, his first instinct was to not answer the door and lie low. But it was only a matter of seconds before his more logical and sensible side told him it was surely better to hand himself in to the police and take the consequences. Rather that option than being loose on the streets and at the mercy of "K" and his comrades. After all, the cold reality was that Roger had already met a brutal end and now there was the question of what the hell had happened to Chris. Surely it would only be a matter of time before it would be his turn. He really had no choice. With a deep sigh of resignation, he walked slowly towards the front door.

*

An hour later, David Jennings and Paul Mason were stood outside the interview room comparing notes. They were just about to interview Brandon Lyons after he had been picked up at his brother's house and brought back to Pikes Hill. Paul Mason was updating Jennings on a report he had just received about the email communication between Roger Turnbull and the mysterious Chris Barlow.

'There's nothing actually stated but it's pretty obvious that Barlow was in Turnbull's employ about something. There are obscure references to getting the job done and completing the process. I think we should bring him in.'

Jennings agreed, 'All sounds very fishy. Let's get all we can on him.' He looked at the closed door to the interview room. 'Now let's see what Mr Lyons has to say.'

They took a bit of time to study the lean and well-groomed man who sat opposite them in the interview room. Hearing that Brandon Lyons had been found and wanted to confess his part in Turnbull's operation, David Jennings had pulled himself away from the exciting developments caused by Ed Farrows and Sarah Harrison's early morning discovery of the abandoned trap house in Milford.

Sitting alongside the station solicitor, Charles Fenton, Lyons seemed perfectly at ease. Jennings thought that if Lyons was nervous, he was doing a good job of hiding it.

Jennings began the proceedings. 'At the moment, Mr Lyons, you're not under arrest or caution. At this moment, you're not even being charged with anything. Do you understand?'

Lyons held a steady gaze and answered, 'I understand.'

The recording was switched on and Jennings began the interview. 'Now, Mr Lyons, before you reveal your side of the story, I'll tell you what we know about you. Feel free to correct me if any of these facts are inaccurate. You operated out of an office in Lymington for several years until you recently moved to a new office site in Lyndhurst

High Street. You lived in Brockenhurst until your divorce and after selling up you now live in Sandbanks while your ex-wife and two teenage children live in Weymouth. In the course of investigating the business proceedings of Roger Turnbull, we noted that you were the primary legal representative in the majority of his property dealings. We now have strong evidence that Turnbull was involved in some heavy criminal activity in which his properties played a pivotal part. A discovery in one of his properties of a trap house earlier today confirmed this beyond doubt. Here's the thing, we've looked into the history and interestingly you played a major part in the legal process in the purchase of that property. We also know from our past police records that you personally have sailed very close to the wind from time to time when it comes to lawful process. I think that you would agree that the fact you have also hidden yourself away at your brother's house since Turnbull's murder looks more than significant. We've also heard today from one of your neighbours that she has seen some suspicious men snooping around your flat in Sandbanks.' Jennings thought he detected a look of anxiety flash across Lyons' features before he quickly composed himself. Jennings leant back. 'You're now free to give your side of the story.'

Lyons gave a brief glance in the direction of his solicitor before speaking. 'I've known Roger Turnbull for many years, both as a client and as an associate. In the early years, I never asked too many questions, I only knew that, as a property speculator, he was as sharp as a needle. Always ahead of the game. He seemed to have a network and contacts way beyond what was normal.

As time went by, the deals I processed for him seemed to get more and more lucrative. He was paying me way above the normal rate and it was pretty obvious that he was into something criminal. I guessed pretty early that it was probably drugs rather than just property speculation. He confirmed this to me one night when we were having a drink. He said he was working with a London drug criminal called Charlie Sayer. He told me that Sayer was spreading out his county lines and trap houses into the more rural areas like Hampshire and he wanted me to be a big part of it. It must have been about a year before the European boys got involved and then the stakes suddenly got much higher. Roger seemed to be excited by it, as if he wanted to be up there playing with the big boys. He asked me there and then if I was in or out, as if I had any choice. The truth was I was already in right up to my neck.'

There was a brief but sombre silence before Paul Mason asked, 'Turnbull could not have been doing this alone. How many others were in the know like you?'

Lyons gave the question some thought before he answered, 'There were many people that did well out of Roger's dealings but I'm pretty sure there were only three of us that knew the full extent of the criminality.'

David Jennings leant forwards. 'Are you going to name the third man?'

Lyons' face suddenly clouded over. 'His name is Chris Barlow, and I fear he may be already dead as we speak.'

Jennings glanced across at Paul Mason. 'Now that's a name that keeps cropping up. What makes you think he's dead?'

'After we heard about Roger's death, I agreed with Chris that we lie low and keep in touch. The worrying thing is he's not been answering my calls, and I've heard nothing from him since last Sunday.'

'What was his part in it exactly?'

'Many years ago, he used to work in the London passport office—'

Jennings instantly made the connection and interrupted. 'We had some mystery fingerprints at a site in Fawley. I take it you're going to tell me that he was the documents man.'

Lyons looked surprised. 'You've found the site at Fawley already?'

Jennings looked pleased at his reaction. 'Admittedly, it was a bit of luck that we found it so quick, but we would have got there eventually. It looks like your friend left in a hurry, which I doubt was the plan. He left behind a whole host of evidence.'

Lyons looked disconsolate. 'Chris must have left in a panic when he heard about Roger's murder. The gang would have not been best pleased, that's for sure.'

'So this Chris Barlow is their precious false documents man. Why would they kill him? Surely he's too valuable to them.'

'Normally that would have been the case, but the game changer was when we recently agreed with Roger we all wanted out. He was going to let them know on the night he was killed. We did warn him not to go alone, but Roger thought he was untouchable. I think he'd somehow lost touch with reality. He really didn't see the danger.'

'What made you all want to get off the gravy train?'

Lyons didn't hesitate. 'It was when we heard through the grapevine about the murder of Charlie Sayer that everything changed. It was then we realised we were in a much bigger and more dangerous league. Apparently, it's what these gangs do as a matter of course. They establish a partnership before ruthlessly taking over when it suits them. We should have realised these kinds of people are not the kind to let you just walk away; we were in much too deep and there was no way out.'

Jennings made up his mind: 'We'll circulate a local search on Chris Barlow. Do you have his address?'

'He lives in one of the flats that overlook the harbour in Poole… number thirty, I think.'

Paul Mason wrote down the details before asking, 'Is he married?'

'No, his wife died a few years back. He has two children that attend an expensive private school near Winchester. He and Roger went back a long way. They'd known each other in London. I think the crippling school fees were the main reason Chris got involved in the operation. Roger could be very persuasive, especially when he saw signs of weakness.'

Paul Mason asked the obvious question, 'What about you, Mr Lyons, what was your motivation?'

Lyons' face looked expressionless as he answered, 'You know, I've asked myself that question many times. The truth is, I don't really know. Greed, boredom, or the plain fact that I'm just plain crooked. It's not a nice thing to realise that about yourself but there you go.'

'Did you ever meet any of the European gang members,

Mr Lyons? I'm thinking particularly of someone who goes by the initial "K"?'

Lyons sighed and gave a resigned smile. 'Oh, you've heard of him. Thankfully I never had the pleasure, but both Roger and Chris met up with him on occasion. One of the reasons I moved office from Lymington was that I always had the feeling I was being watched, strange men hanging around on the street as if they didn't belong. It's hard to explain but I definitely felt it.'

Paul Mason pulled out the police identikit image described by Jack Foster from his folder and put it on the table.

'Does this face look familiar?'

Lyons stared at the image for some time before speaking. 'He definitely looks the part, and he sort of looks vaguely familiar. I remember Roger mentioning something about a tattoo but they're pretty much par for the course amongst gang members.'

Mason picked up the image and placed it back in the folder.

Jennings spoke to the station solicitor. 'Be great if we can get a full written confessional statement, Charles.' He looked back at Brandon Lyons. 'We already have the UK Financial Intelligence Unit going through Roger Turnbull's property dealings in which you played a big part. From what I'm hearing, they've already seen enough evidence of payments to obscure companies and offshore accounts to suggest money laundering. From where I'm sat, it looks like it's going to be a hefty charge sheet thrown at you when they've finished. Somehow, I don't think you'll be seeing a lot of sunny Sandbanks in the next few years, Mr Lyons.

But I can give some assurance that you will be getting full protection while the inquiry goes forward.'

Jennings was sure he detected more than just a trace of relief on Lyons' face as he looked back at him with a resigned smile.

David Jennings had one more question. 'I take it you'd heard of Adrian Ferguson and Jack Foster?'

Lyons nodded. 'Adrian was the planning consultant; yes, I knew him. Jack Foster not so well; I only knew him as the shifty info man on the council.'

'Unfortunately, Adrian committed suicide this week. We wondered if it was connected in some way.'

Lyons looked genuinely affected. 'I'm really sorry to hear that. He was very much a loner but a gentle soul. Roger's death would have hit him hard. I never had any reason to think he was gay, but, you know, in his way I think he truly loved Roger. So, yes, it probably was connected but not in the way you think.'

David Jennings stood up. 'You definitely don't think either of them had any idea of the full extent of Roger's criminal activities?'

Lyons was definite in his answer. 'No chance. Adrian would have run a mile, and I know for a fact that Roger would never have trusted Foster with that knowledge.'

Paul Mason turned off the recording to signal the interview had concluded.

*

After first tracking down Chris Barlow's two teenage children at the expensive boarding school near

Winchester, the investigating team had it confirmed that the children had not heard from their father for several days. Fortunately, the children had not only possessed a recent photo of their father but also spare keys to his flat. The first appeals for anyone who had seen Barlow were broadcast on the local news early that evening and were soon all over the internet. Meanwhile, Paul Mason and a back-up team had wasted little time in getting to Barlow's flat overlooking Poole Harbour. After ringing the bell and not getting an answer, Mason and his team were soon gaining access to the property. The first thing they noticed was the general untidiness, with the bed unmade and piles of washing up on the draining board. A small room off the hallway contained a small office space with two filing cabinets and a desk with a laptop and printer. It was one of the officers who spotted a dark stain on the floor just inside the kitchen area. Paul Mason got down on his haunches to take a look. On closer examination, it became apparent that it was the larger of a few smaller stains that led to the front door. Mason and the officer looked at each other in confirmation; there was little doubt that it was blood.

*

James Cumber and the Loxleys were just about to settle down in front of the TV to watch an episode of *Endeavour* when the phone rang. Joe Loxley pulled himself out of the armchair and made his way to the phone in the hallway.

The voice on the other end was David Jennings. 'Hello, Joe. Have you got time for a quick pint in The Rabbit?'

Loxley was a bit surprised. 'Sounds tempting. Why, have you got something for me?'

Jennings gave a brief chuckle. 'Just a bit. Pick you up in ten minutes at the end of your road.'

Loxley put the phone down. For David Jennings to ring him at this time, it must be important. Intrigued, he rushed to put his shoes on while updating Janet and James about the unexpected invitation.

*

Half an hour later, Loxley was sitting peacefully in the pub garden of The White Rabbit sipping a cool Peroni. Sitting opposite was David Jennings, sinking his nose into a foaming pint of BrewDog IPA. The evening air was pleasantly still and warm, with the sweet scent of the forest hanging pleasingly in the atmosphere. It was only the occasional tinkle of glasses and distant laughter of other customers that reminded them they were not totally alone. Loxley liked David Jennings for a lot of reasons, not least that you knew exactly where you stood with him. He was as straight as a die with no side to him. He could have easily imagined working alongside him back in the day. It occurred to him that he hadn't seen Jennings' wife Angela for some time.

'How's everything at home, David? The wife still treating you well?'

Jennings grimaced. 'You know how it is, Joe, it's never easy. Let's just say she tolerates my antisocial hours, and I tolerate her antisocial moods. It seems to work. The bottom line is, I wouldn't change her for the world.'

Loxley knew exactly where he was coming from. He thought back to his own often difficult experiences and James Cumber's failed union.

'Combining a marriage and a career in the police is bloody difficult. It just won't work if there is no give and take, plus a large dollop of devoted understanding from the wife.'

'You're not wrong there, Joe.' Jennings took another swig of his beer and changed the subject. 'Anyway, I'm sorry to drag you away from Janet, Joe, but I think you will definitely want to hear what I have to say.'

'I'm all ears.'

Jennings looked around him and lowered his voice. 'It turns out Turnbull was into the drug trade right up to his neck. His property development business Burgeon was the respectable front, but you won't believe what was under the surface. Eastern European gangsters, bent councillors and solicitors, money laundering, false documents men, people going missing; honestly it's mind-blowing. Your mate James Cumber had mentioned to us that one of Turnbull's cronies called Chris had not been seen at the golf club recently. It turns out that he was the false documents man. Between you and me, it doesn't look good for the poor sod from what we've found out so far.'

Loxley remembered seeing the early evening news bulletin on the TV. 'We saw the news appeal this evening for a missing person called Chris Barlow. We guessed it might be the missing golf buddy.' He shook his head. 'Turnbull must have gone off his trolley; it's the only explanation I can think of.'

'I can't disagree with you there, Joe. I'm still undecided whether the man was an ego maniac on the rampage or an adrenaline junkie.'

Loxley gave a wry smile and shrugged. 'From what you've found out so far, most probably both.'

Jennings went on, 'Anyway, as a result we've been trawling through Turnbull's New Forest properties for the last few days. Many of the houses looked in various states of disrepair and there was certainly evidence of drug activity in some of them. But it was Ed Farrows and Sarah Harrison who hit the jackpot when they discovered a deserted trap house this morning. The forensic team have been crawling all over it for most of the day. They found fingerprints and DNA samples everywhere, and, as you would expect, amongst them there were plenty of known local dealers and users. Two of them, I suspect, that would be very much of interest to you personally.'

Loxley took another sip of his beer. He had a good idea where this was going.

'Now you really have got me intrigued.'

Jennings leant forwards. 'I was having a very interesting conversation with PC Packer just before I rang you tonight. He told me the names of the two men who have been threatening you and Janet recently.'

Loxley had no trouble remembering them. 'Terry Evans and Trevor Whitelock.'

David Jennings could hardly keep the grin from his face. 'On the findings of forensic today, both of them have been regular visitors to Turnbull's trap house.'

Loxley sat back and quietly processed the information. 'I suppose at first it seems a quirky coincidence, but when you factor in the common theme of drugs, not so much.'

'The good news, Joe, is we should be able to get them off your back in the next day or so.'

Loxley raised his glass. 'In view of everything else that you've had to contend with recently, we really appreciate all you've done for us, David.'

Jennings picked up his pint. 'All part of the service, Joe.' He took a long swill from his glass. 'So, as I understand it, this Terry Evans is the son of a suspect who was wrongfully arrested at the time of a series of high-profile murders back in 1986?'

'Yes, it was all a bit of an unfortunate coincidence at the time. Two men of very similar build stalking the same murder victim. You couldn't make it up.'

'I'll have to read up on it; sounds very interesting.'

'It was certainly one of my most memorable cases.'

Jennings looked wistful. 'I often wish I was around in those days. Policing sounded much better resourced and more satisfying. Nowadays, we have PCSOs having to take up the slack. The PCs often spend most of their time having to act as social workers or paramedics because there are not enough ambulances.'

Loxley sympathised. 'You're certainly not selling it to me. Is it true that nowadays you're not even allowed the pleasure of office banter to relieve the pressures?'

Jennings laughed. 'Banter, what's that? You're not allowed to express personal opinions anymore; someone's bound to report you. In these days of email and tweets you have to be so careful; there's always someone out there ready to jump on you. Believe me, it's a political minefield.'

'I don't envy you.'

Jennings cheered up. 'I must admit, I've enjoyed being crime scene manager on this Turnbull affair, it's probably the most high-profile case I've ever had to work on. We've had the rare luxury of plenty of resource and the novelty of a really heavy-duty investigation. It'll seem pretty boring when it's all over and your mate Keith Simpson goes back to Scotland Yard.'

'Is he proving an asset?'

'It pains me to say it, but I must admit he's come up with some decent stuff. At the moment he's homing in on the gang leader.'

Loxley was confident. 'I know he's not a team player, but he'll get there. He's sure to have some useful connections in London.'

'He certainly doesn't hold back with his theories; he's already suggested the gang might have a police insider giving them the heads up. He's also not wasted much time in establishing a contact with an informant who communicates with the regional drug squad in Lymington.'

Loxley finished off his pint before saying, 'There you go, I rest my case.'

*

Ed Farrows and Sarah Harrison approached what looked like an old fifties council house on the outskirts of New Milton. They and the rest of the investigation team had risen early that Saturday morning to round off the searches of Turnbull's properties. There were several fellow officers out examining similar structures scattered about the New Forest on land still awaiting development. The land they were now checking was the last of Turnbull's property transactions listed on Sarah's sheets. Still buzzing from their discovery of the trap house the previous day, the houses and land they'd visited that morning had so far proved disappointing. Basically following the same pattern – dilapidated, neglected and empty – they showed no sign of recent drug activity. No doubt, if Roger Turnbull had not met his untimely end, the land would have been eventually flattened and properties bulldozed before being replaced with cheap modern housing.

Farrows breathed out an audible sigh of relief. 'You're definitely sure this is the last one on the list? Please don't tell me you've missed a sheet.'

Sarah Harrison playfully pretended to find another sheet. 'Shit. Oh well, we've got nothing else to do on a Saturday morning.'

Smiling indulgently, Ed Farrows studied the pile of property information sheets in his hands.

'I wouldn't have wanted to play Turnbull at Monopoly, that's for sure; he would have wiped the floor with me.'

Sarah looked a bit disgruntled. 'He had one heck of a portfolio. I can't even afford a one-bedroom flat. My parents can't get rid of me.'

They drew nearer to the house to examine it more closely. The front door was hanging off its hinges and a large tractor tyre leant against the wall. Farrows shaded his eyes as he peered through the cracked and grimy outside windows. It was Sarah Harrison who saw the parked van at the side of the house first. Partly hidden by an overgrown privet hedge, its white bodywork was stained with dirt and tree residue. Pointing it out to Ed Farrows, Sarah approached the vehicle and wiped the registration plate clean before keying the number into the police database. Meanwhile, Ed Farrows had left her to it and moved towards the fragile front door and carefully pushed it open. Entering the house, he was immediately struck by the foul smell, a toxic cocktail of stale sweat, human excrement and urine. He made his way further into the house, treading carefully between the discarded food cartons and empty plastic bottles. The flooring was heavily stained, the odd syringe discarded amongst the debris. He suddenly came to an abrupt halt. What at first had looked like a pile of dirty linen appeared to stir into life. A dark head of hair fleetingly appeared before submerging once more into the sheets. Whoever was in that grubby bundle of linen was well and truly out of this world. Sarah Harrison appeared at his shoulder holding her nose. With her other hand, she showed the display window on her phone. In bold bright lettering, it highlighted a name: Trevor Whitelock.

TEN

THE ENEMY WITHIN

David Jennings turned to Ed Farrows and raised his eyes to the ceiling. 'I might have guessed he would show up at some stage.'

They were finishing their machine coffee outside the interview room at Pikes Hill and had just seen Jim Wallace go through the door. He was a well-known legal representative of the criminal classes at the lower end of the scale. The illegal drug trade was definitely one of his favourites, be it dealers, users, or small-time criminal gangs. As a result, he was disparagingly known back at Hampshire Police HQ as "Weasel Wallace". He was not the first legal brief to discover that there was money in drugs, but there was no one quite like the Weasel for crawling amongst the low life and milking the opportunities. Jennings and Farrows entered the room and gave a curt nod towards Wallace, who had already taken his seat alongside Trevor Whitelock. After bringing in Whitelock an hour earlier, they had immediately granted him access to the shower facilities at the station; more for their own benefit than his. The unventilated interview room was stuffy at the best of times. Throw in the unwashed body of Whitelock emitting its foul odour and it would have been unbearable.

Jennings glanced across the table at Jim Wallace as he sat down opposite. 'Still dredging the bottom of the barrel I see, Mr Wallace.'

Wallace gave a wide grin. 'Someone's got to help the poor souls at the bottom. Who else will? Besides, it pays the bills.'

Ed Farrows came and joined them at the table. 'Well, that's alright then.' There was more than a hint of sarcasm in his voice.

Jennings turned his attention to Trevor Whitelock. The shower facilities they had provided had spruced him up considerably from the smelly, scruffy specimen they had found sleeping on the floor earlier. The young man who sat in front of him was small and wiry with quick suspicious eyes, his hollow cheeks and sallow complexion betraying a life of long-term drug use.

Jennings turned on the tape and began his questioning. 'So, Mr Whitelock, what were you doing in one of Roger Turnbull's properties?'

There was a defiant, almost insolent expression on Whitelock's face.

'No comment.'

Jennings pressed on, 'From our initial search, it's pretty obvious that the property was being used for drug dealing. Would that be correct?'

Whitelock stared straight back at him. 'No comment.'

'Have you heard of someone who goes by the name of "K"?'

Whitelock shook his head but said nothing.

Ed Farrows filled in for the silence. 'For the benefit of the recording, the suspect shook his head.'

Jennings glanced across at Jim Wallace. The solicitor avoided eye contact, keeping his head down and possibly pretending to be busy writing notes. Jennings was sure he detected a slight smile playing around his lips. Jennings took a deep breath. Interviews could often become a game of cat and mouse. Sometimes a bit of provocation could do the trick. He often found that making the suspect angry could lead to him giving the most away.

'Here's what I think, Trevor. I reckon that the property has been used as a trap house and there have been times when you have probably been the cuckoo in that property.'

There was just a slight raising of the voice in Whitelock's reply. 'That's what you think. You wanna know what I think?'

Jennings was encouraged to get some dialogue. 'Be my guest, I'd love to hear.'

'If you want to know the answers to your questions, I think you should look a bit closer to home.'

'What do you mean by that?'

'I'm saying you should make sure your own house is in order before you go accusing.'

Jennings thought of Keith Simpson's theory that someone in the know might be keeping the European drug gang informed.

'Have you got any evidence to back up that accusation?'

Whitelock displayed his tobacco-stained teeth in a self-satisfied grin. 'No comment.'

Ed Farrows took a turn with the questioning. 'Where is Terry Evans?'

Whitelock shrugged. 'Who knows.'

'You don't deny you know him?'

'I've seen him about.'

'Oh, we definitely know that you have been seeing a lot of him. In fact, we know that you've both been threatening and harassing a retired police officer.'

'No comment.'

Farrows produced an envelope with some CCTV images inside and placed them in front of him.

'We have a nice little gallery here, Trevor. Images of your vehicle parked outside the retired officer's house at the time of the offences. As you can see, we also have images of you driving away from the house. More significantly, we also have images of you and Evans getting out of your vehicle on the day that the victim's wife was confronted by Evans in her garden.'

As Whitelock studied the CCTV evidence, he began to fidget and bite his lip. He looked across at his solicitor for guidance. There was not an ounce of smugness on the face of Jim Wallace now.

'You don't have to say anything if you don't want to.'

David Jennings pushed home the advantage. 'You know, Trevor, silence is what everyone does when life gets too difficult. If you say nothing, you can't come to any harm. But no one can keep silent forever, Trevor, you get lonely. You have to say something sometime.'

Whitelock looked back at the CCTV images of himself.

They may have been a touch grainy but there was no doubt they were of sufficient quality to be used as hard evidence.

He finally cracked. 'Terry kept going on about this old copper killing his dad. He said he'd found out where he lived, and he asked me to help out in giving the old boy some aggravation and fear. It sounded like fun, so I went along with it. The trouble was, it wasn't fun to him, it was deadly serious. I realised just how serious when I told him I wanted no more of it and he turned nasty and cleared off. I haven't seen him since.'

'Have you got any idea where he may have gone?'

'No idea, but I would not be surprised if he's gone back to London.'

'Why do you say that?'

'He kept talking about it, saying how much he was missing it.'

David Jennings turned to Jim Wallace. 'We will be arresting your client under section four of the harassment act in addition to suspicion of numerous drug-related offences.'

Jim Wallace made a faint effort to protest but Ed Farrows was already reading Trevor Whitelock his legal rights.

*

PC Matt Packer took a grateful swig of his tea before saying, 'From what I heard about the conversation with Trevor Whitelock in the interview room, it sounds like Terry Evans could well have scuttled back to London.'

He was sitting on the sofa in the Loxley lounge after

he had been sent by David Jennings to update Joe Loxley and James Cumber on the arrest of Trevor Whitelock. It was early evening, and a hungry Packer could not help noticing the appetising aroma that was emanating from the kitchen. Janet was once again busy giving James Cumber the benefit of her cooking abilities by cooking a ribeye steak pan-fried on Cajun spices.

Though David Jennings had already told him off the record the extent of his harassers' involvement, Loxley did his best to sound surprised.

'So you're saying they were using one of Turnbull's properties for drug dealing?'

'That's what I'm hearing.'

James Cumber asked, 'So it looks like they might well have had links with the Eastern European gang that shot Turnbull?'

'It's too early to say, but I know DCI Jennings and the team are working on that theory.'

Loxley was in detective mode. 'Our experience tells us that a theory is not always much good on its own. There's always a tendency to lose objectivity because you want to hang on to it. I suppose the good news is that the gang's activities are getting severely disrupted. David Jennings felt they were getting close. With luck, there's a chance it could only be a matter of time.'

Matt Packer sounded upbeat. 'Now that Terry Evans has lost his partner in crime, it looks like there's a good chance you might not be hearing anything from him anytime soon.'

James Cumber was not so sure. 'Hopefully he'll also be rounded up in the next few days.'

Packer stood up to leave. 'He's sure to be on the radar if he's gone back in London; he shouldn't be on the run for long.'

Joe Loxley could feel the tension easing away from him. Though he had tried to disguise it from Janet, the whole harassment episode had got to him more than he cared to admit. In that moment, the delicious aroma of the cooked food coming from the kitchen seemed like the perfect way to celebrate.

*

There was a subdued but purposeful atmosphere in the offices of Pikes Hill that Saturday night. It had been a long day, and the warm, sticky evening air added to the sense of fatigue they were all feeling. There had been some major developments with the Turnbull case throughout the day. It had been David Jennings' idea to call an impromptu progress review meeting with key staff before they all went home.

All of the senior investigators on the Turnbull case were present, the only junior exception being PC Sarah Harrison who had also been invited to tag along with Ed Farrows. For the moment, it was DI Keith Simpson who was holding the attention.

'I think we can almost be certain that our tattooed man is this Ivan Kriska, otherwise known as Serge Ostrog. He is practically on the radar of every country in Europol, but he is a very slippery customer who was not even known to be presently in the UK. Like a lot of these gangs, he and his cronies manage to avoid capture through a combination of fear and corruption. They set out to have some very influential people on their payroll. If that fails then they just scare people witless.'

On a purely selfish note, David Jennings could see the high-profile career opportunities of catching the big fish.

'It would be a real feather in our cap if we could snare him. We have his gang on the run so it's definitely game on. Do you think this informant of yours could prove crucial in nailing him?'

Simpson rubbed his unshaven chin in thought. 'There's always a chance. My contact in the regional drug squad is working on it as we speak.'

'Just out of interest, Keith, who is your contact? I might know him.'

'DS John Craddock.'

Jennings struggled to recollect. 'The name rings a bell, but I don't think I've met him.' He changed the subject. 'This possibility of someone on the inside keeping the gang one step ahead won't go away. Whitelock seemed to suggest in his interview this morning that we have a rotten apple somewhere in our ranks. Of course, it could just have been an attempt to put us on the back foot; he couldn't come up with any names or proof when pushed.'

Simpson nodded. 'That may be so, but as I've said before, it would be no surprise knowing what we're up against.'

Jennings thought of the missing documents man and turned to DC Mason. 'I take it there are still no further leads coming in on Chris Barlow?'

Mason shook his head. 'It doesn't look good. We've

checked his medical records, and the blood found at his flat was definitely his.'

Ed Farrows shook his head. 'It's looking like the men at the top decided they had no further use for him.'

Jennings tried to sound more hopeful. 'Well, we won't give up on him just yet. We have most of the UK police force looking out for him so let's try to keep positive, if only for the sake of his children.' He suddenly thought of the time and looked around the table at the tired faces. 'I think that's it for today, team, get home and get a good kip.'

As they all started to leave, he looked appreciatively in the direction of Ed Farrows and Sarah Harrison.

'Not for the first time in this case, that was good work this morning reeling in Trevor Whitelock, got us off to a flyer.' He suddenly had a thought. 'I would like you to stay behind for a moment, Sarah.'

Ed Farrows gave her a subtle wink as they all filed out of the office.

Jennings sat back down at the desk. 'Take a seat, Sarah. I won't keep you long.'

Sarah sat down struggling to contain the butterflies fluttering in her stomach, the jaded fatigue she had felt only moments earlier miraculously disappearing.

Jennings gave her a reassuring smile. 'As you know, Sarah, there's been a bit of a log-jam since promotions were frozen by budget cuts and you amongst others have been negatively affected by it.'

Sarah gave a nod, not wishing to assume what was coming.

'Well, I'm pleased to say that there has been a bit of movement on that score, and we've got a bit of room for manoeuvre. Earlier today, I was pleased to promote Paul Mason to a DS, which was well overdue. That, of course, now opens up a place for a new DC.'

Sarah could feel her legs trembling under the desk and an increasing parched dryness in her throat.

Jennings went on, 'Well, I'm pleased to say I want to give you that new position. How do you feel about it?'

Sarah felt appreciated, euphoric and relieved all at the same time, but she could not say that. Instead, she heard herself stutter an answer.

'Thanks very much, sir, of course I'm well pleased.'

Jennings stood up and shook her hand across the desk. 'I think you're ready, Sarah, but I'm accompanying your promotion with a bit of well-meant advice. Don't be a blushing violet. Too often I've seen young talented officers get overlooked in this profession; you have to get yourself noticed if you want to move up to the next rung like Paul Mason has done. Otherwise, there is always the danger that some outsider will come in and get in over your head.'

'Thanks very much, sir, I will remember your advice.'

Sarah left the office with the peculiar feeling that her feet were not quite touching the ground. She caught a brief reflection of her face in a glass partition as she passed through the corridor; she was grinning from ear to ear.

*

Alfie Jenkins had decided to visit the trap house in the early hours when it was at its busiest. The large dilapidated building stood alone in an expansive area surrounded by trees and bushes; Jenkins knew it only too well. He knew that it was in these early drug-fuelled hours that the information flowed more readily, when the hard-core users were far less inhibited and more communicative. Much to his financial advantage, he had recently discovered that self-preservation and fear were instincts that tended to diminish rapidly when someone was pumped full of chemicals. If he was to have any chance of giving DS Craddock the information he needed on the mysterious "K", the addled and unsuspecting brains of the addicts were the very first requirement. When he had arrived earlier at the isolated derelict building that passed as the trap house, he had been pleased to see that it was the usual chaotic mix of drug-fuelled clients either dealing and leaving immediately, or the more hard-core electing to hang around to experience their self-inflicted oblivion on the premises. Blending into the crowd, he instantly recognised the young man acting as the cuckoo. "Sniffer Price", as he was known, had been an active participant on the local drug circuit since he had been a boy and was well known to the police. There was a brief nod of recognition between them as Alfie completed his transaction for a gram of crack cocaine before merging back into the crowd.

He spent the next hour or two casually indulging in small talk with the addicts that were randomly lounging around on the smelly soiled mattresses that littered the floor. All the while he was conducting these conversations, he was very conscious not to arouse the suspicions of the shifty-eyed Sniffer Price. Thankfully the cuckoo seemed to be far too engrossed in his lucrative transactions to notice him. Many of the addicts had been familiar to him, but by the time the house had begun to empty, he had failed to find out anything useful regarding the man they called "K". He was not too perturbed; these nocturnal undertakings could occasionally prove fruitless with the sometimes mumbled conversations ending up going nowhere. But you only had to be lucky once and there would be other opportunities. He made his way to the exit and stepped out into the warm, early morning air. It was still dark but there was just a small chink of light beginning to form in the eastern sky. It was as he was getting into his car that he caught the sight of headlights from an approaching vehicle. The car pulled up and two men got out. Even though it was dark, both the size and the look of the men drew his attention. He sensed immediately that the two men were not ordinary punters or dealers. There was more than a hint of menace in their body language. Instinctively, he felt himself sinking low into his driving seat. Fortunately, he had deliberately parked his car in a secluded area tucked away amongst the trees. The men began to walk towards the entrance of the trap house before stopping a little way from the trees where he was parked. Jenkins sat perfectly still in the darkness, hardly daring to breathe. There was a brief moment of mounting terror when he thought he had been spotted, but thankfully his car was well hidden from view, and they were totally unaware of his presence. Though he could feel a tight knot of fear in his throat, he slowly raised his head to catch a partial glimpse of the men through a small gap in the trees. Everything about the men suggested to him that they were significant players at the top of the food chain. Despite his deep anxiety, he sensed an opportunity. Ever so slowly, he cracked open his car door and heard the men's voices travelling loudly through the early morning air. For the next few minutes, he sat there listening to snatches of their conversation. He had some difficulty understanding everything, but by the time they'd finished and continued walking towards the trap house, he was sure he'd heard more than enough that would prove valuable to DS Craddock. Not daring to put his headlights on as he drove away, he realised he'd been extremely lucky to leave the house when he did. It had been a close call.

As Alfie Jenkins drove speedily away, he would have had no way of knowing that his questioning behaviour in the trap house had been noted and aroused the suspicions of Sniffer Price. Even worse for Jenkins, at that precise moment, those suspicions were being communicated to the two men by the resident cuckoo.

*

The investigation team had come back to Pikes Hill fresh and eager after having the Sunday off. David Jennings had just ended a phone call in his office and was digesting the information that had been relayed. The call had been from DI Simpson ringing from the offices of the drug squad in Lymington. He stood up and beckoned to Ed Farrows through the glass partition.

'It looks like we might have a possible breakthrough, Ed.'

Farrows put his coffee down on the table before sitting down. 'I'm all ears.'

'It seems Simpson's contact in the drug squad has been told there's an active trap house in a secluded area just outside Lymington. Not only that, the informant was also pretty adamant that he saw a couple of the big cheeses turn up there in the early hours. He says he overheard them talking about another meet at the same venue tonight.'

'How reliable is this intel?' asked Farrows.

'It sounds pretty solid; it's coming from their main man on the inside.'

'What does DI Simpson suggest?'

'He reckons if the two men show themselves, we should throw the lot at it, stake out the place tonight with a view to raiding with armed response.'

Farrows nodded. 'We've got nothing to lose.'

David Jennings could not conceal a slight grin. As the man leading the investigation, he knew only too well that if he could bag this gang it could have massive implications for his career.

'Let's go for it.' He immediately got on the phone to inform Area Commander Cobbold with a view to selling him the plan.

*

The afternoon sun was at its hottest when the young policeman from the regional drug squad pulled his car off the road and stopped in a secluded area heavily shaded by trees. He pulled a burner phone from a zipped pocket and rung a number he now knew by heart. It rang once before being answered. He had only a brief message to deliver but it was massively significant to the listener.

'Operation Hampshire, disappear.'

He put the phone back in his pocket and mopped the sweat from his brow. It had been a highly lucrative and rewarding few months for him. Certainly, his wife Cathy had appreciated the extra cash and that was only the money she knew about. But with the recent murder of Roger Turnbull and a man from Scotland Yard hanging around, he was beginning to wonder if it was worth the stress. He suspected that this would be his last big payday. It appeared that the net was closing in on the gang and the likelihood it was all coming to an end was probably for the best. He was only too aware that there could only be so many failed drug raids before suspicions were raised within the squad. Questions were already being asked back at HQ as to why the squad always appeared to be one step behind. He started the car and gently reversed back onto the road. He drove off back in the direction of Lymington.

*

You could have cut the atmosphere with a knife at Pikes Hill as midnight approached. From the moment the green light had been given for the early morning raid, the tension and excitement had been rising throughout the day. The investigation team were about to join up with a full-strength unit of arresting officers fully armed with Glock 22 pistols and Tasers. David Jennings was seated alongside DI Keith Simpson in one of the patrol cars as it sped towards the trap house situated just outside Lymington. He could not remember the last time he had felt so much adrenaline pumping through his veins. So much so that he had been unable to eat a thing throughout the day. He was fully aware that it was not only the risk of the operation that made him so excited, it was also the thought of the possible career-changing rewards. Nearing the location, the patrol car slowed as the driver searched for a suitably secluded place to park. They eventually stopped in a small copse secluded by bushes but still in sight of the wide lane that led to the trap house. By now there were up to twenty or so police vehicles parked in seclusion within the vicinity of the house, all connected by radio contact.

Keith Simpson turned to Jennings. 'Now it's just a waiting game.'

'It seems quiet; are we a bit early?'

Simpson looked at his watch. 'Maybe; these types of places tend to keep unsociable hours.'

Jennings got in radio contact with Ed Farrows, who was parked in a concealed area just inside the grounds of the building. He was accompanied in the car by the newly promoted Sarah Harrison and an armed officer.

'Is there anything going on, Ed?'

There was a low crackle before Farrows' voice came through. 'There were a few punters that turned up earlier, but they didn't hang around for long. To be honest, the place still looks a little empty.'

Jennings felt himself deflating. 'That doesn't sound promising.'

Farrows' voice came crackling back. 'How long do you think we should give it?'

Jennings looked to Keith Simpson for confirmation as he answered, 'What do you reckon, about two hours?'

Keith Simpson nodded his agreement.

As Jennings rang off, he tried to reassure himself that it was still early in the operation, but he could not help feeling the beginnings of a sense of anticlimax and disappointment.

*

It was sometime later, and all was quiet in the grounds of the trap house when Ed Farrows finished off his bacon sandwich and turned to DC Harrison.

'I don't think David is going to be a happy man if this raid comes to nothing; he's invested a lot in this operation being a success.'

Sarah Harrison gave a grimace. 'I think he definitely saw this as his glory day.'

There followed a lengthy silence in the car as they watched the trap house, before Farrows asked, 'Do you feel any different since your promotion?'

Sarah Harrison gave her answer some thought. 'To be honest, I've not really had time to think about it. So far, nothing seems to have changed much. No offence but, for instance, I'm still patrolling with you tonight.'

Farrows laughed. 'That must be so tough for you. Don't worry, you will soon be shot of me when this case is closed.'

Harrison went to answer but was interrupted when a small car drove up to the entrance of the house. A solitary man got out of the car and approached the front door. He stood there for a minute or so before returning to his vehicle and driving away.

Sarah gave a slight groan. 'This is not looking good.'

Farrows nodded. 'It definitely looks like the punters who have shown up were expecting the house to be dealing tonight.'

Throughout the next two hours, several more people turned up, but it all ended with the same result. Frustratingly for the police operation, it looked like the trap house was disappointingly closed for business.

After a brief and dispirited consultation between David Jennings and Keith Simpson, it was finally left to the Scotland Yard man to make the final decision to call it a day. This left a crushed and disappointed David Jennings the dismal job of reporting the failure back to Chief Super Cobbold. Not surprisingly, there was a sombre silence in the car as the two officers returned to Pikes Hill deep in thought. David Jennings had certainly not enjoyed having to inform the area commander that the whole operation had proved to be a total non-runner. It was Jennings who finally broke the silence.

'Either Craddock's informer got it completely wrong, or we really do have a rogue cop amongst us.' He turned towards Keith Simpson. 'What's your feeling?'

Simpson had no doubts. 'The strong suspicion the gang had inside info was already there; now I'd say it's pretty obvious.'

David Jennings sat in the back of the car with a face like thunder. He spent the rest of the return journey swearing under his breath.

*

With most of the police vehicles returning to base, Ed Farrows and Sarah Harrison were left to stay behind with a couple of the patrol cars and a forensic team. On entry to the property, they were left in no doubt that it was a full-blown trap house littered with all the unsavoury debris you would normally expect to see. With the early morning sun giving some light as it began to rise, they returned to their car. It was Sarah who noticed the outline of a distant shape in the trees. As they moved closer, they realised it was the burnt-out shell of a car. Farrows approached it carefully.

'Looks like it could be a little leaving card.'

A thought suddenly occurred to Sarah Harrison. 'Do you think the gang are laughing at us?'

Ed Farrows didn't like to admit it. 'It's quite possible. For me, there's no doubt they were tipped off regarding our raid tonight.' He stooped and picked up a charred badge that had dropped off the burnt vehicle. He gave it a close examination. 'Hyundai, wasn't that the make of car that followed Jack Foster?'

Sarah opened her notebook to confirm. 'Dead right, it was a red Hyundai.'

Farrows looked back at the burnt-out shell. 'Can you think of a more efficient way of destroying any forensic?'

Sarah looked despondent. 'Nope.'

They slowly made their way back to the forensic team to report their find. In that moment, it felt very much like game, set and match.

*

Another day had passed since the failed raid on the drug gang at the abandoned trap house and the atmosphere in the small police station that was HQ to the regional drug squad still felt flat and depressed. DS John Craddock had prided himself on the quality of his intel but this time it had failed miserably. The high profile of the failure had felt both disappointing and embarrassing. He had involved the whole of the Hampshire Constabulary and Keith Simpson from Scotland Yard and had let them down. Had his informant made a mistake or been misled in some way? All morning he had been trying to get in touch with Alfie Jenkins on his mobile but so far the bugger had failed to pick up. It was the policy with informers to never leave messages in case the phone got in the wrong hands. As things stood, he was worried, not only worried about Jenkins' safety but also the thought that the squad could have a rotten apple in its ranks. He'd had a brief phone conversation with DI Simpson after the failed raid and the Scotland Yard man was convinced of it. For him, it was just a simple question of where and who. The drug squad consisted of a team of ten and Jennings genuinely found it hard to believe it could be any of them. He concluded that if Simpson was correct in his suspicions, then it must be someone operating from another division. He suddenly jumped as his mobile went off in his pocket.

He recognised the number immediately; it was Alfie Jenkins! The informer sounded a little excited.

'DS Craddock?'

Craddock moved away from the desk and lowered his voice. 'Am I glad to hear from you.'

'Why, what's up?'

'Let's just say your intel about the trap house didn't exactly go to plan.'

There was a slight pause on the end of the line before Jenkins answered, 'I think I know why.'

'Would you care to expand on that?'

'I think I've got something big for you.'

'Can you give me any clues?'

'Oh no, you will have to meet me in the usual place. Say about three o'clock this afternoon. This news is dynamite so make sure you bring a nice fat wedge with you.'

'I'll be there.'

There was another slight pause before Alfie Jenkins went on, 'All I will say is that it looks like you have a bad egg amongst you.'

The suspicion that leaks of crucial info had been coming from within the force seemed to have finally been confirmed.

'Do you have a name?'

'Not until I see you, but the answer to your question is yes, I do.'

Craddock caught his breath.

As Jenkins hung up, Craddock stood still for a second, processing the news. The implications of what his informer had told him could be massive and could go some way to restoring the credibility of his intel. He looked hurriedly for DI Simpson's number; he had decided to bring back the man from Scotland Yard.

*

After the phone call to DS Craddock had ended, Alfie Jenkins put the key in the lock and entered a small rundown cottage. It wasn't much but it was somewhere he could call home. Something he had hardly known in his short and troubled life. It may have been a touch isolated and in some disrepair, but it felt good to return to a base where he felt secure. With the state benefits and informant money making the rent affordable, he felt like he was finally moving up in the world. Despite the failure of the raid on the trap house, he was feeling quite pleased with himself. He was beginning to enjoy the importance that the police were placing on him. Sometimes he fancied that in another life he could have seen himself working alongside people like DS Craddock in the drug squad. In the end, life was all about choices, and he had made more than his fair share of mistakes. He now felt that with the benefit of painful experience, those errors of judgement were becoming less frequent. When he had originally informed Craddock about the trap house, he had deliberately held back on one more crucial nugget of information. A name he had heard crop up more than once in the conversation between the two men on that early morning. He was sure that what he had to say later that afternoon would be worth a pretty buck to DS Craddock. He was looking forward to the three o'clock meeting and picking up his reward. He went to the drawer and pulled out a tin before sitting at the small kitchen table. A self-satisfied smirk played around his lips as he proceeded to roll a joint.

Outside Alfie Jenkins' cottage, concealed deep in the shade of the elms and silver birch, Serge Ostrog, otherwise known Ivan Krista, stared fixedly at the cottage. It was his eyes that gave it away. They were the dead, expressionless eyes of someone without conscience or a single trace of humanity, devoid of all normal feeling other than chilling, cold-hearted cruelty. After the execution of Roger Turnbull, it had been the gang's intention to carry on the

New Forest operation in some form, relying on their usual combination of playing on those two most basic of human frailties: greed and fear. However, the subsequent events that had transpired now made that impossible. The county lines that had stretched far into the hills of Purbeck had to be abandoned. They were getting out at the right time. His policeman on the inside had served him well. It was a setback but no big deal. Right across the country, there were more than enough lucrative lines and trap houses to keep them wealthy and busy for months to come. Still staring at the ramshackle cottage, the man they called "K" had one last task to complete before his business in the New Forest was done. He would wait for his chance.

ELEVEN
FEAR AND GREED

Keith Simpson drove into the car park of the drug squad HQ in Lymington. He had wasted little time in getting there after getting the phone call from DS John Craddock. David Jennings had insisted he take the precaution of taking an armed officer with him in case the informer was a captive of the gang, and it was some kind of set-up. Simpson had needed little persuading in agreeing, as he knew the nature of the men they were dealing with. The stakes were high but if it was true that Alfie had the name of the bent copper, then they had no choice but to follow it up. After parking up, he and the firearms officer got out of the car and made the short walk across the car park to the offices. Simpson's attention was momentarily caught by a man standing next to a couple of vehicles on the perimeter of the car park. Simpson thought he looked familiar and then remembered he was the cheerful young officer who had been giving out the birthday cake on his first visit. The memory gave Simpson a vague thought of wishing he was thirty years old again as he entered the building.

DS Craddock was waiting for him in reception. Simpson could see that the drugs officer looked excited, no doubt grateful for the opportunity to redeem himself after the failed operation at the trap house.

Craddock gave a brief enquiring glance towards the firearms officer standing beside Simpson before saying, 'Glad you could join me for this meeting, Inspector, it sounds like we could well be on the verge of getting some very important information.'

'Wild horses wouldn't have kept me away from this one, DS Craddock, we need to get a name. This bent bastard has caused us far too much damage already.'

Craddock thought back to the recent string of failed drug raids and held out his hands in exasperation.

'Tell us about it.'

'How was your informant on the phone? Did he sound stressed or agitated?'

'No, he sounded fine, a little excited maybe, but apart from that, perhaps more assured than he normally is.'

Simpson waved an arm in the direction of the officer standing beside him by way of introduction.

'We've got some armed assistance along with us in any case. You can't be too careful with these people.'

Craddock looked at the officer and nodded. 'I've had so many clandestine meetings with Jenkins in the past, it would not have occurred to me that this situation might be different. But yes, you're right, with recent developments it seems a sensible precaution.'

After first looking at his watch, Craddock's craggy

features burst into that likeable smile that Simpson had noted on their first meeting.

'I make it forty minutes or so before we leave. Fancy a cuppa?'

Simpson didn't need persuading. 'I won't say no.'

They followed John Craddock upstairs to his office.

*

Loxley and Cumber were relaxing in the garden on the sun loungers, a couple of chilled bottles of Peroni sat on the table in front of them. Though the sun was still shining brightly, the hot temperatures that had roasted most of the country for the previous month had changed to a muggy humidity that suggested a thunderstorm was not too far away.

The two friends had been discussing the fortunes of the English cricket team who were in the middle of an enthralling Ashes series against Australia. Since the news of the arrest of Trevor Whitelock and the suspected fleeing of Terry Evans back to London, the atmosphere in the Loxley household had grown more relaxed with every passing day. Janet appeared at the patio doors that opened out onto the garden. She'd had a busy morning doing housework and now there was the enticing aroma of freshly baked bread emanating from the kitchen as lunchtime approached.

Looking at the two men lying in their loungers, there was more than a hint of mockery in her voice: 'Don't like to break up the party, but the bin bags will need putting out at some stage.'

Joe Loxley picked up on the sardonic tone and slowly hauled himself out of the chair.

'Don't worry, Janet, I'm on it.' He gave Cumber a slight grin before disappearing through the patio doors.

Janet was pouring herself a long cool Pimm's and lemonade as Loxley entered the kitchen.

He nodded in the direction of the garden and quipped, 'I've kept the seat warm for you, pet.'

Janet raised a playful hand as if to hit him. 'You're not too old to get a smack, you know.'

Loxley jokingly put his hands up defensively before giving her a quick kiss on the cheek and going outside to the bins. Making his way round to the side of the house, he wondered idly how the Turnbull murder case was progressing. He made a mental note to try and fit in a chat with David Jennings if the opportunity came to pin him down. He knew only too well that in the middle of such a high-profile murder case, that was not going to be easy. He pulled the sack out of the bin and tied it up. Idly thinking about the state of play in the cricket, he would not have been certain when he first became aware of a figure standing just a few yards away from him. What he realised instantly with stone-cold certainty was that the figure was Terry Evans. His tormentor was staring straight at him and mumbling incoherently. Loxley could see that, in his hand, a flash of steel glinted blindingly in the bright sunshine. There had been many times in Loxley's long police career when he had confronted dangerous situations, but in that moment, he could never remember feeling such raw terror. Evans took one step towards him, his voice becoming louder and more threatening. His eyes had a glassy, glazed look and there was a white sticky film forming in the corners of his mouth. Loxley could see immediately that he was out of his head on drugs. He could feel his heart thumping hard and a cold, clammy sweat forming uncomfortably on the back of his neck. A chilling morbid realisation that this could be his end flashed before him. For a brief moment, he fought against a stupid impulse to run back to the house to be near Janet. Instead, he forced himself to think of his police training. Keep the assailant talking and look for an object to fend him off. He picked up the bin lid. His neighbour's dog, Chalky, had started barking loudly on the other side of the fence.

He heard himself saying, his voice sounding strange like it didn't belong to him, 'What exactly do you want, Terry?'

Evans was becoming increasingly agitated, his words a disconnected stream of rambling gibberish. Amongst the senselessness, Loxley could just about make out the gist of the accusation that he had killed his dad.

Loxley knew that James Cumber was just a few yards away in the garden. He purposely raised his voice.

'It wasn't me that killed your dad, Terry, the truth is he killed himself.'

Evans took another step towards him and swore loudly.

Loxley heard himself shouting, 'You don't want to go down the same route as your dad, Terry, that road leads nowhere.' His mind flashed back once more to his police training. He remembered that in the event of a knife attack, you should go for the assailant's throat, eyes or genitals. It was at this point that he caught the welcome sight of James Cumber over Evans's shoulder. His old compatriot was creeping up on his drug-riddled attacker from behind and appeared to be holding Loxley's old police baton in his hand.

Heartened by the sight, Loxley kept talking. 'We can help you, Terry. Drop the knife.'

Evans went silent as if momentarily considering Loxley's advice, before suddenly and violently lunging with his knife held high. Stepping backwards, Loxley only just managed to block the thrust with the plastic bin lid, which exploded into pieces, before Evans lifted his arm once more for a second attempt. Cumber had seen Loxley defend the first lunge and was determined there would not be another. As Evans went to plunge the knife for the second assault, Cumber knew that his contact with the baton had to be good and true. He moved decisively and caught Evans on the back of his neck and head with a solid and satisfying thud. Terry Evans went out like a light: his body falling heavily to the ground. Cumber kicked the knife away as Loxley leant unsteadily against the side of the house. Janet came running around from the garden and rushed towards Joe Loxley. She had rung the police immediately when she'd heard the shouting, and the distant siren confirmed that they were already on their way. With Loxley repeatedly assuring her he was alright, she slowly led him back to the house. Cumber stood over the stricken body of Terry Evans, his body in a slumped, crumpled heap. Danny Tyler's son had come perilously close to robbing him of his closest friend. He felt his rapidly beating heart gradually beginning to slow. Taking a long, deep, shuddering breath, he calmly waited for the police to arrive.

*

Keith Simpson and DS Craddock were accompanied in the car by the armed officer as they made their way along the approach road that led to the old allotment wasteland that served as the regular meeting place with Alfie Jenkins. They were both eager to hear what he had to say. If his intel was even half as valuable as he had indicated in the phone conversation, then they could be on the verge of a major breakthrough in identifying the snake in their ranks. They both knew that if the information was good, Alfie would want to be generously rewarded. It was for that reason that Craddock carried a bulky package of used notes in his inside pocket.

It was Keith Simpson who saw the car first. Parked a little way back from the road under the shade of a leafy oak tree, he pointed it out to Craddock.

'Isn't that Alfie Jenkins' car?'

Craddock recognised the car immediately, braking instantly and pulling up a few yards ahead of the stationary vehicle. All three men got out of the car with the firearms officer leading the way as they cautiously approached the battered old Ford. There was no doubt that the weather was changing. The air felt sticky and heavy with large black clouds beginning to form in the distant sky. Keith Simpson could not help feeling a deep sense of foreboding as he peered into the car on the driver's side. It didn't look good. The ignition keys were still dangling in the lock. All three men walked to the rear of the car and stopped abruptly. A thick trickle of blood was creeping slowly across the sun-baked earth and on to the tarmac. Simpson gave Craddock a quick glance as if to prepare him, before slowly lifting the lid of the car boot. They all instinctively took a step back, repulsed at what they saw. Arranged neatly in the foetal position, it was the limp and lifeless corpse of Alfie Jenkins. They forced themselves to look a little closer. Jenkins' eyes were disconcertingly wide open, the blood still seeping from the unsightly bullet wound in the back of his head. While a visibly shocked DS Craddock took a moment to steady himself and process the sight and implications of what had happened, Simpson and the firearms officer widened their examination to the immediate area beyond the trees. Amongst the undergrowth, they found a considerable amount of blood spatter already cloying and sticky in the humid atmosphere.

Simpson turned back to the ashen-faced Craddock. 'No doubt he was executed on this spot. Looks like they wanted us to find him. The gang are obviously clearing out of the area, and this is quite literally their parting shot. It's what they do.'

Craddock looked concerned at the realisation. 'So you think they definitely knew we were coming here to meet him?'

Simpson nodded. 'Without a doubt. Who else knew we were meeting Jenkins?'

Craddock thought back carefully to his conversation with Jenkins that morning. There had been around four officers in the office. He supposed it would have been remotely possible someone may have got an inkling of the conversation.

'There were a few of the team in the room but as I remember, they were all talking amongst themselves.'

Simpson had an open mind. 'Could have been any of them. Remember, whoever it was would not have been making it obvious.' He had a second thought. 'What about when you made the call to me?'

Craddock played back the events in his mind. 'I had stepped away from the desk and was looking out of the window.' He suddenly remembered with a jolt that there had been one officer standing nearby, appearing to be preoccupied with his mobile phone but standing alone. 'DS Stainrod was standing pretty close, but surely it's not Nick?'

Simpson vaguely remembered the name. 'Am I right in thinking that was the birthday boy from the other week?'

Craddock nodded. 'That's the one, a really promising officer.'

Keith Simpson was reminded of his brief sighting of Stainrod in the car park earlier that day. He remembered a vague feeling of something not looking quite right but had been too preoccupied with his own thoughts at the time. What was it? He thought back. That was it! Stainrod had been transferring a shoulder bag from his squad car to what Simpson assumed to be his own vehicle. It could have been perfectly innocent, but his investigative instincts were beginning to smell a rat. He would love to know what was in that bag.

He asked Craddock, 'Where is Stainrod supposed to be now?'

'He was sent out to bring in the cuckoo, Sniffer Price.'

Simpson sounded sceptical. 'Somehow I don't think that's going to happen.'

Craddock was still in denial. 'I just can't believe he's our snitch. He seems so straight and honest, really eager to please.'

Simpson gave a resigned smile. 'In my experience, those are the ones you've got to watch.' He turned his attention back to the gruesome sight of Alfie Jenkins. Searching for his mobile to ring David Jennings at Pikes Hill, a distant roll of thunder reverberated ominously across the Purbeck landscape.

*

Nick Stainrod was watching the storm clouds gathering in the sky as he sat alone in his squad car. When he had overheard Craddock's telephone call to the man from Scotland Yard, he had panicked. But, in truth, he'd had no choice but to let "K" loose on Alfie Jenkins. He had no idea how or if the informant had got hold of his name, but he'd had no time to work it out. There was no way he could have taken that chance. He felt bad about it, but the stakes had been far too high. The informer had to be eliminated, otherwise he'd have faced the risk of instant dismissal from the force and a lengthy prison sentence: it had been a simple a case of dog eat dog. He consoled himself with the thought that Jenkins had been on Ivan Krista's hit list anyway. His urgent situation had just brought forwards the inevitable. He only hoped "K" had done the job with his customary efficiency and there would be no comeback. Not before time, the Europeans were pulling out of the area and then he would be in the clear. He'd had his last payday, which was nestling nicely in the boot of his car back at HQ.

It was a seriously substantial sum that opened up all sorts of possibilities. His wife Cathy would not be going short, that's for sure; she was going to be well pleased. To think she'd been worried that there might be less money when they moved down to Hampshire Division from the Met in London. Happily, the opposite had proved to be the case.

He'd been sent out to find and pick up Sniffer Price in order to bring him in. He laughed to himself; fat chance that was going to happen. He turned on his ignition and headed slowly back to HQ as the rain started to fall.

*

David Jennings was sitting on his own in the small partitioned side office at Pikes Hill. Keith Simpson had just given him the news of the murder of the informer Alfie Jenkins and the forensics team were already on their way to the murder site. Simpson had not revealed too much on the phone, but it was pretty obvious he thought it was someone from the inside who had tipped off the gang. What's more, Simpson sounded confident that he had a good idea of who it might be. The Scotland Yard man had annoyingly rung off when Jennings had pressed for more details. He still found elements of Simpson's approach to policing difficult, but he had to admit he was seriously good at his job. He guessed it was mainly Simpson's loner mentality that got under his skin and made him an awkward cuss to work with. Jennings rubbed his eyes and let out a deep sigh. What with the news he'd received earlier about the near fatal attack on Joe Loxley, it was proving a very difficult afternoon. He could not help feeling guilty and responsible that Terry Evans had been allowed to get so close to Joe. From all accounts, if it hadn't been for James Cumber, they could easily have been looking at a very tragic situation that didn't bear thinking about. He felt he owed the Loxleys a big apology. The truth was the Turnbull murder had taken all his attention. He had found the whole business so dammed exciting. Still, at least Terry Evans was now safely locked up downstairs with what looked like a very long charge sheet and jail sentence stretching ahead of him. He took another sip of his coffee, deep in thought. The failed drug raid the day before had hit him hard. If it had been successful, it would have been a career-changer for him no doubt. As it was, it was increasingly looking like the gang were on the move and about to get away with their evil crimes. As for him personally, he knew the Roger Turnbull murder investigation would no doubt be eventually scaled down and he would once more have to get used to a more mundane, low-key existence. After the long adrenaline-charged days of the last two weeks, the prospect did not fill him with much joy. Feeling more than a little deflated, he picked up his case notes once more.

*

Lightning flashes and loud claps of thunder accompanied Nick Stainrod as he drove slowly back to HQ in the heavy rain. The storm had finally arrived with a vengeance.

He was talking to his wife on the car phone. 'Book up any holiday you fancy, I'm feeling generous.'

There was a delighted giggle from the end of the line. 'You're definitely saying I have no limits on the choice?'

'Cathy, the world really is your oyster, go for it.'

'Well, in that case I'm looking at Mauritius or Australia, if you can get the time off.'

Stainrod paused to manoeuvre the car through a narrow gap caused by a small collision between two cars that were having difficulties with the difficult driving conditions.

'I'll see what I can do.'

'The weather outside is terrible. May I ask why you are so cheerful?'

'No real reason. I think I'm enjoying the rain after all that hot weather.'

'I'll order in a curry tonight. What time do you expect to be home?'

Stainrod was drawing closer to HQ. 'Sometime between seven and eight, I reckon.' He was enjoying driving in the storm. 'This is like being in a rally.'

'You be careful.'

'Don't worry, I'm only going about twenty miles per hour at the moment.'

'I'm looking at the holiday catalogue.'

'As I said, don't hold back.' He pulled into HQ and turned sharply into the car park. The visibility was not great through the rain-splashed windscreen, but he could just make out some bedraggled figures standing in the quad. It was only when he stopped the squad car that he caught sight of something that immediately drained his colour and made him feel sick to the stomach. Both DS Craddock and the man from Scotland Yard were standing with a small group of people next to his parked car. Even worse, the car boot was wide open.

Cathy was still talking. 'You want to see the prices – they're astronomical.'

Stainrod answered almost as if he was in a daze. 'We'll speak later, hon, something's come up.'

Keith Simpson and a grim-faced Craddock were walking across the car park towards him. He noticed that the man from Scotland Yard was carrying his holdall. It was at that precise moment he felt his whole world crash around him.

*

It was the following day at Pikes Hill and the station was still buzzing with the news that the Eastern European drug gang had apparently ceased their operations in the New Forest and that an officer from the drug squad had been arrested for corrupt malpractice. As David Jennings had suspected, with the confirmation of the gang's departure, budgets were already being drawn in with both the investigation and the active personnel scaled down. Throughout the day, several of the low-level drug criminals that had been collaborating with the gang had been pulled in and arrested, including chief cuckoo Sniffer Price. The cells downstairs were now a hive of activity as the arresting officers, solicitors and legal advisors processed the individual cases. Not surprisingly, prominent among them and enjoying himself was criminal brief Weasel Jim Wallace.

In the large meeting room upstairs, a sizable group of the investigation team who were brought in from outside were gathered as David Jennings stood up to address them for the last time.

'It's been an interesting two weeks to say the least.' He paused briefly at the murmured laughter his comment provoked. He went on, 'The murder of Roger Turnbull has unearthed a cesspit of corruption in the New Forest that has been truly shocking. The harsh reality is we still haven't caught his killer or any of the major players of the gang that perpetrated the act. We also have a missing person, Chris Barlow, a father of two children who, if not already dead, seems to have been forcibly kidnapped by the gang. So I can't stand here and pretend the investigation has been a total success. But thanks to your diligent police work, we have managed some small victories, not least getting close enough to scare off the gang. More significantly, with the valued assistance of DI Simpson from Scotland Yard, we have identified and charged the rotten apple amongst us who was hindering our investigation at every turn.'

Simpson was standing nearby and looked slightly embarrassed.

David Jennings was in full flow. 'The biggest positive we can take is that, once again, we're county-line free in the New Forest. Of course, the reality is these psychopathic bastards are still out there in the UK, free to carry on peddling their evil trade in financial corruption, fear and drug dependency. We cannot afford to be complacent. Sometime in the future, gangs like this will be sure to try their luck in this area once more. When that day comes, we can only do our best to be ready for them.' Jennings rounded up his speech by thanking everyone for their efforts and wishing everyone good luck.

There was a generous round of applause and a few half-hearted whoops before everyone began to disperse.

*

It was not until the early evening that Pikes Hill felt something like close to normal. With all the processing of the offenders pretty much completed, a relative calm and quiet had once more descended upon the station. Jennings was still discussing the conclusions of the investigation with Ed Farrows when they were interrupted by Keith Simpson. The Scotland Yard man was holding his hat and coat.

Simpson held out his hand. 'My work here is done, gentlemen. From here on, I think my investigations into this case will be better served back at Scotland Yard.'

Both Jennings and Farrows rose from the desk and shook his hand.

All three men had been present at the unpalatable interview with Nick Stainrod when the disgraced police informer had confirmed that they were definitely on the right track in thinking that Serge Ostrog was the mysterious "K".

Jennings asked Simpson, 'Did you ever have any doubts that "K" and Ostrog were the same man?'

Simpson shook his head with some certainty. 'Going from the physical description, the fact of his unknown whereabouts and the alias of Krista, it pretty much made it a sure thing for me. It just remains for us to catch up with him. It's not going to be easy, but believe me, I will make it my mission. The day will come when we will eventually flush him out.'

David Jennings took some comfort from Simpson's words.

Ed Farrows also had a question. 'What made you so sure that Stainrod was the rat in the kitchen?'

'If you want to know the truth, I wasn't, but you must know as a detective you sometimes just have to follow your gut.'

'You certainly hit the jackpot.'

'I had seen him earlier in the car park putting a bag in his boot and Craddock's recollection of his telephone conversations did the rest. Easy, two and two make four.'

Jennings thought back to the interview with Stainrod and could not ever remember feeling so repulsed by the man sitting in front of him. He knew only too well that it had been Stainrod's corruption that had robbed him of his moment of glory. He could not help revealing his feelings.

'The bent bastard.'

There was a momentary silence before Simpson unexpectedly gave Jennings a grin.

'Thanks for the honourable mention in your speech, by the way, but there really was no need. I was only doing my job.'

Jennings sounded genuine, 'I meant every word. If you're telling me that you were only doing your job, all I can say is you're bloody good at it.'

There was just a fleeting moment when Simpson's expression looked suitably pleased, but it was gone in a flash.

'Obviously I'll keep you updated of any further developments on the case.' The man from Scotland Yard then turned abruptly on his heel and was gone.

As David Jennings watched him leave, he felt a complicated mix of emotions: jealousy, envy, dislike, but also an admiration and a respect so strong that, in that moment, he felt he wanted to be him. Standing there watching Simpson's retreating back, he was only too aware that an exciting chapter in his career had come to an end.

Suddenly, Pikes Hill seemed very quiet.

*

A FEW DAYS LATER

The sun was shining brightly but there had been a more refreshing feel to the air since the storm had ended the heatwave. James Cumber was sitting outside the coffee shop in Lyndhurst High Street with Joe Loxley and was making the most of his last hours in the New Forest before his drive back to London the following morning. His daughter Kelsey had messaged that she would be heading back to her Notting Hill flat in a few days, so he wanted to make sure he got back to spend some time with her. The two retired policeman were slowly coming to terms with the crazy series of events that had unfolded in the duration of Cumber's stay.

Cumber was asking Joe Loxley the question, 'What do you think will happen to Terry Evans?'

'Well, hopefully they will throw the book at him. Phil Shaw gave a positive identification that he was the bastard he saw walking away from my house after terrorising Janet. No doubt we will be called as witnesses in relation to the deranged assault with the knife. As for the other charges, pick any from harassment with menace, possession of a knife, an intent to murder, plus a whole host of drug-related offences.'

Cumber looked satisfied. 'It sounds like he could be banged up for some time. There will probably be a need for a court order when he's eventually released to keep him away from you.'

Loxley felt a cold involuntary chill run down his back as he thought back to the demented attack.

'Don't remind me.' There was still a discernible tremble in Loxley's hand as he picked up his coffee cup. 'Look at that, I'm a nervous wreck.'

Cumber wore a slightly concerned expression. 'I'm not surprised. Evans looked totally out of control.' After a brief reflective pause, he smiled. 'And to think I originally came down here for a chilled week in the New Forest.'

Loxley could not help giving a faint chuckle. 'I suppose we should have known things were going to be different for this trip when you almost ditched your car on the first day.'

Cumber recalled his near-fatal collision, and his expression turned serious. 'The bad news is that David Jennings and his team never got to catch the wicked monsters that have been doing the killing.'

Loxley nodded resignedly. David Jennings had recently updated him on the conclusion of the case when he had visited Loxley's house to apologise for allowing Evans to get so close. He had picked up on David's obvious disappointment with the eventual outcome of the case.

'I think we have to accept that it's more difficult now. The old is not like the new, James. Drug crime today is on a completely different scale to our time. The financial rewards are life-changing. It's so much easier now for drug gangs to get significant people in their pocket. You only have to look at the corruption in this case: Roger Turnbull, the councillor Jack Foster, a bent solicitor and not least a bad apple in the local drug squad. Added to that, you've got the police not being able to patrol as they should, as we used to do. The money and the manpower are just not there. David was saying that in some areas they now have to rely on private security companies and local neighbourhood watches to fill the gaps.'

Cumber shook his head and took a sip of his coffee. 'You sure don't paint a good picture. I wonder if they are still holding out any hope in finding the missing documents man, Chris Barlow?'

'We can only hope. But dead or alive, I think it's a long shot whether they ever find him.'

Cumber shook his head. 'Those poor children. How do you ever accept your dad suddenly disappearing without trace and never knowing what happened to him?' There was a brief reflective silence before Cumber attempted to sound a more positive note. 'At least the drug gang were driven out of the area and the low-hanging fruit rounded up.'

Loxley nodded. 'Yes, that's something; the New Forest for the moment at least is drug-gang free. It'll never be cleared up completely. As our old boss used to say, James, the police can only get little victories, but if you want to live in a free society, the war on crime can never ultimately be won.' Loxley's face suddenly clouded over at the thought of his old friend and mentor. 'You know, James, I still feel pretty rotten about not seeing enough of Bill in his last years.'

Cumber reached over and gave Loxley a comforting pat on the back. 'It's not worth beating yourself up, Joe. After all, we're all destined to go our separate ways in the end.'

Loxley smiled wryly. 'That's certainly true enough, though not a particularly cheerful thought.'

There was a brief reflective silence as the two men pondered on this sobering reality, before Loxley asked, 'Fancy a pint on the way back?'

Cumber's face brightened. 'You bet. We'll have one to the memory of Bill Kemp and maybe another to Tottenham Hotspur Football Club eventually winning the Premiership.'

Loxley laughed. 'If that glory day ever arrives, do you think we'll still be around to see it?'

'We Spurs supporters have to be the eternal optimists; we've got no choice.'

Loxley grimaced. 'I only hope that Bournemouth don't beat Spurs to it and win a trophy first; my neighbour Phil will be unbearable.' As Loxley stood up and stretched, he looked down at Cumber benevolently. 'I suppose, on balance, you have earned the right to a couple of free pints; after all, you probably did save my life.'

'Well, modesty forbids me to make that claim, but I have to admit your chances didn't look too good.'

They both laughed.

Comfortable and easy in each other's company, the two old friends left the coffee shop and strolled leisurely down the Lyndhurst High Street towards the pub.

*

Many miles from Lyndhurst, Chris Barlow forced himself to look away from the window. The clear blue sky outside only tormented him with the illusory promise of freedom. He had no idea what part of the country he was in; he only knew the car journey had been long and uncomfortable. Badly beaten up and forced down on the back seat wearing a blindfold and nursing a head wound, there were times in the journey when he had wished there and then that he could have ended it all. But the harsh reality was that his living nightmare had only just begun. He looked across the room at the two Eastern Europeans pondering their next moves on a chess board before forcing himself to concentrate on what was in front of him. The all too familiar fake documentation papers were laid out before him on the table.

This was his life!

The gang members brought his meals to him and his bed was comfortable enough, but the stark truth remained: he was now an unwilling captive member of the gang. He looked out of the window once more and glimpsed some green hills far away in the distance. He thought of his two teenage children. It had all been for them! What a fool he had been. The day would eventually come when the gang would decide he had served his purpose. But he knew that in this life, there would be no escape for him.

There could only ever be one outcome.